# Velvet
## undercover

## ALSO BY TERI BROWN

*Born of Illusion*
*Born of Corruption*
*Born of Deception*

# Velvet undercover

## TERI BROWN

Balzer + Bray

*An Imprint of* HarperCollins*Publishers*

Balzer + Bray is an imprint of HarperCollins Publishers.

Velvet Undercover
Copyright © 2015 by Teri Brown

Library of Congress Cataloging-in-Publication Data
Brown, Teri J.
 Velvet undercover / Teri Brown. — First edition.
  pages  cm
 Summary: "A World War I era spy novel about a bright British girl who is
sent undercover into the heart of enemy territory to rescue Britain's most
valuable (and secret) spy"— Provided by publisher.
 ISBN 978-0-06-232127-5 (hardback)
 [1. Spies—Fiction. 2. Undercover operations—Fiction. 3. World War, 1914–
1918—Fiction.] I. Title.
PZ7.B81797Ve 2015                                          2015006603
[Fic]—dc23                                                        CIP
                                                                  AC

Typography by Ray Shappell
15  16  17  18  19   PC/RRDH   10 9 8 7 6 5 4 3 2 1

First Edition

This book is for my children, Ethan and Megan, who always believed in me, and my hubby, Alan, who has both my heart and my back.

# PART I

*Asset*

# ONE
## RQH

*Talent Spotter: Someone who brings potential agents to the attention of recruiters.*

I stand at the podium, ramrod straight, awaiting the challenge questions. The Lenard Auditorium, which is more a dingy neighborhood dance hall than an actual auditorium, is filled mostly with Girl Guides and their parents. To my right is pretty, droll Sarah Wheeler, whose dimples hide a sharp mind. To my left is painfully shy Evangeline Green, who has already had a book of poetry published.

I barely hold back a dismissive snort.

*Poetry!*

Dame Richards, the leader of England's Girl Guides, paces in front of us, a sheaf of papers in her hand. The Girl Guides are England's answer to all the exclusionary boys' clubs popping up all over Britain. Since girls certainly couldn't join the boys—at least according to the powers that be—a group was created just for us.

From the solemn look on Dame Richards's face, she takes her job very seriously. "How are you girls doing? Ready for the challenge?"

Like marionettes, the three of us bob our heads and smile blindly at the people in the front row.

"Samantha Donaldson."

I straighten. Every year, Dame Richards asks the final three girls about themselves to increase the excitement of the competition.

"Yes, ma'am?"

"Now that you're graduating from the Girl Guides, what are your plans for the future?"

Smiling brightly, I give the answer I'd been rehearsing. "Currently, I'm working for the government until the war is over, and then I plan on specializing in mathematics at the University of London."

"Mathematics! How very ambitious of you! Your parents must be very proud."

I nod as she moves on. Automatically, I glance over to where my mother is sitting, her posture so perfectly upright that her shoulder bones barely skim the back of the chair. My chest tightens at the empty seat beside her. We'd reserved the seats months ago, before my father's disappearance on a sudden trip to the Arabian Peninsula.

*Don't worry about that now. Focus on the task at hand.*

My throat tightens at the familiar sound of my father's voice in my ear. Intellectually, I know it's not truly my father, that my brain is just playing tricks on me because I miss him so much. Nonetheless, his voice is comforting, and I follow his instructions now by returning my attention to the left of the stage, where the Markel Cup sits, a giant gold chalice etched with the Girl Guides' clover symbol.

I've had my eye on the Markel Cup ever since my mother made me join the Guides six years ago. I'd been half-afraid the war would disrupt the competition—after all, how important is a Girl Guide contest when young men are dying in the bloodiest conflict the world has ever seen?

I'm rather ashamed at how relieved I was when it was announced that the competition would commence as usual.

Dame Richards finishes up her questions and then turns to us, a small smile on her face. "The next challenge is in language. Each of you will be given a stanza of poetry in French. You must translate it into English and then into the language of your choice. You'll have five minutes to do so."

I pick up my pencil and wait as she hands me the slip of paper. The contest consists of five tasks, in five different disciplines—math, science, history, geography, and languages. Each answer is judged and given a certain number of points. Whoever receives the most points wins.

My lips curve slightly as I'm handed the paper. I may not know as much about poetry as Evangeline Green, but very few people my age can say they've mastered four languages, with a smattering of several more.

When Dame Richards rings the bell, I turn the paper over and read the lines. I recognize the poem, "Autumn," by Alphonse de Lamartine.

I scan the original French before translating it into English. Translation is somewhat of an art. If I convert it word for word from one language to the next, it'll be gibberish. I have to take into consideration subtle differences in meaning and subtext.

> *Earth, sun, valleys, sweet and beautiful nature*
> *As I am nearing death, I owe you one last tear*
> *The air is so fragrant, and the light is so pure*
> *The sun is so beautiful when death is so near*

I pause a moment, wondering whether or not I should translate the poem into German. From my years in Berlin as a child, the German language is second nature to me, but because of the war, anti-German sentiment is high right now. I glance over at the judges, wondering if they'd mark me down because of it. I could always do Portuguese. . . . I shake my head. No. I know German even better than I do French or Dutch.

German it is, then.

> *Erde, Sonne, Täler, schöne und liebe Natur,*
> *Ich schulde dir Tränen am Rande meines Grabes!*
> *Die Luft ist süß! Das Licht ist rein!*
> *Für den Sterbenden ist die Sonne was wunderbares!*

I finish the translation and hand the paper back to Dame Richards. The judges go over our answers while we're given another challenge.

My confidence ebbs as the competition moves into geography. Despite traveling extensively as a child, topography has never held the same appeal for me as math or languages, and my knowledge of capitals and landforms is sketchy at best.

Even though I'm unsure of myself, I quickly mark down answers as if I'm a geographical genius. Once, as a child, I upended a chessboard, scattering the pieces across the floor when I realized I couldn't win. Instead of punishing me, my father took me on his lap and explained why such behavior was unacceptable. One should exude assurance, he said, even in the face of sure defeat. When I asked why, he told me that confident bluffing can triumph over seemingly impossible odds, whereas showing your hand with temper or despair never does. "Don't give up until you're well and truly checkmated," he would tell me.

Remembering his words, I keep a smile pasted on my face as I answer Dame Richards's rapid-fire questions:

"The Great Victoria Desert is located in which country?"

"What are the intersecting lines on maps and globes called?"

"What is a cyclonic depression?"

Sweat trickles down my back as I write. What would Father say if I lost?

I take in a relieved breath as geography wraps up. Science and math whiz by. History is trickier, mostly because the question about the colonization of Queensland is subjective in nature. But I still finish confidently.

"Thank you, girls." Dame Richards takes the papers. "You've done a wonderful job and have made us all proud.

You may take your seats until the judges tally up the points."

I take a seat on a bench on one side of the stage. Next to me, Evangeline looks as if she's going to faint, and even pretty Sarah Wheeler looks tense. The Markel Cup is a feather in any Girl Guide's cap and I know they must want it as badly as I do.

I watch as the judges confer with one another. Every year they bring in guests to referee the competition—usually officials from different universities or members of the government. I bite my lip as Captain Parker, assistant to the head of Military Intelligence 5, frowns at the papers. Like many of the older Girl Guides in London, I'm employed as a messenger girl for the government and actually work in the same building as Captain Parker, though he didn't give any sign of recognition when I was introduced. He probably doesn't even know who I am.

My gaze returns to my mother. She must be as aware of the empty seat beside her as I am, but her pretty face is composed as she catches my eye and gives me an encouraging smile. The past few months have been difficult for her, but you'd barely know it. Only the clouded sadness in her blue eyes and the lines etched around her mouth betray her grief and worry.

I'm so lost in thought that I don't even notice Dame Richards standing in front of the podium until she begins to speak to the audience.

"Ladies and gentlemen. Thank you so much for coming.

As many of you know, the board of directors and I were of two minds as to whether holding the Markel Cup Competition was appropriate or not, given the circumstances. But our young women have studied so diligently that it would be wrong not to reward them for their hard work. The Girl Guides you see before you"—she motions for us to join her—"exemplify the values that Girl Guides stand for and that our young men are fighting for. These include honor, integrity, and intelligence. All have had a distinguished career in the Girl Guides and we will miss them as they graduate from our organization."

One of the judges hands her the envelope.

"Now for the results that you've all been waiting for."

My heart pounds with excitement. All the hours I spent studying with my father and tutors are about to bear fruit.

If only he were here to witness this.

Dame Richards casts a stern eye over us. "Now remember, girls, that you should all be very proud of yourselves. And with that, here are the results."

My mouth dries as she unfolds the slip of paper.

She stares at it, her brows rising ever so slightly as if she's surprised. On my left, Sarah grabs my hand in a show of solidarity. I'd look ungracious if I snatched it back, so I leave it, even though her hand is as limp and damp as a day-old oyster.

"In third place is Sarah Wheeler!" Sarah smiles and waves halfheartedly at the polite clapping of the crowd. She drops my hand and I surreptitiously wipe it on my skirt as she walks off the stage. Evangeline glances at me, her face a stiff mask, and I know we won't be holding hands. Which is fine—I'm not really the hand-holding type.

I stare at the cup, wishing with all my heart that my father were here to see this.

"And the winner of this year's Markel Cup is . . ."

Dame Richards pauses dramatically and I hold my breath. Why doesn't she just say my name!

"Evangeline Green!"

I step forward with a smile before her words fully reach my brain. My lips stiffen and I do a half turn to give the stunned Evangeline an awkward hug before walking off the stage. My stomach somersaults and I'm very much afraid I'm going to be sick before I can reach the water closet. Instead of taking a seat in the front row, I turn and slip out a side door. I can hear Evangeline's family and friends whooping as I hurry down a narrow hallway toward the bathroom.

*I was just beaten by a poet!*

Hot, humiliated tears run down my face as I lock the door, and I don't care that I look like a sore loser for running off.

I *am* a sore loser.

I should be the one holding the Markel Cup in front of everyone, getting my photograph taken for all the news stories. I pace the small room, overwhelmed with hurt and anger.

I want my father so badly it's like a physical ache. Just the thought of him makes me cry more—hard, ugly sobs that rip furiously out of my chest. Father would know what to say to make me feel better. I love my mother, but for most of my life she only existed on the edges of the studies, codes, and puzzles my father and I shared.

A knock sounds on the door. "Sam, open up. It's me."

Cousin Rose's voice reaches me and, with a sob, I throw open the door. If I can't have my father, then Rose is the next best thing.

Her skinny arms embrace me and she pats my back as if comforting a child. "I know, I know," she croons as I cry against her shoulder.

"Now then. That's enough," she says after a minute. "Donaldsons must sally forth, no matter what!"

Rose's voice mimics our deceased grandfather's so perfectly that I giggle through my tears. We're the best of friends even though she's two years younger than me and all sunshine and frolic, while I'm more solemn and studious. We balance each other perfectly.

She helps me splash water on my face and tilts her head to look at me critically. "You rather look like hell. All this over a stupid cup!" She shakes her head, setting her curls to bouncing.

"It's not stupid." I sniff. "I really wanted to win." I well up again and she pinches my arm.

"Stop that. And I know you wanted to, but it's not like you needed the scholarship money that comes with the cup. Perhaps Miss Snooty Poetess does. Think of that. Come on. Let's go keep up appearances."

I take a shuddering breath and dry my hands and face on the towel provided before following her down the hall.

I paste a smile on my face and we rejoin the others. The chairs have been cleared away and someone is playing records on the Victrola.

My mother joins us. "I am so proud of you, darling. You did splendidly."

Even though my mother knows how deep my disappointment must be, she doesn't betray that knowledge with a single look or action. To do so would make my pain cut even deeper. We're alike in that way.

"Thank you, Mother." I take a casual sip from the cup she offers as if I hadn't just gone to pieces in the restroom.

Rose links her arm in mine. "I don't care who won that ugly cup. Sam is still the smartest person I know."

I give her a grateful smile, even though the loss burns in my stomach.

"Congratulations, Miss Donaldson. That was a spectacular showing. I'm gratified you work for MI5."

Startled, I turn to see Captain Parker behind me.

And I thought he didn't know who I was.

Then I realize that standing next to him, blinking rapidly behind thick glasses, is none other than my flighty boss. "Miss Tickford! I didn't know you were coming!"

She takes my hand and gives it a warm squeeze. "I wouldn't have missed it." She clears her throat before lapsing back into her customary silence.

Then I remember that the captain just spoke to me and I'm practically ignoring him. "Thank you, sir," I say, and make introductions.

"You should be very proud, Mrs. Donaldson," Captain Parker says. "Your daughter has an extraordinary mind."

Miss Tickford makes a little noise of acknowledgment before dropping her eyes again.

My mother smiles. "I agree, Captain Parker. Her father and I have always been proud of her."

Like that of most military men, Captain Parker's bearing is stiff, and though I suppose many women would think him handsome, with his strong jaw and dark eyes, I find him intimidating. I wonder if Miss Tickford came with him or on her own. Surely such a mousy little woman wouldn't attract a man like the captain. But then she *is* in charge of the Girl Guide contingent at MI5. It makes sense that she would attend the Markel Cup.

"I was sorry to hear about your husband. He was a very good man," Captain Parker says.

A jolt runs through me. He knows me *and* my father?

My mother's expression remains tranquil, but there's a tremor in her voice as she answers him. "*Is* a good man, Captain. My daughter and I are very sure that George will be returning to us soon."

"Of course," Captain Parker says smoothly before moving on. "I'm glad I ran into you, Miss Donaldson. I'd love to speak to you sometime about your position at MI5. I was very impressed with your performance today, and I'm sure your skills could be better utilized than for just delivering messages."

Miss Tickford blinks. "Delivering messages is very

important," she says, her hands fluttering. "Communication is the lifeblood of the realm."

"Of course it is, Letty. You know I didn't mean that."

*Letty?* I look from one to the other. How very interesting.

"I just feel that Samantha's talents could be of better use to the cause elsewhere," the captain continues.

Miss Tickford's mouth droops and even the severe bun at the back of her head seems to wilt. "You're right, of course."

My pulse kicks up a notch. I've often thought that I could be of more use elsewhere—someplace where I could utilize my brain rather than just my legs—but Miss Tickford never seemed amenable to the idea.

I straighten. "I'd like that very much, Captain Parker." I bet Evangeline Green won't be offered a promotion in such an important organization.

Next to me, Rose fidgets, bored with the conversation. "Oh, there's Priscilla. I must go say hello. Excuse me." She shoots me a sly smile as she makes her escape.

Dame Richards taps me on the shoulder. "You're needed at the prize table, Samantha, to receive your certificate of achievement."

"I'll be right there." I turn to Captain Parker. "It was nice meeting you, sir. I'll see you in the morning, Miss Tickford."

He glances at his watch. "Yes, I must be going, as well. We'll talk soon, Miss Donaldson. Are you ready to go, Letty?"

She nods and turns to me. "Captain Parker was kind enough to give me a lift after we finished work. Congratulations on your performance, Samantha."

Frowning, I watch them go. How very strange that they came together. But then, I suppose it's no stranger than me losing out on the Markel Cup. I lift my chin. As Grandfather Donaldson would say: It's time to sally forth!

No matter how shattered I am inside.

# TWO
## WZR

*Clean: Someone who has never been involved in espionage and is unknown to enemy intelligence.*

I spend a fitful night, dreaming again and again of the moment Evangeline Green's name was called instead of mine. My nose wrinkles as I hurry downstairs. Porridge again. Doubtless with no sweetener, unless our housekeeper, Bridget, "found" some honey on a back shelf. Mother's never actually accused her of buying from the black market, but Bridget seems to discover things that even Cook has no idea we had. Bridget has a bit of a sweet tooth and rationing is hard on her.

My mother and Rose are already seated at the table. Mother is eating and Rose is pretending to, a book propped up on the table in front of her.

Mother looks up and gives me a smile. "Good morning, dear."

Since Father's disappearance, Mother has transformed into a more formal version of herself, and though I don't blame her for being so self-contained, it does make my life lonelier. That's one of the reasons Rose spends the night with us so often now—her lively chatter fills the silence.

"Good morning! That looks good, Bridget, but I won't have time to eat this morning."

Rose glances up at me. She's looking unfairly bright and shiny in spite of the fact that she was up as late as I was last night, listening to me rant. "You're not partaking of this delicious breakfast?" she asks, widening her eyes in mock surprise. "Why ever not?"

"You work too hard, Sam," Mother says, ignoring Rose.

"And you don't?" I ask.

"I read to soldiers and write letters for those who can't do it themselves. I'd hardly call that work."

"You're at the hospital five days a week. I'd call that work." I shrug into my wool coat and pick up the lunch pail Cook left on the counter for me. "I have to run. I'll be home in time for supper." I kiss Rose on the cheek and waggle my fingers at my mother on my way out the door.

I ride the Underground to the city center, trying to shake off the fine film of melancholy that coats my skin like invisible ash. Most of the women on the train are wearing black—a reminder that my loss is only one in a nation full of losses. It makes my disappointment over the Markel Cup seem trivial.

I shove the thought from my mind and hurry through the crowded streets. Miss Tickford frowns on tardiness.

"Excuse me," I say, bumping into a young woman in overalls. She elbows me aside and hurries on toward the docks. She's probably late for a job she wouldn't have dreamt of having just a year ago. Before the summer of 1914, men, in their black suits and derbies, were the rule on the streets of London. They scurried about, filled with the self-importance of the privileged, masculine citizens of the greatest nation in the world.

Then everything changed, as if an enormous hand reached out of the sky and swept them all away. The remaining men have exchanged their proper English garb for uniforms, and doubt has crept into their once overconfident faces.

Worse, though, are the men no longer in uniform. Their ill-fitting civilian clothes hang on sharp, skeletal bodies, and far too many shirtsleeves or pant legs dangle empty—a mocking testament to healthy limbs no longer there. These men linger in the dark, smoky doorways of pubs or make-shift rehabilitation houses, watching the world through eyes sad beyond comprehension.

What a horrible waste of humanity. So many men have been lost.

Including Father.

A twinge of pain compresses my chest as I hurry toward the brick building I now work at six days a week for ten to twelve hours a day. Before the war, I went to school, attended Girl Guide meetings once a week, and spent hours with my parents.

Then my world changed along with everyone else's.

After showing my identification to the guard at the entrance, I hurry down the narrow hallway toward the room that has been commandeered for our use. The other girls have already been dispatched on various errands, so the room is empty. Before I can make myself a cup of tea,

Miss Tickford pokes her head around the door.

"You're late, Miss Donaldson." Miss Tickford's breathy voice sounds pained, as if she's upset that she has to reprimand me.

"I'm sorry, Miss Tickford. It won't happen again."

She blinks rapidly. "After last night's excitement, it's a wonder you're here at all. Captain Parker wishes to see you first thing."

My heart jumps. *Already?* I follow Miss Tickford from the room. When Captain Parker told me that he wished to speak to me about another job, I had no idea he meant so soon.

"Don't dawdle," Miss Tickford says, walking rapidly down the hall.

Our identification badges are examined at three different checkpoints along our way. I keep mine hidden under my bulky black sweater, especially when I'm running messages outside. No Girl Guide has ever been accosted while working for the Security Offices, but nobody wants to take that chance—we have no idea what is in the messages we're bearing.

As I follow Miss Tickford down the hall, I wonder what she does for fun. Perhaps she doesn't have any? She raises her hand to knock on one of the many brown doors lining the hallway and then hesitates. Her large, childlike green eyes blink furiously behind her thick spectacles and she places her hand on my arm. "Conduct yourself well and bring credit to us all, my dear."

Before I can ask her what she means, she raps on the door.

"Come in."

We enter a small, cramped office with an enormous battered desk squatting in the middle. The woman sitting at it has her dark hair pulled back in an uncompromising bun, and her glasses, like Miss Tickford's, are perched on the tip of her nose. I wonder if it's some sort of unofficial uniform for important women, because I can tell by the aggressive set of this secretary's head that she thinks herself very important indeed.

She looks me up and down. "Is this her?"

Miss Tickford nods. "Samantha Donaldson. GG number one twenty-eight. He's expecting her."

Hesitating for a moment, I draw in a breath for courage, and then I walk in. Once I'm inside, the scents of dust and pomade tickle my nose. Captain Parker is sitting at a desk as large and battered as the one in the anteroom. It's precariously stacked with mountains of papers and official-looking green journals and it shoots a hole in the notion that military personnel are tidier than everyone else.

The look he gives me is friendly, and I feel myself relaxing.

"Sit, Miss Donaldson. We have quite a lot to discuss."

"Thank you," I murmur, taking the seat he's indicated across from his desk.

"How are you and your mother getting along without your father, then?"

I blink. "As well as can be expected. We keep faith that we will hear word of him soon."

The captain nods. "I'm sure you will." His dark eyes regard me seriously and I resist the urge to squirm under his scrutiny. He straightens. "We've had our eye on you for quite some time, Miss Donaldson. I've been told by your superiors that you are smart and respectful, and that you carry out your tasks promptly. Last night, I had a chance to see just how intelligent you are, and I feel quite confident that you are able to accomplish any task set before you. I take it you are amenable to being reassigned?"

"Yes, I am." I lift my chin, grateful for his words. Last night's loss bruised my ego more than I care to admit. I wonder where they'll send me. Military Press Control? The Propaganda Section? A thrill of excitement runs through me at the possibilities. Cryptography would suit me best, but they won't send a seventeen-year-old girl to Room 40. I just hope I won't be going to Censorship. Reading through hundreds of letters a day is not my idea of fun.

"I understand you spent the first part of your childhood in Germany, yes?"

Even though he poses it as a question, I can tell that the captain already knows the answer. I nod. He sits silently and an uncomfortable moment stretches out before I realize he's waiting for me to explain myself. "As an ambassador, my father worked in many different countries. He received a long-term assignment and we moved to Berlin as a family in 1902, when I was four. I'm sure this is information you already have?"

*Mind your tongue, Sam.*

The captain raises an eyebrow at my tone and I shift in my seat. I don't mean to be disrespectful, but I'm tired of explaining myself. My mother and I avoid discussing our

Berlin years publicly, and indeed the years we spent in Germany almost kept me from getting a position at MI5, even though I'd been a member in good standing with the Girl Guides for over five years. It wasn't until my mother called in a favor from a family friend that my application was accepted.

"I know your written German is flawless. How is your spoken German?" His voice is casual, but the sharp way he looks at me is not.

I can't help but show off. *"Ich spreche fast perfekt Deutsch. Ich spreche auch fließend Portugiesisch, Italienisch, Französisch sowie ein paar Brocken Niederländisch."* I grin. "I have my father's gift for languages."

Captain Parker raises his eyebrows and returns my smile. "Ah yes, I seem to remember that about your father. Tell me. Do you have his proclivity for mathematical puzzles as well?"

It's my turn to be surprised. I'd always thought my father's love of cryptography was private—something we played with at home or when on one of our outdoor excursions. On the other hand, this *is* Military Intelligence. If they're offering me a job, my life, as well as my father's, has probably been thoroughly investigated. According to popular thought, there are German spies in every nook and cranny of Britain, and as a onetime resident of Germany, I'm sure I'm suspect.

"I'm very adept at math, but I am also well read and I have adequate outdoor skills," I tell him cautiously. There's a fine line between being honest and being too honest. "I am a Girl Guide, after all."

"And what a fine organization they are. All that camping, archery, and boating. We took the liberty of obtaining your school transcripts and believe that you are destined for far greater things than stenography or running errands."

My throat tightens. After last night's loss, I'm grateful for the praise. "Thank you, sir."

Captain Parker clears his throat and thumbs through some papers, which I can only assume are about me.

What did the captain mean when he said I was destined for greater things? I stare idly out the window behind him and remember the time my father said almost the same thing.

I'd been almost seven and we were sitting in the parlor of our house in Berlin. It must have been winter, because a cheerful fire crackled in the fireplace and the diamond-paned windows were covered with frost. My father had been reading through a French newspaper while my mother knitted. I lay on the rug in front of them playing one of the puzzle games my father designed for me. The game had dozens of pegs of all different shapes, sizes, and colors. Each peg had to be fitted into its corresponding hole in a wooden box. I managed to shave seconds off my score every time I played as he timed me on his watch.

"What? You think she is going to marry a crown prince someday?" my mother asked, amused. "If that's your plan, you'd be better off teaching her how to dance than testing her intelligence."

I didn't take the time to look up to see my father's

expression—that would have cost me precious seconds—but I listened with all my heart.

"No, Eunice. Our daughter is destined for far greater things than marrying a mere prince," he said.

I remember how I glowed at that remark. I'd just finished reading *Grimm's Fairy Tales* in the original German, and the exciting adventures in "The Six Servants" were more to my taste than the story of Cinderella.

"Miss Donaldson?"

I jump. "I'm sorry, what did you say?"

"I was saying that we have had our eye on you for quite some time." He leans forward and his face is so serious that I swallow, suddenly nervous. "Have you heard of La Dame Blanche?"

My breath catches and the hair on my neck prickles. "Not officially," I tell him with some hesitation. Admitting that you've heard of an undercover espionage group could be tantamount to admitting you're a spy. But the mostly female spy organization was a favorite topic of gossip and conjecture among my fellow Girl Guides.

Captain Parker stares at me, his dark eyes grave. "Miss Donaldson, I'm pleased to inform you that you've been selected to join La Dame Blanche. We would like you to leave for training with the objective of joining the Third Company in Luxembourg. Are you interested?"

# THREE
## WKUHH

*Eyes Only: Top secret documents to be read by only one specific person.*

My head jerks up. Captain Parker's eyes drill into mine. During one of our many chess games, my father taught me that rushing a move without taking the whole board into consideration is like surrendering the game right from the get-go, so I stare back at the captain and hold my peace.

My silence clearly unnerves him, and he continues talking, which is precisely what I want. I half listen to what he's saying while my mind races. Here it is, finally, a chance to do something important—far more important than winning some silly cup.

*La Dame Blanche!*

There isn't a Girl Guide in my company who wouldn't give up all her badges to be conscripted into this shadowy organization where women actually take oaths just as if they were in a real army. What LDB actually does is not entirely known, but the thought of being a female spy is wildly intriguing.

Exhilaration pulsates through my veins. Not only does La Dame Blanche exist, but Captain Parker wants *me* to join. What does he think I can offer that he can't get from dozens of other girls? I *know* I have a lot to give, and have long yearned to prove my father's faith in me. I just didn't realize anyone *else* knew.

"Why me?" I ask, interrupting him midsentence.

He pauses and raises an eyebrow at my rudeness. My face heats.

"I told you that we've had our eye on you for some time now. The university entrance exams you took last fall were exemplary, and your former Girl Guide leaders say that your skills in languages and maths are the best they've ever come across, bar none."

Even though my father told me I was special my whole life, I find it hard to believe that someone of Captain Parker's caliber thinks so as well. I give him a faint smile. "So you want me to be a spy because of my ability to win games?"

"No one ever said we were going to send you to *spy*, Miss Donaldson. The women at La Dame Blanche do many things, including tracking the railroad schedules, helping Allied soldiers escape to unoccupied France, and keeping tabs on troop movements."

I cross my arms. It seems to me the captain is playing a game of semantics with me. He doesn't know that my father and I treated wordplay as if it were swordplay. "Isn't that, by definition, spying? Sir?"

The corners of his mouth curl upward. "Your father

always said you were a pistol. Spying isn't nearly as exciting as the novels would have you believe."

Again the question that popped into my head last night at the reception comes to mind. "Exactly how well do you know my father, Captain Parker?"

"I met him several times in the course of our duties," he says matter-of-factly. "Are you interested, Miss Donaldson?"

Of course I'm interested. But isn't spying incredibly dangerous? My mind leaps ahead to the moment when I'll have to tell my mother that I'm leaving. She's already lost a husband—can I really deprive her of her daughter? I chew my lip, considering my options.

"Exactly what would I be doing, Captain? If you don't mind my asking."

"I really can't go into details, but rest assured your particular set of talents is in great demand." His brows draw together as if he's considering his next words. "You know that La Dame Blanche isn't exactly a British organization, correct?"

I nod. That I did know. "It was originally started in Belgium, wasn't it?"

Captain Parker nods. "Yes. British Intelligence leapt at the chance to collaborate with them when they approached us. They were already well organized; they just needed additional funding, as well as access to some of our intelligence. They share with us and we share with them." He pauses. "To a point."

I file that away for later. Then something occurs to me.

"You're the head of MI5, which is primarily involved in catching out spies in Britain. MI6 gathers intelligence from abroad. Why are you recruiting for them?"

He seems taken aback at the question. "The two organizations overlap quite often. Now, if you're quite finished with your questions, I'd very much like an answer. Are you interested in training to become a member of La Dame Blanche?"

I waver. With all my heart I wish I could tell him yes. Working for La Dame Blanche, becoming a spy for my country—I don't know if I've ever wanted anything so badly except for my father to come home.

But my family has already sacrificed enough for king and country. I can't make my mother suffer more. Emotion tightens my throat as I give him the only answer I can. "Thank you for thinking of me, Captain Parker, but the answer is no. I'm quite happy where I am and my mother needs me." I stand. "I will of course keep the details of this offer in the strictest confidence."

The captain's jaw works. This is a man who doesn't like to be told no. "Sit down, Miss Donaldson."

A shiver runs down my back. That's an order if I've ever heard one. I slowly resume my seat.

Captain Parker stares at me. He is tapping his fingers on the desk, apparently in no hurry to continue. I attempt to meet his eyes, but his gaze is so steady that I'm forced to look away. Tension runs across my shoulders, and still he waits. Any idea I may have had that I could beat this man at wordplay or anything else flees my mind. Finally his fingers stop tapping and he sits back in his chair. "Miss Donaldson, I'm hoping you'll reconsider. I think you could be an important asset to the Allied agenda."

I look away, unable to meet the intensity of his gaze. "If I do reconsider, I'll let you know. But I wouldn't count on it. I must think of my mother. I'm all she has now. Thank you for your offer, though."

"That's very commendable, Miss Donaldson. But I believe that duty to one's country is at least as important as love of one's mother."

He sounds sincere, and for a moment I'm tempted. Under other circumstances, I would jump at the chance, but as things are . . .

"Of course. But I don't think my father would want me to leave my mother alone."

His brows rise. "Are you so sure of that? George Donaldson spent his life in the service of his country, as did his father before him. For that matter, your mother, before she married your father, was a lady-in-waiting to the queen, and your great-grandmother served with Florence Nightingale in the Crimean War. You might say that service is in your blood, Miss Donaldson. Are you so very sure that your parents would tell you to forsake your country because of family?"

My mouth drops open. *And I thought he didn't know who I was.*

Captain Parker leans back in his chair with an air of

smugness, as if I couldn't possibly argue with that. He's quite right, I can't, but then again, I don't have to. I lift my chin.

"Perhaps, or perhaps not, but that's for me to decide, Captain Parker, and I've made my decision."

"Miss Donaldson, I understand your position, but as I said, there are reasons La Dame Blanche and the Allies need skills like yours. I was hoping you and I could make an even trade."

I frown. "What do you mean?"

"We thoroughly investigate all La Dame Blanche candidates before offering them positions with the organization. As I was going through your history, I came across some discrepancies in the reports concerning your father's disappearance. If you accept our offer, I would be happy to look into the matter further."

It's as if someone suddenly punched all the air out of me. I *knew* something about my father's disappearance wasn't right.

His contingent had been waylaid in the Arabian Desert while on a diplomatic mission to Tripoli. But while most of the delegation made it home, my father did not. In fact, he was the only one taken by Ottoman soldiers. The report stated that he was most likely targeted as the official ambassador of the group.

I spent the first several months after his disappearance haunting the War Office searching for any information they might have overlooked. At first, the office staff was sympathetic and helpful and even let me go over some of the eyewitness reports, but they must have lost patience with me, because eventually doors began to slam in my face. Even formerly helpful aides shooed me off.

But now I know I was right. There was more.

Captain Parker and I stare at each other. "And I take it you won't investigate my father's disappearance unless I join La Dame Blanche?"

He sighs. "Miss Donaldson, there's a war going on. My time is valuable. If you're willing to sacrifice your time for me, then I'd be willing to sacrifice a bit of my time and my staff's time for you and investigate the incident further. If you choose not to join us, I'd have to spend that time searching for another candidate to take your place."

My mind races. As an officer and a member of Military Intelligence, Captain Parker would be able to find out more than I ever could about my father's disappearance. The question is, Can I trust that he'll follow through or is he merely saying this to get what he wants? But why would he do that? Another thought strikes me—yes, my mother would be devastated if anything happened to me, but wouldn't her relief if we actually got some solid news about Father be worth the risk? My heart drums in my ears as I make my decision. Standing, I place my hands on his desk. "How do I know you'll do as you say?"

Instead of being insulted by my question, he nods, as if expecting it. "First off, you have my word as an officer in the king's army. Secondly, you're a smart girl." Pushing a packet across his desk, he leans forward, his eyes gleaming at his little victory.

"Checkmate."

The next hour passes in a blur. I leave Captain Parker's office, make my way to the Girl Guides' break room to snatch up my coat and lunch pail, and take the Tube home. It isn't until I pause at the bottom of the front steps that I take stock of the situation.

One, I'm being bullied into being a spy.

Two, I'm going to be a *spy*.

Three, I'm equal parts resentful and excited.

I believe that covers it.

Shaking my head, I hurry up the steps, impatient to look inside the folder Captain Parker handed me so casually. Bridget must have heard the door, because she's there in moments, clucking her tongue.

"You'll catch your death if you keep gadding about, you poor dear."

"I'll be fine, Bridget, thank you."

She hangs up my things and shoos me off to the sitting room. "Your mother is reading, I believe," she tells me. "Or pretending to."

I take a minute to draw a couple of deeps breaths and compose myself. I wonder if I'm being too optimistic about Captain Parker's promise to look into my father's disappearance. What can he possibly discover? I know I'd like to believe that my father is alive somewhere and that Captain

Parker will find him and bring him home, but is that just wishful thinking? What if Captain Parker is leading me down a rabbit hole for his own ends?

I take one final, cleansing breath and go to face my mother.

She looks up and gives me a weary smile. "You're home early. What a nice treat. I haven't had tea yet, would you like to join me?"

Even though I'd rather run up to my room and open the packet Captain Parker gave me, the wistfulness in my mother's expression compels me to join her.

"Is Rose back from school?" I ask.

My mother shakes her head. "Your aunt Elaine collected her, saying she was on the verge of forgetting what her daughter looks like."

I breathe a sigh of relief. Rose would know in a minute that something was going on with me.

"What's that?" Mother nods toward the packet still under my arm.

I bite my lip. "Just something from work."

Bridget brings in our tea and a plate of almond biscuits. Mother and I fall into our customary silence as we eat. The packet, which I'd tucked next to me in the chair, feels as if it's burning into my thigh, and the knowledge that I'm about to leave my mother, when she has already been through so much, hurts all the way to my toes. Yet what choice do I have? If Captain Parker knows something about my father, I *must* find out what it is.

How am I supposed to tell my mother about my impending

absence? Captain Parker didn't give me instructions about that. He just handed me a packet and told me a motorcar would be picking me up at five a.m.

Then he bade me good day and waved me out.

"I had a meeting with Captain Parker today. He offered me another position." I think quickly. "I'm to be Miss Tickford's assistant."

Mother folds her hands in her lap. "Congratulations, darling. I know you were a bit bored being a messenger girl. When do you start?"

"Immediately. We'll actually be leaving in the morning for a short trip." I take a bite of my last almond biscuit, which suddenly tastes like dust.

"And where would you be going?" Only the fine quiver of her bottom lip betrays her surprise.

Lying has never been my forte, but if I'm to join La Dame Blanche, I suppose I'll have to get used to it. "Liverpool and Plymouth."

I make a note to myself to inform Captain Parker about the cover.

"How long will you be gone?"

"I'm not sure. Several weeks, at the very least."

Mother's smile becomes fixed. "You'll be wanting to go pack, then."

Which means that she wishes to be alone to take in this new development. My heart squeezes tightly in my chest as I stand. "Yes. I'll be down for supper."

Once in my room, I open the packet and dump the

contents out on the large desk my father had built in the bay window. Bridget must have had the maid light a fire while I was having tea, because the room is cozy and warm.

Taking a seat, I inspect each item carefully. There's a typewritten letter, travel papers with a fake name, and a packing list. I turn to the letter first. There's no signature, but I can almost hear Captain Parker's voice as I read.

*Dear Miss Donaldson,*

*Enclosed you will find the papers necessary to complete the first leg of your journey. I have no doubt that you will be a credit to your family and your country. You can be assured that you'll be properly compensated for any inconvenience in the manner in which you most desire.*

*We'll be sending updates on the wonderful job you're doing to your mother. Packing instructions are included.*

*Thank you for your service.*

I throw the letter down, frustrated. I'm going to get into a motorcar to go God only knows where, to be trained to do God only knows what, all so Captain Parker will investigate my father's abduction. For all I know, he may not find out anything new. Clenching my teeth, I pick up the list of things to bring. They include toiletries and warm clothing, which are basic and included on any trip. At the very bottom are several words that make no sense at all. It takes me a moment to realize they must be in some sort of code.

*Ghvwurb diwhu uhdglqj*

I snatch up a pencil and paper and my fingers race. In addition to playing our math games, my father used to leave coded little notes for me around the house. After several minutes I grasp that it's an easy three-shift Caesar cipher, where the letters are simply shifted down the alphabet by three. I scoff. It's one of the first puzzle codes my father taught me.

*Destroy after reading*

Bridget knocks on the door and I startle. Her disapproval is evident in the tightness of her jaw and the stiffness in her back. "I hope you know what you're doing," she says, leaving a large leather satchel on the foot of my bed. Her tone implies that she doubts very highly that I do.

Somehow I make it through the rest of the evening, though I'm so nervous that even the scraping of cutlery on the china makes me jump. My mother doesn't seem to notice that anything is wrong. Or does she? After supper she gives me an uncharacteristic hug before inquiring politely about my travel plans. I tell her what I know, that a car will be picking me up in the wee hours of the morning, and she nods.

"We'll say good-bye now, then."

My chest tightens as my mother presses her cheek against mine and pulls me in for a warm embrace. "Sleep well, my dear," she says.

But sleep eludes me. After checking to make sure I have everything, I carefully burn the papers in the coals left in the fireplace, keeping only the travel documents.

At a quarter to five, I wrap my wool coat around me, pull my tam over my head, and walk down to wait in the foyer. My hands are so slick with sweat that I can barely maintain a grip on the satchel.

The stone statue of Diana in the corner, the potted palm, and even the bookshelf full of books take on a strange and unfamiliar quality in the early morning light. There's a light tap on the door and, taking a deep breath, I open it. The driver reaches for my things with barely a glance in my direction.

I follow him to the motorcar parked in front. He places my bag in the boot and then opens the door for me without a word.

I start to crawl in but hesitate a moment when I see a woman already in the backseat. As I slide in, an expensive French perfume assails my nose. Glancing sideways, I note that the woman is wearing a fashionable fur coat and her felt hat has a sweeping brim that partially obscures her face. The dim light reveals carnelian-red lips and matching fingernails. A gleaming chignon of dark hair sits low on her neck. The woman leans forward and taps on the glass separating the driver from the passengers. The little silver bells hanging from her pierced ears tinkle enticingly as she moves.

She turns to me and I see that her green eyes are daringly rimmed with kohl. Her allure is so potent, so chic and modern, that I blink.

"Are you hungry?" the woman asks. "I think we can get tea at the station."

I frown as her voice, tantalizingly familiar, tickles my ear. Except something about it is just slightly off, like looking the wrong way through a spyglass. "Who are you?" I ask.

Even her laugh is charming. "Samantha! Don't you know me?"

She faces me and removes her hat. It takes my stunned brain several seconds to recognize who it is, and when I do, my heart slams into my chest.

Miss Tickford.

# PART II

*Spy Craft*

# FOUR
## IRXU

*Swallow: An attractive female agent used to seduce people
in order to obtain intelligence information.*

"What? How?" I'm pretty sure I look as idiotic as I sound.

Her mouth twists. "My alter ego's disguise must be very convincing." She sticks out her hand. "Perhaps we should reintroduce ourselves. My name is Letty Tickford and I'll be your handler."

My world tips for a moment as I try to grasp this new reality. I shake her hand automatically and blurt out the first thing that comes to mind. "What on earth is a handler?"

She smiles. "Your trainer and point of contact when you go in the field. I'll be your handler, so you'll be sending messages to me and I'll be sending them to you, through various people and methods, of course. It's important for you to remember that you must trust only me and the people I trust."

My suspicion gets the better of me. "Trust you? I don't even know who you are!"

She folds her hands in her lap, her lips twitching. "Tell me, what do you wish to know?"

"Is Letty Tickford your real name?"

"You don't believe me?" she asks, amused. "Why not?"

I cross my arms, feeling as if I've been had. "I find all this a bit disturbing, especially so early in the morning."

Her grin widens. "You always were like a little old woman inside a young girl's body."

My cheeks flame. "Are you making fun of me?"

Her smile disappears and her expression becomes serious. "No, little one. Your maturity is actually one of the reasons you were chosen for LDB. There are assignments that only someone with your talents can carry out."

I raise an eyebrow. "Captain Parker said the same thing. What sort of assignments do you mean?"

Miss Tickford shakes her head. "We'll discuss that later. First, I must make sure you understand the gravity of the situation. While you're perfectly suited to help us, MI6 isn't in the business of sending girls to their deaths. But it *is* important that you understand that most of our agents are now considered officers, not spies. Think of LDB as an auxiliary, albeit secret, military operation. Once trained, you'll be considered an officer."

I frown. "Why is that so important?"

She regards me, and I notice that her green eyes are no longer childlike, but instead crackle with intelligence and energy. "Because the punishment for betraying your country is much more severe for an officer in the king's army than it is for a common citizen."

I straighten. "I'd never betray my country!"

She pats my hand and nods. "I know. But the lines of loyalty and betrayal are often blurred in our line of work."

Miss Tickford lets that sink in for a moment and then continues.

"I was delighted when Captain Parker told me that you'd be joining us. I think you're an extraordinarily talented young woman—and our organization is in desperate need of talented young women."

I wait, knowing there's more.

She tilts her head to one side as if deciding how much to reveal. "While I can't tell you about the type of assignments you'll receive, I can tell you that you'll be undergoing a short period of rigorous training. Only after you've successfully completed that training will you be given your first assignment. Now you may ask me a few questions, if you like. I may not be able to answer them all, but will if I can."

"How long have you been a part of La Dame Blanche?"

Her brows arch in surprise as if she hadn't expected me to ask anything personal. But why wouldn't I? Her transformation is dizzying.

"For a little over a year. Because of my background, I was uniquely qualified to be a liaison between La Dame Blanche and MI6. I accepted immediately."

I want to ask her what her background is, but I know from experience that she dislikes talking about herself, so instead I ask her what she's doing working at MI5.

"Recruiting."

I nod. That makes sense. "Where are we going?"

"Our first stop is Verdun. Your training will begin there."

"And then?"

"We will move to another location for some specialized training."

"After that?"

She shakes her head. "After that we shall see."

I digest that, then ask curiously, "What will I be learning during this training?"

"You'll be learning everything you need to know as an officer of La Dame Blanche."

I refrain from snorting. She's telling me nothing, really, so I change tactics. "What do you know about my father's disappearance?"

She startles and I grin. She's not the only one who can surprise people.

"I don't know anything about his disappearance that you don't already know." She reaches out and her gloved hand touches my arm. I look up and her green eyes are soft with sympathy. "I wish I did, Samantha. But I don't."

I detect no deceit in her voice, but then, until a few minutes ago, I had no idea that mousy Miss Tickford was a beautiful spy, so I should be on my guard.

The motorcar pulls up to King's Cross Station and the driver hops out to open Miss Tickford's door. I scoot out after her while he gets the bags. He pulls out our cases and follows us into the train station.

Most of the people milling about are soldiers, and I marvel at how awake everyone is. Of course, they probably slept last night, which I most assuredly did not.

The train trip to Dover is uneventful. Miss Tickford takes out a small pillow and dozes in the cramped compartment. In spite of my lack of sleep, I'm oddly awake. What sort of assignments am I uniquely suited to? Yes, I'm good with puzzles, codes, and languages, but surely MI6 has other employees who are also good at such things.

Fog obscures the early morning light as we reach our destination. The damp chill seeps through my coat and I shiver. My legs inch forward like blocks of concrete and a giant yawn almost splits my head in two. A porter takes care of our luggage while Miss Tickford guides me through security.

Crossing the Channel by ferry isn't as common as it used to be. Though our submarines and military vessels are regularly patrolling the waters, we know that the Germans have U-boats out as well. Travel between countries, except by military personnel, is rare now. I hold my breath as I hand the officers my fake papers, but they don't question them at all.

Once we're in the comparative warmth of the salon, Miss Tickford buries her nose in her book. I walk over to the window and look out. The mist is rolling over the water in eerie waves and I pull my collar up around my neck. Shivers dance up and down my spine as the ferry slides noiselessly through the water. There could be U-boats stalking us at this very moment. The sun is beginning to burn through the fog, causing glittering streams of light. The beauty doesn't ease my anxiety, so I take a seat and shut my eyes.

Miss Tickford seemed surprised when I brought up my father. I hope that's the truth. I desperately want to trust her.

When the ferry arrives in France, we're instructed to wait to take our leave until the servicemen and nurses have disembarked. Again, my papers are not questioned. I wonder if Miss Tickford is also pretending to be someone else or if it's just me. Why don't they want anyone to know I've left the country?

So if I don't return, I can't be traced?

I shiver. Part of me wants nothing more than to bolt back home as quick as I can, but I shove the thought from my head. I must concentrate on completing my training and assignment, so Captain Parker will investigate my father's abduction.

After the train departs from the station for Verdun, Miss Tickford orders tea from a passing porter. I wolf down the biscuits, longing for something more substantial, but beggars can't be choosers.

When we're finished, Miss Tickford leans toward me, her eyes serious. "You must listen carefully and remember everything, all right?"

I nod and she continues. "The Germans have a far more advanced espionage network than the British or the French do. The Abwehr—their intelligence organization—has been key to the Germans' military success. I'm afraid that we're playing catch-up."

Her head is close to mine and the urgency in her voice is clear. "The women of La Dame Blanche are largely responsible for what intelligence success we've had. As one of us, the work you'll be doing is crucial."

A little kick of elation erupts in my chest and I lower my eyes to avoid showing her the excitement that seems so inappropriate. Men are dying and here I am, thrilled to be chosen to spy.

She seems to know how I'm feeling, though, because she reaches out and tweaks a loose curl. When I look up, startled, she smiles, her green eyes glittering.

"You may have found playing errand girl for the men of MI5 dull, but trust me, little one, being a spy for La Dame Blanche is far, far from boring."

# FIVE
## ILYH

*Ears Only: Material and information too sensitive to be put in writing.*

**B**y the time we reach Verdun, I'm stiff from sitting, and my muscles protest as I follow Miss Tickford off the train. I glance around, struck by the tension in the station.

"Everyone is getting ready for the spring offensive," Miss Tickford murmurs as we gather our cases. "Come along, we're going to walk."

The Germans had invaded France last summer with their sights set on Paris, but were stopped just outside of Verdun. The civilians and the military personnel of this small city look equally grim.

I follow close behind Miss Tickford. I'm glad for a chance to stretch my legs. The fishy scent of the river Meuse wafts through the air of this tiny city of church spires and quaint gables. The trees on the hills surrounding the city are still bare of leaves. It's hard to believe that the front is just a few miles away.

I shudder as if the proverbial ghost has crossed my grave.

"Where are we staying?" I ask.

Miss Tickford slows a bit. "A little farm just outside of town. We have training houses all over France and we alternate our use of them so we don't arouse suspicion. It's a short walk, and I wanted to go over some of our expectations during this part of the training."

I nod.

"You won't be allowed to roam about on your own. It's important that we keep our presence here as low-key as possible. There are informants everywhere."

"In France?" I ask, surprised.

"Everywhere," she says firmly, and then continues. "While here, you'll talk to no one except myself and your cryptography instructor. And, of course, the housekeeper. Beyond codes, we'll be teaching you how to use a gun, how to defend yourself physically, how to make dead drops, brush drops, and live drops, among many other necessary skills. After that, you'll be smuggled into Luxembourg, where we'll prepare you for your first assignment."

I nod. Luxembourg's been occupied for almost eight months and is completely overrun by the German military.

We turn into the wide, circular drive of a large white farmhouse surrounded by stone outbuildings. The shutters on the multipaned windows are blue; the door is a sedate green. I spot a pond behind the house, and in the yard, chickens peck at the ground in search of bugs.

Standing outside the front door, as if he'd been expecting us, is a tall middle-aged man in a plaid cap. He frowns at me and I look to Miss Tickford for guidance.

"Monsieur Elliot, how nice to see you again. This is Rosemary James. She'll be our guest for the next several weeks."

*Rosemary?* Of course, the name on the papers. "It's a pleasure to make your acquaintance, Monsieur Elliot."

The man tips his hat, revealing a round, bald head fringed with dark red hair. Then he turns to Miss Tickford and speaks in rapid French. "This is what you're bringing us these days? She's not only wet behind the ears, I bet she's in nappies as well. What am I supposed to do with this? What could such a baby know of codes and ciphers?"

My face burns and I realize that this man who looks like a French farmhand is my cryptography teacher. I answer in French before Miss Tickford can reply. "I assure you, monsieur, that while I may be wet behind the ears, I am *not* wearing nappies. I can also assure you that I have a working knowledge of almost every common code in existence, including the Vigenère cipher. I look forward to our studies."

Monsieur Elliot raises an eyebrow and bends over my hand. "Touché, Mademoiselle James. My apologies. We'll meet in the library right after supper to see just how much you know."

He takes Miss Tickford's bags and goes inside.

The rooms inside the house are small and cramped, but the walls look as if they have been freshly whitewashed and the red tiles on the floor are immaculately clean.

Madame Ducat, the stern-looking housekeeper, shows

me to a small, tidy room. The bed is narrow and pristinely white, with two soft down pillows. I place my satchel on a trunk next to the door and, barely pausing to kick off my shoes, stumble across the room to the bed.

By the time a knock on the door wakes me for dinner, the sun has disappeared. I run a brush through my hair and twist it into a low knot at the back of my head, doing my best to calm the unruly curls. Slipping on my shoes, I try to press the wrinkles out of my dress with my hands, and I hurry to join the others for dinner.

In a house full of tiny rooms, the dining room is an exception. A cheerful fire crackles in a large fireplace on one wall, while a large, dark cabinet holding glasses and pottery fills the other. The gleaming table could seat a dozen or more people, though at the moment, only two are sitting together at one end.

"Did you sleep well?" Miss Tickford asks.

I nod, taking a seat. "I did, thank you."

The housekeeper serves a beef consommé with thin shavings of carrots and leeks floating in it. I concentrate on not wolfing it down and let the conversation wash over me. I almost miss it when someone says my new name. I look up, startled. "Excuse me?"

They exchange looks and I wonder if I just failed some sort of test. What if Miss Tickford is already regretting her choice? I straighten. "My apologies. What did you say?"

Monsieur Elliot clears his throat. "I was wondering why

you agreed to join La Dame Blanche, mademoiselle."

"Please, call me Rosemary." I'm proud of myself for not even hesitating over the name.

He inclines his head. I dart a glance at Miss Tickford, but she continues to eat. I chew on my lip, feeling as if my answer will be weighed and scrutinized. My father, ever the diplomat, told me that in any new situation it's best to get people to root for you, whether they agree with you or not. In a case like this, where I'm dependent on other people to teach me what I need to know to survive, it's even more important. "As I'm sure you are aware, I was part of the Girl Guides. We'd all heard about a female espionage group, though we couldn't confirm it, of course. I couldn't pass up the opportunity to become a member and help my country in a more concrete way."

From the expression on his face, Monsieur Elliot isn't overwhelmed by my patriotism. "So you're ready to die for your country, mademoiselle? Be tortured for your country?" His voice echoes harshly in the sedate and proper French dining room and my heart slams against my ribs.

Miss Tickford's spoon clatters on the table.

"That's enough," she says. "There's no need to terrify her."

"There's not?" His features are stark in the gaslight and I can't believe I ever thought he looked like a genial farm-hand. "Shouldn't she know why we're recruiting children? Because so many of our more mature, experienced agents are missing. The more she knows, the more seriously she'll take her lessons."

He leans across the table toward me and I force myself not to back away.

"You'll be pretending to be someone you're not, and for the most part, you'll be doing it alone. If you're caught, you'll be thrown into prison, tortured for information you probably won't have, and quite possibly killed. Does this sound like a school vacation, mademoiselle?"

My eyes sweep to Miss Tickford, whose calm gaze is trained on me.

It's time to bluff.

I lift my chin. "Of course not, Monsieur Elliot. I'm well aware of the gravity of the situation, don't worry on that account. And I have *always* taken my lessons seriously, as you're about to discover."

I pause to butter my dinner roll. Only a slight trembling of my fingers shows my agitation. "It's true I have a lot to learn, but I think you'll find there are reasons why my superiors thought I'd be an excellent candidate. And please, call me Rosemary."

I take a bite of the roll, which tastes like sawdust, and give Monsieur Elliot a stiff smile.

Miss Tickford calmly resumes eating. The man across the table stares at me before bursting into surprised laughter.

"We shall see, Rosemary, we shall see."

# SIX
## VLA

*Plain Text: The original message or word before it is encrypted.*

After dinner, I met with Monsieur Elliot for two hours of decoding history and practice with a cipher disc. I actually enjoyed the lesson, in spite of Monsieur's disdain, and once even earned a grunt of approval that made me beam with pride.

Then I studied invisible inks and chemistry with Miss Tickford, whose specialty, it turns out, is poisons. Her other talent, not surprisingly, is disguises, but she said she would be teaching me more about that subject once we're in Luxembourg.

This morning, Monsieur Elliot is to teach me basic self-defense, which is why I'm standing in loose cotton trousers and an even looser artist's smock in a freezing outbuilding behind the house.

His face is serious as I join him. "You know what jujitsu is, don't you?"

I nod. "Isn't it from Japan, originally?"

"Yes. I took lessons several years ago from the Garruds, who studied the art in Japan and then opened their own jujitsu gymnasium in London. It's actually quite involved, so I'm only going to teach you a few basic moves in case you're attacked."

*They expect me to be attacked?* I shove the thought away and nod.

"Unfortunately, if you're attacked, you'll no doubt be wearing skirts, but I want to start off teaching you in trousers so I can see how you move. We'll have you practice in a dress before you go to Luxembourg. I'm teaching you four basic moves: the body drop, the escape wrist grab, an escape front strangle, and an escape back strangle.

"Let's begin with the escape wrist grab."

"Why not the body drop?" I ask. It sounds like the most fun.

"Because you'd be too sore for the rest of the lesson." Monsieur Elliot reaches out and catches one of my wrists. "What would you do if I grabbed you like this?"

Instinctively, I try to yank my wrist away, but his grip increases. I move to hit him with my other hand, but he catches it easily.

"Now I have both your wrists. What are you going to do?"

I bring my knee up swiftly, but he jumps back and twists one of my wrists. Within seconds I'm on my knees.

I glare up at him. "Uncle."

He immediately releases my wrists. "You'd be immobilized

in seconds, and they won't let go just because you scream or sob. Stand up."

I stand, rubbing my wrists.

"Now grab mine."

I do so as best I can even though his wrists are too large for my hands to encircle completely.

"The men who attack you are going to be bigger than you and stronger than you. You are only going to have two things on your side."

"What's that?" I ask sullenly.

"Surprise. They won't expect you to fight back."

"What's the second thing?"

He leans forward and his blue eyes bore into mine. "More surprise. They won't expect you to know *how* to fight back. Now tighten your grip."

I do as he commands and then he suddenly claps his hands. While they're together, he steps closer and jabs his hands into my stomach, causing me to lean back. In that moment he yanks his arms backward and I lose my grip.

I shake my head, frustrated. "I'll never be that fast."

"Yes, you will. Now let's do it in slow motion so you can observe the mechanics. Then you can try."

After I learn that technique to his satisfaction, he teaches me how to respond if grabbed from the front or from behind. By the time we finish, I've been on the floor six times and am not only sore but annoyed. Why don't I get to knock *him* to the floor?

"I think that's enough for now," he says. "I don't want you to overdo it."

Resentful, I lean in close. "There's something you haven't showed me."

Puzzled, he looks at me. "I told you, I'll teach the body drop later."

"Not that." Grabbing his shoulder, I pull him close to me, then sweep my leg under his, causing him to fall straight back onto his backside. I grin down at him. "That."

To my surprise, instead of getting angry or annoyed, he laughs. "Apparently, you don't need any instruction in *that*."

I snatch up my clothes and walk out of the barn with my nose in the air. The sound of his laughter follows me into the house.

I spend the next several weeks learning basic surveillance techniques with Miss Tickford, followed by more jujitsu. Most of the time, I feel completely inept, but when Miss Tickford and Monsieur Elliot take me out to teach me to shoot, I know the time has come to show them a thing or two.

"You'll be issued a small muff pistol and it's important that you know how to use it," Miss Tickford tells me. Monsieur Elliot stands behind us with his arms crossed, a sour look on his face. "Don't mind him," Miss Tickford says. "He doesn't think a lady should know how to shoot."

Monsieur Elliot snorts.

In response, she shoots off several rounds, getting respectably close to the center of the target.

"Women should stick to their poisons," Monsieur Elliot tells us. "They're better with them than they are with guns."

Irritation ripples through me. "Is that so?" I ask, quickly reloading the weapon. Bringing it up, I shoot it six times in quick succession, hitting the bull's-eye with every shot. Smirking at his stunned expression, I turn and hand him the gun. "I'm not a woman, I'm a girl, and my father taught me to shoot when I was nine."

This time it's Miss Tickford who's laughing as I walk back to the house.

My confidence grows daily with each new skill I master and each new challenge I overcome. I learn which kind of invisible ink works best with which paper, how to do a brush pass, and how to pick basic locks. Even though I worry about my mother, I have to admit the truth.

I'm having the time of my life.

But it is exhausting. I'm up before the sun each morning and I work far into the night.

I'm glad for the respite that studying codes with Monsieur Elliot affords me every evening. We're working in the library, which, with its comfortable chairs, giant stone fireplace, and low beams, is my favorite room in the house. With a pang, I'm reminded of all the hours I spent studying with my father. I swallow against the sudden pain and focus on my work, which has become increasingly challenging. We're now working more on theoretical codes and mathematics than on practical coding. I look up.

"Monsieur, can you answer me a question?" I ask.

His brows rise. "That depends on the question, does it not?"

I frown. "Do you always answer a question with a question?"

"Is that your question?" His voice is clearly amused.

I refrain from rolling my eyes. "No. We've been working on deciphering codes since I arrived. The work you've given me is getting more and more challenging. I'm good at this, I know I am. Now you know, too. But what are the chances of my actually getting a message in this kind of code?" I wave a paper filled with algebraic equations at him.

He can't quite hide the smirk on his broad face.

"Aha! I'm right! Why give me challenges I'm not going to use?"

He shrugs. "Do you know how rare it is to get a student as proficient as you? Have you not enjoyed the tasks?"

I smile and he continues. "After your work with LDB is finished, I'm going to recommend to Captain Parker that you be reassigned to a position more in line with your talents. Now off with you. I wish to read."

I stand to go and then hesitate. "So you think I'll survive spying for La Dame Blanche? You didn't when I first came."

He stills, his lined face falling into a tired mask. For the first time he looks older than my father. Usually his expression is so fluid and lively that it's difficult to tell, but now age marks his features like the sun marks a grape.

He waves me away. "Don't ask such stupid questions. Of course you'll return."

He sticks his nose in a book, dismissing me.

I go to my room but am too wound up to sleep. My mind

goes round and round with all the questions I have. After an hour, I give up. Perhaps a cup of warm milk and a book from the library will help me sleep. The house is still as I tiptoe down the stairs and I wonder if everyone is already in bed. I'm just rounding the corner to the dining room when voices from the library reach me. I'm biting my lip, unsure whether I should announce my presence or not, when I hear my name.

I glance back at the staircase, knowing I should return to my room, but I hesitate. Aren't I a spy now? Perhaps it's time to put my new skills to use.

Keeping close to the wall, I move toward the raised voices, stopping just before I get to the library.

"This is a ridiculous waste of time. You know that, don't you?" Monsieur Elliot's voice is tight, like he is trying to control himself.

"That's not for me to decide, Elliot, nor for you."

"*Merde!* She has brilliant ciphering skills, and yet instead of giving her a job where she can be of some use, they send her on a suicide mission!"

My breath catches and I strain to hear Miss Tickford's much quieter voice.

"You're being dramatic, Elliot. It's not a suicide mission."

"So you really expect her to return from Berlin? Or is your boss so blinded by the fact that she's the only one who can gain his objective that he doesn't care? What is it you're not telling me?"

There's a long silence and my heart races. *Berlin?* Surely

not. And what objective? What can I do that no one else can? I wait, trembling, for Miss Tickford's answer. When it comes, it doesn't exactly alleviate my fears.

"Don't be silly. I'm not going to just cut her loose. Once the goal has been achieved, I'll do my best to protect her."

"But that isn't your priority, is it."

"Of course not," she snaps. "We're at war. You know as well as I do that war is full of choices that would be unthinkable during peacetime. I value my agents and it is my intent to keep them safe at all times, but if it is one life against many, you can be sure I will choose the many, and so would you. She is the only way we're going to . . ." Her voice quiets and I strain to hear her words.

I swallow. They're sending me to Berlin and they don't expect me to come back. I've learned everything they've asked me to and more. I've earned the right to know what's going on.

Sometimes you *have* to upend the chessboard.

I stride into the library and stand in front of Miss Tickford and Monsieur Elliot, my body trembling. "I think it's time you clued me in to what's happening, don't you?"

Miss Tickford's face registers surprise.

Monsieur Elliot shrugs. "I thought you should have been told immediately, but what do I know?" He gives Miss Tickford a bitter look.

Miss Tickford regains her composure and twitches a shoulder. "Fine. Sit down and I'll tell you."

"Everything?"

She waves a hand. "Don't be absurd. We're spies. Of course I can't tell you everything."

She has a point, but still. "I think I'll stand."

Her lips curve as if she finds me amusing. "As you like. In the morning, we'll be leaving for Luxembourg, where you'll assume your new identity. You'll also be taking the oath to become a member of La Dame Blanche. After that you'll be traveling to Berlin."

"Berlin," I repeat.

"Yes, Berlin," she confirms. "We have received your assignment and we must get you to Luxembourg as quickly as possible."

Talking about this in such a calm manner seems almost obscene to me. My chest tightens with fear and I struggle to keep my voice even. "And just what will I be doing in Berlin?

Both Miss Tickford and Monsieur are silent and I know he is waiting for her to take the lead.

"You'll be extracting a valuable spy whose life may be in danger. Her handler has disappeared. Her code name is Velvet."

# SEVEN
## VHYHQ

*Cover: The persona and fictitious image constructed and maintained by an agent for the purpose of espionage.*

The cliffs of Luxembourg overshadow the entire city, and I stare out the window at the remains of the ancient fortress built precariously onto the side. How bold and brash of human beings to think it could be done and how astonishing that they actually accomplished it.

Miss Tickford and I arrived at the safe house late last night after a cramped and nerve-racking twelve-hour ride up the Moselle River in a grain container and another four hours of jolting along in the back of a wagon, hidden under a pile of hay.

Upon arrival, we stumbled to our beds and collapsed. Turns out, fear is exhausting.

My stomach rumbles and I wish Miss Tickford would return with some food. We haven't eaten since yesterday.

I wonder if Velvet has enough to eat. I've been obsessing over her ever since I learned of her existence. A young woman, perhaps not so different from me, practiced in the art of espionage but still needing help.

My help.

The responsibility is almost overwhelming.

I push the thought of Velvet out of my head and stare out over the streets of the city. The people of Luxembourg seem to have adapted to occupation far better than the French— perhaps because the Germans allowed them to retain their government. They didn't come to pillage the tiny neutral country; they came to use it as a strategic entry point to France and Belgium. That fact shows on the streets as people go about their business in a much more relaxed manner than they did in France. Just then the noise of a motor hums above me and I duck my head to look upward. My throat tightens as two German aeroplanes fly overhead, making their way toward France. Tears sting my eyes and the war seems very real all of a sudden.

I spot Miss Tickford hurrying down the street and rush to open the door for her as she comes up the stairwell. The warm, yeasty scent of bread from the basket she carries tantalizes my nose.

"Food is definitely easier to obtain here than in France," she says as I follow her to the kitchen, salivating like a dog. "The difference between resisting and playing footsy with the enemy."

Right now, I'd play footsy with the kaiser himself for something to eat.

She takes out the bread, a crock of butter, a small wheel of goat cheese, a bunch of leeks, and a bottle of milk.

We eat right there in the kitchen at a small table covered in a lace cloth. In my advanced state of hunger, I find that butter has never tasted sweeter, cheese has never been creamier, and milk has never been so good and cold. It isn't until the loaf is half-gone that Miss Tickford gets up from the table.

After digging around under the sink for a minute, she produces a worn leather packet.

"Start with this," she says. "This is your cover."

I eye it suspiciously, half wishing I could just continue eating my meal and forget my mission for a few more minutes. Sighing, I wipe my fingers on the cloth napkin and untie the bindings on the packet. Unrolling it, I find a sheaf of papers, and lay them out according to their type—official travel and identification papers in one pile, pictures in another, statistics in another. Then I pick up the travel papers.

Sophia Thérèse von Schönburg, born 1895 in Bonn, Germany.

I look up. "I'm supposed to be twenty years old?"

Miss Tickford waves a hand. "Simple."

"Really?" With my blue eyes, pale skin, and curly blond hair, I look more like a Dresden doll than a twenty-year-old woman.

"Trust me, Samantha, we can make you twenty. Now go on."

I glance at the dossier and read aloud.

"Her parents were both killed in a carriage accident when

she was four and she was taken in by her father's eldest sister, the baroness Eugenie, whose husband, the baron von Schönburg, died early in their marriage. The aunt lived in a small town outside Cologne. She later married Captain Franklin Prosser of the British army."

I look up. "Who are the von Schönburgs? If the German aristocracy is anything like the English aristocracy, I'll need to know the lineage."

Miss Tickford nods. "I have more information on the family line that I'll give you later. All you need to know at this moment is that they're the distant relatives of the duchess Cecilie and therefore considered wellborn even if they don't run in the same circles. That connection is what is important here."

I stare at Miss Tickford, uneasiness crawling up my arms like ants. Duchess Cecilie is the wife of Crown Prince Wilhelm, the kaiser's firstborn son and the heir to the German throne. I glance over the paper, assimilating facts.

Sophia Thérèse was privately educated by an English governess provided by her new uncle, and she attended a small Lutheran church near the family estate.

I turn to the photographs. The first one is of a stern-looking couple. "Her parents?"

Miss Tickford nods.

The next photo is a woman with fair hair and broad cheekbones. "The aunt?" I ask, even though I already know the answer.

After another nod from Miss Tickford, I study a small

hand-colored portrait of a child who looks to be about nine years old. Like the others, she's fair, though the colorist has pinkened her cheeks unnaturally. I suppose there's enough of a resemblance to me if no one has seen her since childhood.

The next photograph is of a group of young people at a picnic. There are several girls in the picture and I have Miss Tickford point Sophia Thérèse out to me. Her cheekbones, like her aunt's, are wide, and she's grown stouter.

"Where is she now?"

"Captain Prosser snuck the family into Switzerland. They currently live in Davos."

I frown. "But how am I to—"

Miss Tickford interrupts me. "Sophia Thérèse died of influenza soon after she arrived in Davos. Mail service has been so disrupted since the war began that no one in Germany knows of her passing. You will assume her identity."

I sit back, the food I just consumed turning in my stomach. I'm to become a dead girl. I don't know why it didn't occur to me sooner, but it makes perfect sense. The dead tell no tales, after all.

"How did we get this information so quickly when we just learned of the assignment?"

"A ghoul put the packet together while we were still in Verdun."

"A ghoul?" I ask the question even though I'm not sure I want to know the answer.

She nods. "An operative who scans the obituaries and

death notices for someone whose identity we can steal."

I knew I shouldn't have asked.

Miss Tickford rises and goes back into the room where I slept last night—the maid's room off the kitchen. When she comes out, she's carrying a dusty bottle. "I thought the time was right for wine."

She uncorks the bottle and pours us each a glass. Raising hers, she toasts: "To Sophia Thérèse. May your passing save the lives of others and do good unto the world."

I toast, feeling a bit better.

"Come, let's finish this in the sitting room, yes?"

I take my glass and the papers, while she takes the bottle.

"So. Your assignment." Miss Tickford kicks her shoes off and tucks her feet up underneath her skirts. Her dark, abundant hair has loosened, and tendrils fall about her face. I've never seen her look so relaxed, and her beauty is incandescent in the evening light.

"I told you that the German intelligence network is far superior to ours, did I not?"

I nod.

"La Dame Blanche is one of the most successful answers to the Abwehr so far. There are a few others, of course, but as LDB has obtained the cooperation of several governments, it's the most effective. Not to mention the fact that the other networks are primarily made up of men—there are some things that women just do better."

I nod. "That makes sense. Men don't suspect us as easily."

Miss Tickford tilts her wineglass in my direction. "Correct.

When women scurry about with their marketing baskets, men assume they're getting food for their children rather than counting train cars or soldiers. You'll assume Sophia Thérèse von Schönburg's identity and travel to Berlin to assist the governess who teaches the kaiser's grandchildren. Just as with English royalty, the kaiser's personal servants are all family members or highly placed aristocrats. So your dear cousin Cecilie was more than happy to discover that her young relative wishes to serve the royal family. You will, of course, have to memorize who all the children are. She has run heavily to boys, as is common in the House of Hohenzollern."

"How many?" I asked, alarmed. I know very little about children other than the fact that they're rather loud and messy. Especially boys.

Miss Tickford grins, as if sensing my thoughts. "Three boys, as well as several other children of relatives who live in the City Palace."

"So while looking after a bunch of children, I'm also supposed to be helping a spy named Velvet to escape?"

"Precisely. But remember, Velvet is only her code name."

I lean back in the chair. "Oh, that's right. What is her real name?"

She hesitates. "That's the problem," she admits. "We don't really know."

I stare at her. "What does that mean?"

Miss Tickford takes a careful sip of wine, her face blank. "It means, little one, that you must discover who Velvet is on your own *before* you approach her. Her handler knew who she was, of course, but gave us precious few details and seems to have disappeared. Colonel Landau, a French operative and liaison between La Dame Blanche and the French intelligence agency, knew who she was, but . . ." Miss Tickford pauses, with a shrug.

"But what?" I ask, a cold, nameless fear starting in my stomach and moving through the rest of my body.

"He was found dead in his bed four weeks ago. The victim of an accidental, or not so accidental, overdose of laudanum."

My jaw drops. "You're not serious."

From the look on her face, Miss Tickford is deadly serious.

I lean back in the chair and close my eyes for a moment. When I open them, I ask, "So there are no paper records? What about her next of kin? Won't they be notified if something happens to her?"

For a moment I think she's not going to answer, but when she does, her voice is as empty as her face. "All records related to Velvet's identity seem to have been . . . misplaced."

"This is bloody impossible!" I explode. "You're sending me on a suicide mission, just like Monsieur Elliot said."

She takes a deep breath and gives me a small smile. "Of course not. We wouldn't send you into Berlin without a plan, or without confidence that you can successfully complete your assignment. We do have some idea who Velvet is—of course we do. Just think of it as the most perplexing puzzle you've ever been challenged to solve."

A hysterical giggle erupts from my mouth, though I find

nothing funny about the situation. "What you're telling me is that everyone who knew Velvet's identity is dead."

"We don't know if her handler is dead," Miss Tickford says sharply.

I snort. "That's comforting." The wine and food churn in my stomach. "Just what kind of information has Velvet been passing to us?"

When she hesitates, I stand, my fists clenched by my sides. "If you don't tell me, I'll walk out of here—see if I don't. If you're sending me in there blind, the least you can do is give me what little information you have."

"And where would you go, Samantha?" Miss Tickford asks, her voice quiet. "You're in an occupied country."

*Stand your ground, Sam.*

I bend so my eyes are level with hers. "If you have so little faith in me that you don't believe I could make my way back to England, how on earth do you think I'll be successful in Germany?"

She lifts her chin and her green eyes bore into mine. The room is so quiet I can hear the ticking of the grandfather clock.

After a long moment, Miss Tickford shrugs. "Fine. Now have a seat and quit standing over me like a disgruntled schoolteacher. I'll tell you what I know."

I sit, only partially placated.

Miss Tickford continues as if the little confrontation hadn't taken place. "We know that the information she passed on could come only from a firsthand source. So she's

71

either very close to the kaiser's family, so close that her presence wouldn't be out of place at either the palace or the Reichstag building, or she's the mistress of someone who has intimate knowledge of German strategy."

I raise an eyebrow. "She could be both."

"Right," Miss Tickford agrees. "Germany's aggressive ground tactics have been devastating, but Velvet's detailed information on troop movements has saved countless lives. The project she's working on now is even more important."

"And what is that?"

"German scientists are developing a new weapon. We believe it has something to do with explosives, and according to the information we've received thus far, the results are going to be devastating."

My mind is racing. "And Velvet's trying to find out what it is?"

"Yes, we believe she is very close."

"And she's in danger?"

Miss Tickford nods. "As you said, everyone who knows who she is has been neutralized in some way. We're concerned that she may fall into enemy hands."

I digest that for a moment. Then something occurs to me. "Are you more concerned about Velvet or about getting information on the weapon?"

Miss Tickford's face stills. "La Dame Blanche and the British government do everything in their power to ensure the safety of their agents and their citizens. Though, clearly, obtaining both Velvet *and* the information on the new weapon would be preferable."

My eyes narrow. I bet it would.

"We're in the middle of a war, Samantha. Don't be a child."

I press my lips together and keep quiet.

Miss Tickford clears her throat. "We've come down to two likely candidates. It will be your job to ferret out exactly which young woman it is."

"How did you narrow down the field?" I can't believe I'm accepting all of this as if it's not the most ridiculous thing I've ever heard.

"Some of the women who were possibilities were ruled out immediately. Their loyalty to Germany is beyond question or they simply don't have access."

"Isn't loyalty beyond question a good quality to have in a spy?" I ask. "She wouldn't have access to such valuable information if she weren't considered loyal beyond question."

Miss Tickford gives me an approving nod. "Of course, you're right. We're just making educated guesses at this point."

"So you're sending me to find someone based on educated guesses?"

"I never claimed the assignment would be without risk," she says sharply.

I nod, biting back the bitter words that threaten to spill over.

*Patience, Samantha. Remember, the end goal is checkmate.*

I sigh and hold my tongue.

Miss Tickford stands and walks over to an imposing dark cherry wood secretary stuffed with china. Opening the cupboard, she fiddles with the bottom shelf until it comes loose. Then she pulls out a dark leather folder and glances through the contents.

"Go over these and then start working to complete a biography on Sophia Thérèse. I'm going to retire. Remember when I told you that the person you're impersonating has to be fully realized?"

"Yes. That's how you were able to be someone else for so long."

"Precisely. Now you must do the same for Sophia Thérèse. Figure out how much of her is going to be you and vice versa. Remember, it's up to you to study her legend."

"Legend?" I ask, puzzled.

"Her history. Now I need to go lie down. I'm not as young as I used to be and sneaking into an occupied country is hard work." She smiles at her little joke and takes her leave.

I watch her go, nerves swirling in my stomach. Do she and Captain Parker really expect me to flush out a spy that the Abwehr has somehow missed? Shrugging off the feeling that I'm in completely over my head, I turn to the folder and study the women who may or may not be Velvet.

Marissa Baum is a pretty nineteen-year-old expatriate from the United States. Marissa's mother is related to the kaiser's wife, the empress Auguste Viktoria, and her father is a German immigrant who made his fortune in Chicago.

According to the file, she's a favorite of Prince Wilhelm's wife, Cecilie; the women are practically inseparable and have the run of Berlin. In spite of the fact that the duchess is married to the prince, the two women have been causing minor scandals with their hijinks—they dress up as men and sneak into private clubs and once even posed as café singers.

One can only imagine what the German royal family thought of that.

The other possibility seems to be the polar opposite of Marissa. Lillian Bouchard is the mature, quiet governess to the kaiser's grandchildren—and the woman I'll be working with most closely. She's half French, half German, and has been a trusted employee for the past several years. She's highly regarded by the Hohenzollern family and therefore can come and go as she pleases both at the Berliner Stadtschloss—the City Palace—and at the Marble Palace in Potsdam, just outside of Berlin.

I finally call it a night when I realize that I can't possibly shove one more fact into my head. One thing bothers me, though. How am I going to get close to Marissa? If she's a friend of the duchess, I hardly think we will be running in the same circles. Did MI6 or La Dame Blanche even think of this?

My stomach knots. If I can't trust *them* to think the mission through, that leaves me no one.

No one at all.

# EIGHT
## HLJKW

*Dead Drop: Secret location where materials or
information are left for another operative to find without
direct contact between the two agents.*

Not wanting to leave sensitive information lying around
the apartment, I take the packet into my room with
me and set it on the antique nightstand next to my bed.
My bedroom is narrow, with a large window behind the
bed and a giant red lacquer wardrobe on the opposite wall.
Miss Tickford has given me two drawers in the wardrobe.
Like the rest of the apartment, the room is sumptuously
appointed, with heavy velvet draperies, feather pillows, and
an ornate gold-framed mirror that's practically the size of
the wall it's leaning against.

Where does La Dame Blanche get its money? I run a finger along the silky-smooth finish of the wardrobe. Who pays
to let a beautifully furnished six-room apartment on one of
the most prestigious streets in the city sit vacant most of
the time?

As fatigued as I am, I'm too restless to crawl into bed
yet. Instead, I quietly open the different drawers and

compartments of the wardrobe, looking for clues to the room's prior occupant. Most contain normal guest room items—extra blankets and pillows, sachets filled with lavender. I'm just about to close the third drawer when I spot the corner of an envelope peeping out from underneath a pillow. Curious, I pull out the envelope and sit on the edge of the bed. I frown at the word scrawled on the front. *Leticia.*

I pull out four photographs. By the look of the clothes, they seem to have been taken about twenty to twenty-five years ago. One is of a young man with dark, slicked-back hair. Another is of the same man in a uniform, but I can't tell what sort it was. It definitely doesn't look British or French. Maybe Luxembourgian? Prussian? The next photograph is of a boy in a sailor suit sitting with a young girl wearing a hair bow as big as her head. I turn the photograph over. *Lawrence and Leticia.* Siblings, no doubt. I peer again at the picture. Yes, there's a certain similarity in the shape of their faces and in their coloring. The last picture is of a family—a mother and father posed with the same two children that were in the last photograph. Startled, I take another glance at the woman and gasp.

Miss Tickford.

Well, not exactly. The woman in the picture is stouter and older and the clothes are too old-fashioned, but the features are so similar that the woman in the photograph could be her mother.

I look at the other pictures again, my pulse racing. The young man and the little boy in the photographs are clearly the same person and there's a strong family resemblance among all of them. I peer closer at the photograph of the little girl.

It could be no one except Miss Tickford, which means the woman must be Miss Tickford's mother. But why are the photographs hidden away in a drawer? And why are they here? Could this be Miss Tickford's home? If so, where is her family?

I replace the photographs carefully in their envelope and crawl into bed. Instead of studying the papers, I turn off the light and ponder the mystery that is Letty Tickford.

The next morning, I try to put the pictures I found out of my mind. They aren't any of my business, but the questions they raise about who Miss Tickford is linger. Is this really her apartment? Where is her brother now?

I shake my head and focus on Sophia Thérèse. For all intents and purposes, the young woman whose identity I'm going to assume led a quiet life much like mine. She comes from a good family, is active in her community, and, though she's not overly social, seems to have a small, select group of friends. But how am I supposed to become her? I don't know her favorite color or food, or even her favorite book. Does she have a young man who is off fighting in the war right now with no idea that his sweetheart is dead? What sort of secrets would she share with her best friend, the way I share mine with Rose?

"Remember that the duchess has only met her young

cousin once, many years ago. She doesn't know any of Sophia Thérèse's mannerisms, either," Miss Tickford says when I bring up my concerns.

She joins me at the table and sets out a wooden box containing several small pots. "But there is one thing that you must learn immediately," she says.

"What's that?" I frown as she takes the lids off the pots, revealing two different rouge-color ointments and one powder. "Don't tell me that Sophia Thérèse was devoted to cosmetics?"

"No. But you're about to be."

I frown. "I don't understand."

"Sophia Thérèse had a small crescent-shaped birthmark on her right cheekbone."

My mouth opens. "I can't fake a birthmark!"

Miss Tickford smiles. "Oh, yes, you can."

I shuffle through Sophia Thérèse's photographs again. "I don't see one . . ." I stop, realizing that her face was always angled so that the camera caught only her left side. Then I come across the one of her as a toddler. I point. "She doesn't have one here."

"That photo was hand-colored," Miss Tickford says. "Her parents must have had it tinted out. We'll practice until you are comfortable duplicating the same mark over and over. And don't worry, you'll get used to it. Now put that stuff down and hold still."

I do as she says, and before I know it, I'm staring in the mirror. The mark isn't too big but it's definitely visible, and it makes me feel self-conscious. I wonder if Sophia Thérèse felt the same way and remember that her parents had the birthmark tinted out of her baby picture. My throat tightens in sympathy. No wonder she always turned her face away from the camera.

"Now let's go. We have to pick up a few things for you to assume your new identity."

"Like this?" I ask, and am immediately ashamed of myself. Poor Sophia Thérèse.

"You might as well get used to it," Miss Tickford says matter-of-factly.

Luxembourg City may be shadowed by the fortress that overlooks it, but the city itself is quite modern. Miss Tickford is wearing a smart gray walking suit with a black toque set atop her upswept hair. I feel out of place in the same wrinkled dress I've been wearing for the past two days. At least my coat covers most of it. We've already ordered a whole new ready-to-wear wardrobe for my new identity. Two walking suits, four simple blouses, and three fitted skirts with matching jackets.

Miss Tickford takes my arm and steps briskly down the street. "Now we go to the hairdresser."

"The hairdresser?" My voice rises at the end.

Her lips quirk upward in a smile. "How do you think we're going to make you look like a woman of twenty?"

I screw up my face, wondering what she means. Sophia Thérèse had white-blond hair, much like I do. Miss Tickford can't possibly mean she is going to have mine dyed. That wouldn't make any sense at all.

A few moments later, she takes me into a hair salon on a small alley just off the Boulevard Royal. A tall, slender man cries out and rushes toward us, babbling something in Luxembourgish. Miss Tickford replies, speaking so quickly that I know she must be fluent.

She touches his cheek briefly, then switches to German. "Antoine, this is Sophia Thérèse. I've brought her to pay homage to your genius."

I yelp as Antoine plucks out my hairpins and untwists my hair. Unbound, it falls to my waist.

"She wants to look older," Miss Tickford says.

"We'll go with a bob, then. With that bone structure and those curls, she'll look just like a golden-haired Polaire."

I blink, not at all sure my traditional mother would appreciate the comparison to the famous French actress and café singer.

"You're going to love it, you'll see." Then he picks up his shears and they hover over my head.

I squeeze my eyes shut, both thrilled and terrified. The scissors make a soft whoosh in my ears as they lay waste to my curls. My head lightens with every cut until I'm sure it's going to go floating off into the Luxembourg sky.

Antoine turns the chair away from the mirror and I open my eyes. I search Miss Tickford's face for a clue as to whether she likes it or not, but her expression is noncommittal. I look away, disappointed. Her feelings about my hair are irrelevant, as are mine. We're not preparing for a ball; we're spies working at making me look older so I'm not exposed as a traitor in an enemy country.

Because if I am, it won't matter what length my hair is.

Antoine holds out his hand and his assistant quickly gives him a pair of scissors so small they look as if they're used to clip the wings of fairies.

He snips here and there, taking his time. Then he takes a comb, parts my hair on one side, and scrutinizes it. Finally he nods. "I think we're done." He turns to Miss Tickford. "What do you think?"

She smiles. "The difference is extraordinary."

Antoine turns the chair around and I face myself in the mirror. My curls, which have always been weighted down, now spring about my face like silvery, flaxen flower petals.

"Well?" Antoine asks.

I see my lips curve in the mirror and it looks like the smile of a grown woman. A pretty, modern, grown woman. "I love it," I say simply, unable to explain how free I feel.

My eyes seek out Miss Tickford's and for a moment I see the delight in them, as if she were my mother and oh, so very proud of me. She blinks and turns away, pulling some notes out of her pocketbook. "Thank you so much, Antoine. You did a wonderful job."

"I always do. Now, when are you going to let me bob *your* hair?"

Miss Tickford gives a charming laugh. "Oh, I'll never cut my hair!"

We leave the shop and Miss Tickford wastes no time

getting back to work. "Now let's talk about the different types of surveillance and how to tell if someone is following you."

The lighthearted feeling I had in the shop dissipates and reality crashes in as we begin another lesson in spy craft. My life and the lives of others depend on how well I learn. I concentrate on her words.

"So remember, even if you notice someone following you, it is best if you give no indication of it."

"Why is that?" I ask.

"Because if he knows that you know he's following, you force his hand. He has to do something. Most of the time, he'll just disappear, but he may also confront you. You don't have any idea who he is or who he works for."

I nod.

"First off, if you're being followed, you do nothing. It's very important that you behave normally and nonchalantly, as we are right now. Watch to see if there is more than one person tailing you." She pauses to look in the window of a bakery. "Right now there are three."

"Three what?"

"Three people watching you. You can go back to the apartment as soon as you spot them."

I shoot her an uncertain glance. "Is this a test? Part of my training?"

"Of course." Miss Tickford turns to me with a smile and touches my sleeve. "Remember all you've learned of surveillance and don't forget that you're in an occupied country. If you make a mistake, the consequences could be irreparable. Once you've spotted all three people, you can come back to the apartment. It's on the rue Beck. Good luck."

"Wait!" I clutch at her sleeve. "How will I know?"

My voice trails off at the smirk on her face. She gently removes my hand and walks away.

My heart pummels my rib cage. Knowing that the first rule of being watched is not to let your follower know that you're aware of him, I force myself to move down the street.

Two German soldiers pass me by in their dun-color uniforms. One gives me a friendly smile, but I avoid his eyes and move quickly on.

I must collect myself. I pause on the street corner, trying to think. I'm completely alone in a strange city with only a vague sense of how to get back to the apartment, but at the moment, I have other things to worry about.

I glance behind me. I know I'm being obvious but can't help it. Panic threads its way through my body. This is my first big test and it looks as if I'm about to fail it completely.

All I see is men and women hurrying about their business like they do in any city of size. Most of the residents are wearing decent, if plain, clothing, and the streets are well cared for, as if the stoops and storefronts are scrubbed on a regular basis.

How am I supposed flush out the spies if I have no idea what to look for?

Then I spot a man smoking on a stoop just down the block from me. Unlike the other industrious, well-groomed

Luxembourgians, this particular man seems to be loitering, and his clothes are rough. I take a deep breath to fight off my anxiety and snap my fingers as if I'd forgotten something. Then I swiftly backtrack toward where the man is lounging, the brim of his hat pulled down low on his head and a newspaper tucked under his arm. He stands as I approach, then, without sparing a glance in my direction, tosses his cigarette into the gutter and hurries across the street, narrowly missing being run over by a trolley.

By the time the street clears he's gone, and I'm fairly sure I can tick off one of the people watching me. One down, two to go. How can I spot the others?

When I see a café across the street, I get an idea. Maybe I can have my tea and drink it, too.

I cross, dodging the motorcars and horses, and enter the café after a sweeping glance behind me. I don't see anyone watching me, but then I didn't really expect to. I order a cup of tea and then take a table next to the window. The two other patrons in the café pay me no mind and I force myself to sip my tea.

As I watch the people pass by the window, I'm hoping to see something out of the ordinary, like last time, or perhaps someone who looks familiar, like I've seen them pass by more than once. A young boy saunters by the window and I notice him looking inside. When he sees me, he glances away quickly, and I frown.

Would they enlist a child for this? No, it must be a coincidence. But then I see the same boy bouncing a ball slowly across the avenue and my suspicions get the better of me. I wait until his back is turned before slipping out of the café and across the street.

When he turns around and sees me, he flushes and darts away, but not before I notice that he has a rolled-up newspaper stuck in his back pocket.

A picture of the first spy walking away with a newspaper under his arm flashes in my mind. *That's* why Miss Tickford asked for a description. Each person watching me will be carrying a newspaper. Triumph erupts in my chest.

There's nothing more satisfying than figuring something out.

I glance around but see nothing peculiar. From the look of the sun on the horizon, it's been about two hours since Miss Tickford left me. I don't want to make my way back to the apartment in the dark. Besides, Luxembourg probably has a curfew, and the last thing I want is to get arrested for breaking it.

So how can I make the third tail reveal himself? I stroll toward the old part of the city, racking my brain. The metallic scent of ancient stone splashed with the blood of centuries floods the alleyways and thoroughfares. Spires rise above the city, casting needle-sharp shadows on the cobbled streets below. I shiver, forgetting my mission for a moment. The permanence of Luxembourg seems to mock occupiers and citizens alike, for what is another war to a city that has witnessed so many?

I shake my head, trying to dislodge the spell of the city.

There has to be a way to end this. Then my lessons on surveillance come back to me. You watch someone to note what they do, who they meet, et cetera. Every seemingly innocent action could be a sign to a fellow spy.

Even if this *is* just a test, how would they react if they thought I was making a dead drop? If it looked as if I, the student spy, were trying to contact someone outside of La Dame Blanche?

The curiosity would be too much. They would have to go see what I'd done and, by doing so, reveal themselves.

I hurry into a little stationery shop on the corner and buy a sheet of paper and an envelope. The dead drop must be clumsily done, as if by an amateur, but not so obvious that it looks like a trap.

I borrow a pen from the stationer—a short, dimpled girl no older than I am—and scribble a quick note. I seal the envelope and stick it into my purse. The city seems more like a modern metropolis now than a medieval outpost, though I'm sure that'll change after the sun retreats.

Making my way toward a patisserie with a large sign hanging on the façade, I look around as if wary of being observed.

Then I study the sign as if trying to decide if I want to go in to purchase myself a meat pie. I'm actually looking for a place to hide the envelope. Heart pounding in my ears, I stick the envelope behind the sign, just above one of the bolts attaching it to the stone wall. Then I bend and pick up a rock and casually set it atop the sign.

I look around again and then hurry back to the stationer's. The dimpled girl is still there and I smile. "I'm so sorry to bother you again, but there's someone out front whom I don't wish to see. A young man. Do you have a back way out of the store?"

An older person might have been suspicious, but the girl just smiles at me. "But of course," she says in French. "We girls must help one another, yes?"

With a swish of her skirts, she leads me through a cramped back room that smells of liverwurst, fresh bread, and ink. She points at the door.

"Thank you," I say.

"I adore your hair," the girls calls as I go out. "I've been longing to bob my hair forever, but my father says no. I'll do it when I'm eighteen, see if I don't!"

"You'll love it," I assure her and then step out into the twilight.

I stand in the shadows around the corner of the building and wait to see who, if anyone, will take the bait. They may be suspicious of a trap, but I'm counting on the distrustful nature of our work to lure them in. They're going to want to know what a La Dame Blanche trainee is doing leaving clandestine notes.

My eyes scan the quickly darkening streets. Whoever it is must still be watching the stationer's to see if I come back out. At some point they're going to realize that I've slipped away, and they'll go to pick up the note, I'm sure of it.

The minutes tick by. I stare at the sign, willing the person to come out and get it. My fists are clenched so tightly that my nails are digging half-moon-shaped grooves into my palms.

Just when I think it's not going to work, a man saunters up to the sign, pauses for a moment, and then walks on. If I hadn't seen the flash of white from the envelope, I wouldn't even have known that he had taken it.

Heart in my throat, I follow him down the street, almost running to keep up with his long strides. I try to remember what Miss Tickford taught me about trailing someone, but I'm too busy just trying to keep pace with him.

When he disappears down an alley, I hesitate. It could be a trap. I'm hoping he was so focused on the envelope that he didn't think to check if he was being tailed. I take a deep breath and edge around the corner of the building into the alley.

The man stops in a doorway and I watch as he pulls the envelope out of his pocket. I can't see his face, but the movement reveals a knot of silky dark hair under the collar of his jacket. I clap a hand over my mouth to stifle a gasp. My stalker isn't an unknown male at all, but rather a female, and one I know very well.

Miss Tickford.

# NINE
## QLQH

*Allegiance: Giving an oath of loyalty to one intelligence organization above all others.*

My shock turns into satisfaction as Miss Tickford reads the note. She's so daunting that I can't help the sense of pride that washes over me at having beaten her at her own game. She tosses the note away and then jumps as I say the words the note contained.

"Caught you."

Annoyance flashes over her face before she breaks into a reluctant smile. "Indeed. How did you know it was me?"

I shake my head. "I didn't until I saw your hair under your collar."

She nods. "Good eye. I didn't have much time to change into my disguise."

A thought comes to me. "Were you the first man, too?"

"Yes. I had to make a complete change while you were distracted by the floater."

"Floater?" I ask.

"Yes, the boy. That's what we call someone who is

unknowingly used in an operation only once." Her mouth twists into a smile. "The fake drop was an excellent idea, by the way, and you pulled it off well. Not many people get the better of me."

I glow at her words.

"Now, come along." She pulls her collar up to better hide her hair. "We should turn in early tonight. We have a busy day tomorrow."

"What are we doing?" I ask, even though I'm dreading her answer. Every time I master a new skill, I'm another step closer to being ready for the assignment, and the thought both terrifies and excites me.

"You'll be assuming your new identity, little one," she says matter-of-factly as she walks out of the alley. "Tomorrow you must become Sophia Thérèse von Schönburg."

Even though I'm exhausted, I have trouble falling asleep. The responsibility of the task ahead presses in on me.

I roll onto my stomach, trying to get comfortable. After returning from our outing, Miss Tickford changed her clothes and we ate a simple dinner of sliced beef and bread while she quizzed me about Sophia Thérèse. Afterward, she read for a bit before retiring to her own room. I wanted to ask her if the apartment is hers and what had happened to her brother, but there's something about her that discourages such questions.

I stare into the darkness, the apartment so quiet that my own breathing fills the space like a lonely ghost. Somewhere out in the world, my father is alive, I know it. Is he hurt? In pain? Is he as lonely and afraid as I am?

Suddenly the staccato beat of heavy footsteps splinters the stillness. I raise my head, staring hard into the darkness. Moments later, blinding light illuminates the room as my door is thrown open. I freeze in stunned disbelief and in that moment lose any chance to react. Rough hands yank me out of my bed. My attacker shoves a coarse, stifling hood down over my head and I'm half pushed, half pulled out of my room and down the hall. My heart slams against my rib cage.

"Take her into the kitchen," a female voice commands in guttural, almost incomprehensible, German.

My breath comes out in short gasps as fear squeezes my chest. I lift my feet in an attempt to topple the man holding me, but he rebuffs my feeble attempts as if I'm a child.

*What do they want? Where is Miss Tickford?*

As if reading my thoughts, the woman says, "We've already gotten rid of your friend, so she can't help."

*Gotten rid of her? What have they done?* My body shakes convulsively.

*The Germans have me.*

"Tie her to the chair."

The man silently, but firmly, sits me down. I struggle as he ties my hands and feet to one of the kitchen chairs Miss Tickford and I had sat in just hours before, studying Sophia Thérèse's life.

"What is your name?" The woman's voice is harsh and I whimper.

Frantically, I try to remember if Miss Tickford gave me any instructions on what to do or say if I was captured. Am I supposed to give my fake name or remain silent?

Someone grabs hold of my inner thigh through my night-dress and pinches so hard that tears spring to my eyes. Terror, hot and corrosive, shoots through me as I realize that my captors can do whatever they like to me.

I'm completely alone.

"I asked your name." The woman's voice is softer, and treacherously close to my ear.

Fear crawls across my skin.

*Stop and take a deep breath, Sam. And most importantly, think.*

My father's voice is clearer than it's ever been, and I take a shaky breath. He's right. I need to calm myself and think this through. I have no doubt they can make me talk if they want. The question is what I'll tell them.

"Who are you?" I ask in German, trying to keep my voice from trembling.

"*Nein.* You do not ask the questions."

Another pinch on my thigh renders me speechless. "Now tell us your name. Don't make me set Rickard loose on you."

*Think.*

I need to buy myself some time. I may not be able to do anything about it, but trying is better than giving up. "Sophia Thérèse," I tell her in German. "Now, who are you? What have you done with my friend? And what do you want with me?"

"Your friend will probably be killed. Luxembourg is not at war with Germany, and yet she betrays her own people by spying," the woman says. "The question is, Sophia Thérèse, what are you, an English girl, doing in Luxembourg?"

Thinking quickly, I switch from German to Portuguese. "How do you know I'm English?" I switch to French. "You didn't even know my name." I return to German, which I notice I speak with more precision and a much better accent than she does. "I could be from anywhere."

I suddenly freeze, my mind racing. The woman had said, "She's a traitor to her own people," *"Sie ist eine Verräter von ihr Volk,"* but the grammar was poor—she'd used *eine* instead of *ein* and *ihr* instead of *ihrem*, and she didn't pronounce her *v*'s as *f*'s as a true German would. It suddenly hits me so hard it almost knocks the breath out of me. Why can I speak German so much better than a supposed German? Because she's trying to hide an accent.

*The woman is not German.*

Then where is she from and why is she speaking in German? Because she wants me to think she's German. But why?

My mind races. Why didn't I hear anything before they rushed into my room? I wasn't sleeping and the house was silent. A surge of anger rushes through my body as it dawns on me who it is. I open my mouth but then snap it shut, afraid of what will come out.

There's only one reason someone would come into Miss Tickford's home and pretend to be German. To test me.

"Who's Lawrence?" I blurt.

The silence that greets my question tells me that I've hit the mark. I'd be elated if I weren't so furious.

After a few moments, the hood is pulled from my head. Miss Tickford is dressed in the same white blouse and moss-green skirt she'd been wearing earlier. *She didn't even go to bed*, I think, *while here I sit, embarrassed, in my thin white night-dress. She sat and waited until she thought I was asleep to strike.*

"You can untie her, Rickard." Her eyes, as flat and still as a brackish green pond, never leave mine. Anger emboldens me and I don't flinch under her gaze.

"You've been snooping." Her voice is devoid of emotion.

"I've been *spying*."

She crosses her arms and this time I look away. Perhaps in this case—riffling through someone else's wardrobe—spying and snooping are interchangeable.

I rub my hands as soon as they're free and glare at Miss Tickford. "At least I didn't drag someone out of bed and make them feel as if they were about to be shoved in front of a firing squad." I stand on wobbling legs.

"You still have no idea how serious this is, do you?" she asks.

I hold out my wrists, showing her the burn marks left by the ropes. "This looks pretty serious to me. Wasn't there any other way to teach me about interrogation?"

I glance at the man, a burly fellow with a soft brown beard. He meets my eyes without any emotion. "My apologies," he says with a thick French accent.

No wonder he'd been silent.

I ignore him and turn back to Miss Tickford, who doesn't look discomfited at all. "It's my job to make sure you're ready for your assignment," she says. "Don't be such a child."

My chest tightens. "So the apartment *is* yours. I should think that as a spy you'd know better than to keep personal effects where they're so easy to find. If a novice could discover them so easily, the Abwehr would have located them in minutes."

Miss Tickford's pale skin flushes. She glances over at Rickard, who raises his eyebrows.

"The apartment belonged to my brother and me. Like you, Lawrence had a knack for languages." She walks over to the sink and runs water into a teakettle. I watch, scarcely daring to breathe. "He rose up the ranks quickly in the Luxembourgian military even without royal connections. Everyone loved him, you see. He just had this quality about him. After the war began, MI6 recruited him right away. They wanted someone with Luxembourgian military experience."

Miss Tickford turns, her hands clenched. Dread tightens my stomach and I know what's coming.

"He disappeared on an assignment in Paris. He was found in the Seine a week later, his body mutilated. It was a warning to British Intelligence."

She pauses so long, I think she's done, but then she turns with a hard smile. "Being a woman, I'm not allowed to join the armed forces, so I did the next best thing and became a spy. Turns out, I'm very, very good at it. Aren't I, Rickard?"

The bearded man nods. "One of the very best."

Miss Tickford takes several cups out of the cupboard and sets them on the counter. "Now, I could give you reams of information about how to survive an interrogation, but in reality there are only two skills you must know."

I swallow, trying to adjust to the abrupt change of conversation. "Just two?"

She nods. "Interrogation is terrifying. If they want to break you, they will."

I think of how frightened I was while tied to the chair and I nod.

She continues. "The first skill you've proved you already possess—the ability to control your own fear. Secondly, you must know how to leave your captors feeling like you have more information than you really do. That you're more valuable alive than dead." She stops there and gives me a look that chills me to my soul. "That is, until you come to the conclusion that you really are better off dead."

My stomach churns as I think of her brother in the river. The teakettle whistles and I startle.

"Go get into your robe and you can take your oath," she says.

I blink. "Now?"

She nods. "It's time. An opportunity has arisen that we must take advantage of. Prince Wilhelm is here and the grand duchess is throwing a reception for him tomorrow evening. It's the perfect time for you to ease into your new persona. I've already sent a note to the prince's secretary to tell him of your presence in the city, and you've been issued a formal invitation."

I turn to leave the kitchen.

"Samantha," she says.

I pause in the doorway.

"You understand why I am so very, very hard on you, don't you? I don't want any more bodies left in the Seine."

Her voice is pleading for me to understand and I give her another nod before going to my room. The bedding is strewn across the floor and I shudder as images of being dragged out of the room replay in my mind. I sit on the bed, hoping the trembling passes before I have to go back out into the kitchen. For some reason it's important to me that no one knows just how terrified I actually was. Taking a deep breath, I grab my robe from the hook behind the door, and return.

Somehow, I'm not as thrilled as I thought I would be taking the La Dame Blanche oath. Perhaps I've already expended my allotment of emotion for the evening. My words feel flat as I repeat after Miss Tickford:

> "I declare and enlist in the capacity of soldier in the Allied military observation service until the end of the war. I swear before God to respect this engagement, to accomplish conscientiously the offices entrusted to me, to comply with instructions given to me by the representatives of the Direction, not to reveal to anyone (without formal authorization) anything concerning the organization of the service, even if this stance should entail for me or mine the penalty of death, and not to take part in any other activity or role that might expose me to prosecution by the occupying authority."

A chill runs down my spine as I finish. I've just promised to face a firing squad rather than reveal anything about Miss Tickford, Captain Parker, Velvet, or La Dame Blanche.

"Congratulations," Miss Tickford says. "You are officially a member of La Dame Blanche. Now sit. You have some official papers to sign."

After I'm done signing the papers, Miss Tickford leans forward, her green eyes serious. "Rumors have surfaced about the schematics for a new weapon becoming available on the black market. We believe it's the same weapon Velvet has been hinting about. Either Velvet has turned or someone has discovered that she has access to the plans and is somehow using her to obtain them. We must find her quickly."

My pulse speeds up, but I try to match Miss Tickford's calm demeanor. "You said her handler had disappeared," I say. "Do you think it's connected? Do we know yet what sort of weapon it is?"

Miss Tickford shakes her head. "At this point, we're just dealing with unverified reports."

"So you believe there's a possibility that Velvet has turned and yet you're sending me in anyway?" Why am I not more surprised by this?

Miss Tickford gives me a sharp look. "Velvet's loyalty has never been questioned before. We're not about to cut her off over rumors, but it does make it imperative that we get to her as soon as possible."

My mind races. "So what happens if the weapons do go on the black market? Either our enemies discover them and get their own arms back, or the Allies buy them for their own use, right?"

Miss Tickford nods. "Yes, but it's not that simple. What would happen if the Japanese or the Chinese or even the Russians get ahold of them before we do? It could change the power structure of the entire world for decades. It's difficult to tell without knowing exactly what sort of weapons we're talking about."

My stomach churns.

Miss Tickford pats my arm. "Do not worry. I have no doubt in my mind that you're ready for this. Now, off to bed. Tomorrow is going to be here before we know it and you must rest."

I glance at Rickard, but he is busy going over the papers I've just signed, so with a nod at Miss Tickford I take my leave.

I think I'm never going to get to sleep, but nod off almost immediately.

The next day is spent learning German royal etiquette, the Hohenzollern family tree, and what my duties might be as an assistant to the governess. I've just closed the book Miss Tickford gave me on the Hohenzollern dynasty when I hear an odd tapping on the window. I freeze, hardly daring to look behind me. When I do, I see nothing through the stiff lace curtain covering the glass. I wait but there's no sound. I've almost decided it's my imagination when it happens again.

*Tap. Tap-tap.*

I leap to my feet, unsure as to whether I should go to the window or run from the room. But before I decide, Miss Tickford appears in the doorway.

"I think someone's knocking," I tell her.

She nods and then walks across the kitchen and over to the window as if such tapping were the most natural thing in the world.

I stare, openmouthed, as she opens the window, reaches her arms out, and pulls in a pigeon.

"I hope you like birds," she says, petting his head.

I throw my hands up. "Just when I think that I'm beyond being surprised . . ."

"Life will always surprise you." She holds the pigeon out toward me. "Bird, meet Samantha."

"Bird?" I reach out and run my fingers over his silky back.

"I call them all Bird. It saves me from having to remember names."

"You know so many?"

Her lips quirk upward. "Not really. But they'll be used a lot during this war, mark my words. They're incredibly useful in passing information along when radio or telephone transmissions are either compromised or too risky."

I nod as the bird settles, warm and unafraid, in her hands. "I knew the troops had them, but I didn't know they were used in espionage. It makes sense, though."

"The palace has a pigeon roost. Three of the birds are plants, and each bird will get the information to several different operatives within the city. Use them only in an emergency, though. Most of your communication will be through the Hess Bakery."

My heart tightens. "On the Nürnberger Straße?"

She nods. "Do you know it?"

"I visited it as a child."

"Oh, good. We'll use that in your signal."

The bird coos, recapturing my attention. "How will I know which pigeons are ours?" I ask.

In answer, Miss Tickford sets the bird on the table, then snaps her fingers three times. The bird flies to her shoulder after the third snap. "All LDB birds are trained to respond to that." She points, and for the first time I see a small silver tube attached to his thin leg with a wire so fine, it looks more like a strand of hair than metal.

"I'll give you several of these before you leave. Use invisible ink if you can for the message. If not, LDB code will do." The bird sits patiently as she unwinds the wire and takes off the tube. Then she unscrews the lid and pulls out a thin roll of paper. It's blank. "This one is for training purposes," she explains. Taking a pen, she scratches something on the paper, rolls it back up, and hands it to me. "Here. You try."

I pop the scroll into the tiny tube, screw on the lid, and then attach it to the bird's leg, careful not to tie it too tightly. His leg is rubbery and cold. "You need stockings, don't you, poor bird," I say to the pigeon, who coos softly in response.

Miss Tickford smiles and then puts him back through the window.

"What constitutes an emergency?" I ask as we watch the bird fly away.

"Imminent discovery, imprisonment, or death," she says.

A chill runs through me as the bird becomes a speck in the sky.

"Now, come. We must transform you into Sophia Thérèse."

Several hours later, I'm sitting in the back of a luxurious motorcar that was mysteriously procured for my use. Miss Tickford said the prince would expect nothing less of Sophia Thérèse. I'm wearing an antique blue charmeuse gown trimmed with snowy lace. The kimono-style sleeves are pleated up to the shoulder and a soft sash ties just above my waist. The gown is too big on me and has to be taken in with pins, but along with my new bob and the new crescent-shaped birthmark on my left cheek, I barely recognize myself.

I won't be returning to the apartment. A suite was rented under Sophia Thérèse's name a week ago at the Hotel Luxembourg. The motorcar will take me there after the reception and I'll receive my final preparations.

After tonight there is no turning back.

# TEN
## WHQ

*Window Dressing: Materials used in a cover story to prove to others that what they are observing is real.*

A Luxembourgian guard opens the door of the motorcar and I stare, unmoving, at the entrance. The façade of the palace is from an ethereal fairy tale, an ode to the Renaissance, with its steeply pitched gables, lacy wrought iron, and graceful spires that seem to reach to the sky.

"Fräulein?" The guard reaches his hand out to me and I take it in spite of a rush of fear and dizziness that threatens to pitch me straight into his arms.

"Thank you," I murmur.

Other guests, women in lovely formal dresses and short capes and men in uniforms or suits, are entering the palace and I tag along, ignoring the German guards lined up in the entryway.

"Name?" a servant asks as he takes my invitation. I tilt my chin.

"Sophia Thérèse von Schönburg," I say as another servant takes my evening coat.

A man standing at a small reception desk inspects the invitation and then marks something in a book before nodding to the men guarding the arched doorway. The long hall is lined with stiff portraits of former grand dukes, and as I move through the corridor, I throw off my former self.

I am not Samantha Donaldson, better at studying than socializing. I am Sophia Thérèse, a young woman who may not be used to such events, but who was raised to know very well how to behave at them. I send a quick blessing to the young woman who died so prematurely and hope that I'm not completely dishonoring her memory.

I move at a slow, measured pace, mimicking the guests surrounding me. The sparkling jewels that encircle the throats and wrists of the women reflect the electric lights like rainbows dipped in dew. The scent of cigars mingling with French perfume hangs heavily in the hall, and if it weren't for all the German uniforms, you'd hardly know there is a war on.

Miss Tickford told me to introduce myself first to Prince Wilhelm, then mingle among the other guests, and take my leave. As a distant cousin who will basically be joining the royal staff, I won't be expected to stay for the late supper.

As each step takes me closer to the moment when I will fully assume my new identity, the glow from the chamber beyond grows more and more dazzling. When I walk into the reception room, I barely refrain from gasping at its brilliance. From the gleaming parquet floor to the domed ceiling painted with cherubim and angels, the entire space shimmers with grandeur.

Taking a deep breath to relieve the tightness in my chest, I join the long line of Luxembourgian elite waiting to introduce themselves to the German crown prince. It's difficult to believe in this opulent room that all these well-dressed guests are actually a conquered people. The grand duchess Marie-Adélaïde, the prime minister, and the congress are walking a fine line trying to maintain their own government while under German occupation.

I spot the young grand duchess greeting guests and wonder if the strain of occupation has contributed to the dark circles under her pretty blue eyes. The line moves slowly and I try to be mindful of both my persona and my training.

Prince Wilhelm stands stiffly in his commandant's uniform, badges gleaming on his chest. In his early thirties, he's a handsome man in the prime of life, and the arrogant tilt of his head shows that he's fully aware of this. The kaiser's eldest son has a reputation as a philanderer, and I can see its accuracy in the attention he lavishes on the younger, more attractive Luxembourgian women.

*My poor cousin*, I think, handing the card Miss Tickford had made up to one of the young soldiers flanking the prince.

"Sophia Thérèse von Schönberg," the soldier says.

My heart is beating so loudly, I think it must be audible to everyone in the room.

I set my chin. I will not be intimidated. My family has served kings. I was at the top of my class at school. I was recruited to be a spy for the British crown. I can do this. I give a low curtsy, for the first time grateful for the lessons my mother forced upon me.

And immediately trip on the hem of my gown.

I don't quite fall on my face, but I come close. There's a moment of stunned silence all around me before I collect myself and offer the prince my hand. "My apologies, Your Highness. Grace is not my forte."

"No need to apologize, Fräulein. It happens to the best of us." He takes my hand, but his eyes are on my modest décolletage.

"Pleased to meet you, Prince Wilhelm," I say in my best German.

"Likewise," he says. "Von Schönberg?" His eyes rise to my face. "Why does that sound familiar?"

I repeat the words Miss Tickford made me memorize. "I'm a distant cousin of your wife, Your Highness, from a little town outside of Cologne. I'll be joining the family in Berlin to help care for your children."

Recognition dawns on his face. "Yes, of course. My wife told me you were coming. I think you'll find that I'm a very involved father, Fräulein von Schönberg. My sons are going to be very pleased with their pretty new governess." His eyes gleam as they sweep over my bare arms.

I give him what I hope is a modest Sophia Thérèse smile, rather than a nervous about-to-be-sick Samantha one. "I'm sure I'll enjoy looking after them very much."

"Will you be traveling back to Berlin with us?"

Miss Tickford hopes I'll be able to leave for Berlin some-time this weekend, though it's hard to be certain—so many of the trains have been preempted for war duties. "I'm not sure; my plans have not been finalized. Very few trains allow nonmilitary passengers now. It's difficult to tell when I'll be able to leave."

"Well, you must come with us. It doesn't make any sense for you to travel alone when my train is so much more accommodating. Plus, you'll get there much sooner."

He snaps his fingers and tells the handsome young guard to his right, "Have my secretary make the necessary arrangements."

The guard's dark eyes sweep over me before he nods, and for some reason a hot flush stains my cheeks. "Thank you, Your Excellency," I say.

Prince Wilhelm inclines his head in response, though his eyes have, mercifully, moved on. I bow, making sure to back away until he is engaged with the next guest. My heart rate returns to normal as I join the others out on the main floor. A three-piece ensemble plays Mendelssohn in a corner of the room while people gather in little knots. I pretend to look at the wall hangings while keeping an eye on the guests. I'm not fond of parties—I'd rather curl up with a good book—but even I can tell that there is something off about this reception. When I first entered, I was dazzled by the lush beauty of the palace and elegance of the guests, but on sec-ond look, there's too much tension in the room for a normal party, or at least any that I've attended.

"Excuse me, Fräulein. Are you enjoying yourself?"

I swing around to find the young guard who had been standing with Prince Wilhelm. He is holding his helmet in one hand and a cup of punch in the other. His dark blond hair is cut neat and short and he's so handsome that my tongue immediately ties in spite of the stern, soldierly look on his face.

Then I lift my chin and accept the cup of punch he offers me. I'm not Samantha, I'm Sophia Thérèse, and surely Sophia Thérèse knew how to talk politely to handsome young men. "Thank you. Are you finished with your duties for the evening?"

He shakes his head. "No, but I was sent to find out where you are staying."

My heart slams against my ribs and I stare at him until I realize that he means the hotel.

He tilts his head as if puzzled by my reaction. "We will need to send you the information on when the train is leaving. The prince isn't sure when his business in Luxembourg will be concluded."

"Of course," I tell him, and he bows his head but seems in no hurry to leave.

"Have you been to the Ducal Palace before?" he asks politely.

*Have I?* I shake my head, deciding to stick as close to the truth as possible. "No. This is my first time. You?"

"No. It's quite overwhelming, isn't it?"

My lips twitch and I glance at him. "Is it that obvious?"

He gives a small smile. "The palace was built to impress."

"It achieves that goal."

He nods. "That it does. I must return to my duties. I'll be in touch with you soon about your travel arrangements, Fräulein."

"Wait." On impulse, I reach out and catch his sleeve as he turns to go. "You didn't tell me your name."

"Corporal Maxwell Mayer." His eyes are trained upon something else and I get the feeling he has more important things to attend to.

"It's nice to meet you, Corporal Mayer," I say, letting him go.

"Likewise, Fräulein von Schönburg."

He clicks his heels together and bows his head before returning to his place by the prince.

I take that opportunity to slip out the door. Surely I've stayed long enough. I need to tell Miss Tickford about this new turn of events.

The hotel I'm to stay at is nice and respectable. I sail through the attractively appointed lobby, ignoring the night clerk as if I've been there before.

The door to my room is, as Miss Tickford promised, open.

"You should have stayed longer." I jump at Miss Tickford's voice. "And you neglected to do the first thing you should always do when staying at a new place."

I close my eyes, allowing my pulse to return to normal.

"What is that? I'm too tired to guess."

"Always search the room upon entering."

"How did you get in?" I ask crossly. I don't like being made to look foolish.

"I took the rooms next to yours. They have connecting doors," Miss Tickford explains. "This way, I'll be able to finish giving you what you need to complete your assignment."

Brushing off my irritation, I tell Miss Tickford what transpired at the palace.

"Excellent. I was hoping that would happen," she says.

"You were?" I ask, surprised.

She nods. "It simplifies things. Your clothing will be delivered in the morning." She sets a black bag she's been holding onto the bed. Opening the bag, she hands me a small red book that has a pencil attached to it with a ribbon. "Keep this with you at all times, and I mean all times. Sleep with it under your pillow and take it with you even if the house is on fire."

"What is it?" I ask.

"The La Dame Blanche code cipher. You'll need it to read any notes sent to you by LDB. I don't need to go over it with you. Monsieur Elliot assures me that you'll have no problem with it."

I open it and glance at the numbers, letters, and symbols that line its pages. I swallow. The well-being of an entire organization would be compromised if this fell into the wrong hands.

She takes out a wooden box that looks as if it's made to hold jewels. The box is about six by six inches and about three inches deep. She opens it and, sure enough, it contains a strand of pearls, several bracelets, a locket, and a cameo ring.

First she removes the ring and snaps it open. "This can contain a note if you make it small enough, as can the locket." She dumps the rest of the jewels out onto the bed. "This box has a false bottom. Watch carefully." She pulls the velvet lining aside and runs her finger along the inside. A piece of the box swings out when she pushes on it, and the bottom comes out.

I frown at the contents. "What are those?"

She takes out a small paper packet sealed with wax. "This is sleeping powder. Empty it into someone's drink or mix it in their food and they will be sound asleep within a few minutes. It'll take less time if they're small." She points to a vial. "I'm sure you've heard of syrup of ipecac. It's given to children with croup. It's also used to make someone sick. It won't hurt them, but they'll become nauseous and dizzy and sweat profusely. It can be very handy if you wish to incapacitate someone for any length of time. It's sickly sweet, though, so is best hidden in something strong, like sugared tea or lemonade."

My eyes widen in horror. "Oh, I don't think I could ever poison someone," I say.

Miss Tickford shrugs, but her shoulders are too rigid to pull off the nonchalance she's attempting. "Did you think that espionage is all about drops and surveillance? Lives are at stake." Her voice grows shrill. "It's not a game. I'm risking your life to save another life. Do you think I'd be doing this if I had a choice? What if you're captured and you need to escape? I certainly hope you could poison someone if you had to!"

Her face is red by the time she finishes and she avoids my eyes. The only sounds in the room are the street noise from outside and her breathing.

My chest hollows at her agitation. I need her to be in control.

I can see she is trying to get ahold of herself, so I ignore her outburst and point to the next packet. "What's that one?"

She picks it up. "This is to be used as a last resort." She looks up at me, her green eyes sharp as glass. "It's arsenic. Just a small amount is lethal."

I stare at the small, deadly packet, wondering if I will ever have enough guts to use it.

She holds the two brown packets up closer for my inspection. "Look at the seals on them very closely. The plain blue seal is for the sleeping powder. The one imprinted with the scarlet $A$ is the arsenic."

I suppress a shudder.

"The trunk you'll be using also has a false bottom. It'll contain false passports and travel papers to help you escape if necessary, as well as a blueprint of the inside of the palace. I'll show you how to open it in the morning. For now, we should get some rest." Miss Tickford hesitates and then does something completely unexpected. She reaches out and pulls me in for a warm embrace. "You really did look lovely tonight, Samantha." Then she leaves the room quickly, as if embarrassed by her actions.

I put away the jewelry box and slowly undress, making sure to hang up the beautiful gown Miss Tickford let me borrow. I should be proud of myself. I made it through the evening with flying colors and even managed to secure myself transportation to Berlin. But I'm not.

I get the feeling that nothing about my training has been standard procedure. I'm proud to be a member of LDB, but I wonder if my father would be, or if he would be angry that I'd left my mother. But why would he be? He left us to do his duty. Why should it be any different for me?

I sit on the edge of the bed, so angry that if he were here in front of me right now, I'd scream at him. Why was it so easy for him to walk away from us, knowing there was a risk that he wouldn't return?

I cross my arms, as mad at myself as I am at him because all I want in the world is for him to tell me that everything is going to be all right.

Even if it's a lie.

The next morning, Miss Tickford leaves to run some errands, instructing me to stay put in case the prince contacts me. She says we'll wait twenty-four hours before sending him a little note reminding him of my existence.

I study Sophia Thérèse's backstory some more, but at this point I know her history as well as I do my own. I push the papers away, wondering what Sophia Thérèse thought of the war and if she, like me, was completely shocked by the events that led to it last summer. How could the assassination of an Austrian archduke in Serbia lead to such bloodshed? Within weeks, Serbia and Russia were at war with Germany and Austria-Hungary. By August, Britain entered the war and, one by one, the other countries fell like a house of cards. Did Sophia Thérèse read the newspapers with growing horror or did she applaud her country's actions? How did she feel when her new uncle took the family to Switzerland?

I pace the room, wishing I were already on the train heading to Berlin. As much as I dread it, at least then I'd be moving forward with the assignment. The waiting is killing me. Too much time to think.

A knock sounds on the door and I jump. Quickly shoving the papers under the mattress, I glance about the room. It's probably just a maid, but I don't want to take chances. The knock repeats and my heart pounds. "Who is it?" I finally call, hoping they don't notice that my voice cracked in the middle.

"It's Corporal Maxwell Mayer. I'm looking for Fräulein von Schönberg."

Relief floods through me so quickly I'm light-headed as I open the door.

He's standing straight and handsome in his field-green uniform and matching cap. His face is as stiff and professional as his uniform.

"Good morning, Fräulein. Did you enjoy the reception?"

I hesitate. "I enjoyed the palace. . . ."

He nods and for the first time I see the corner of his mouth twitch. "I understand. A bit too much pomp and circumstance, perhaps?"

I smile and wait for him to tell me the reason for his visit.

He clears his throat. "I've been dispatched to give you

your travel papers. The royal train leaves tomorrow morning at ten sharp. You should be there a bit earlier to load your trunks. You've been given a sleeping compartment, so keep a small bag with you."

I nod and take the papers from him. "Thank you. This does make getting to Berlin much easier."

Corporal Mayer stands silent for a moment and I wait, puzzled.

He finally takes a deep breath. "I know this is improper for me to say, but you seem like a very nice young woman."

Still he hesitates and I finally prod him.

"Yes?"

He continues, clearly uncomfortable. "His Excellency seems to have taken an interest in you that may not be entirely . . . family related. I thought it prudent to let you know so that you could be prepared to tactfully rebuke him, if you were so inclined."

My eyes widen as his meaning hits me. "Oh. Oh! Of course I'm so inclined. I wouldn't . . ."

He nods, his cheeks a brilliant shade of red. "I didn't think so. I mean, I wouldn't assume . . ."

"Of course not," I put in quickly. "I wouldn't assume that you would assume . . ." My voice trails off and my face flames.

The corporal straightens. "Well, then. That's good." Swallowing, he stares up toward the ceiling as if something brilliant were written there. I wish it were something that would rescue us from this conversation.

"Yes," I say inanely.

"I suppose I should be going."

"Yes," I say.

With a sharp nod, he's gone.

I slump against the door the moment it's closed. Pressing my hands against my heated cheeks, I groan. That was the most awkward conversation I've ever been involved in. Possibly even worse than the one when my mother tried to tell me where babies came from. Her mortification had been palpable, and telling her that I'd known since I'd visited a horse farm at the age of eight didn't seem to help much.

"Well, that muddles things a bit," Miss Tickford says, coming into the room.

I jump and my face flames again. "How long have you been there?"

"I arrived just as your shiny, earnest young German knocked, so I let myself into my room and listened through the door. Why would he warn you about the prince, though?"

"Well, I tried to be friendly last night at the reception," I tell her. "Perhaps it worked?"

Her brows rise.

I feel compelled to explain myself. "He's a family guard and I thought it would be wise to make friends."

She nods. "Very smart. Just be careful. And as far as the prince goes, I must admit that I was a bit worried about that, considering his reputation. You're very pretty and the prince likes pretty girls. Don't worry. I brought a Bible for that very purpose."

I look at her confused. "A Bible?"

"Yes. Sophia Thérèse is a serious young woman who taught Sunday school. You need to keep the Bible with you at all times. If you behave piously when the prince is near, it should keep him at bay. If it doesn't, and he insists, you can always use your religion as an excuse to rebuff his attentions. I don't think he will, though. You are, after all, his wife's cousin, no matter how distant."

A Bible. All right, then.

"Let's get to work now. You leave in less than twenty-four hours."

A cold wave of panic runs through me. This is really happening. Part of me wishes to turn and run out of the hotel and not stop until I'm somewhere safe, but the possibility of an investigation into my father's disappearance keeps me going. Plus, somewhere in the heart of Germany, a young woman is in trouble.

I may not be able to help her, but I have to try.

Miss Tickford says her good-bye at the hotel the next morning. The thin early morning sunlight streaming through the curtains accentuates her wan features and I wonder if she slept at all.

She reaches out and takes my hands. "Remember to stay observant at all times. Don't let your objective be muddied by all the court intrigues going on around you. It is of the utmost importance that you stay focused on saving Velvet and obtaining information about the new weaponry—it could very well change the course of the war."

I bite my lip, the weight of her words descending on me like a pallet of bricks. I'd been so intent on getting information about my father that I had lost sight of what this assignment might mean to the bigger picture.

*What if I can't do this?*

As if sensing my thoughts, she gives my hands a squeeze. "You are an extraordinary young woman, Samantha. I have all the faith in the world that you'll be able to complete your objective."

I give a slight smile and nod before taking my leave. All I can think of as I take the lift downstairs is, *If she has so much faith in me, how come it looks as if she's been crying?*

The driver opens the door for me and I climb into the back.

My pulse races as we drive through the streets of Luxembourg. When I exit this vehicle, I'll cease to be Samantha Donaldson and I'll become Sophia Thérèse von Schönburg, German aristocrat. Or Rosemary James, LDB agent, depending on the circumstances.

I have a hard enough time being one person, let alone three.

By the time we reach the station, my nerves are screaming.

"Fräulein Sophia Thérèse!" a voice calls.

I look up to see Corporal Mayer striding toward us, his wide smile at odds with his upright, soldierly bearing.

"Corporal Mayer, how nice to see you again," I say, my heart lightening at his friendly greeting. As silly as it seems,

I almost feel as if I'm being greeted by a friend. "I do hope I'm not late."

"Right on schedule. Are these your things?" He nods toward the trunks the driver is holding.

I nod.

"You travel light. Most women I know would have three times this number, at the very least."

I smile as he takes the trunks. "I came to Luxembourg in rather a hurry and knew I was going to be traveling to Berlin right after, so it seemed practical to bring only a few things. I can send for some more once I'm settled."

Corporal Mayer nods. "Very wise. Your compartment has been prepared for you. Please follow me, Fräulein."

# PART III

*Operations*

# ELEVEN
## HOHYHQ

*Infiltration Operation: Moving an operative into a target area without detection.*

I follow the corporal through the busy train station. He doesn't look to the right or left, but marches resolutely toward the train—which is pretty impressive, considering all the people rushing here and there.

"Watch your step, Fräulein," he warns as I hurry up the platform steps after him. "Some of the boards are loose. The Luxembourgians don't keep up their public buildings the way we Berliners do."

His words irritate me. "I'm sure they have more important things on their mind, considering the circumstances."

He raises his eyebrows. "Not a supporter of our peace agreement with Luxembourg, I take it?"

I shrug, wishing I could take my words back. "I really don't have an opinion on the matter."

"The agreement is mutually beneficial to both our peoples, Fräulein. They have their own government." His voice is neutral and he gives me a sideways glance. "If you do have opinions regarding the matter, it might be wise to keep them to yourself," he says quietly.

I nod, chastising myself for my stupidity.

The guard at the top of the platform stops us and checks Corporal Mayer's papers before turning to me. Heart in my throat, I pull my own papers out of my handbag and wait while he scans them. It seems to take forever, and I'm sure my sigh of relief is audible when he hands the papers back.

I return them to my handbag and follow Corporal Mayer onto the train.

"I hope you don't mind that you will be sharing a compartment with Mrs. Elsa Tremaine. She's an Australian opera singer the prince is taking back with him to Berlin." The red creeping up the back of his neck tells me far more about who Mrs. Tremaine is than his words do.

I take a relieved breath. Perhaps I won't need the Bible after all.

The train itself is as luxurious as one would expect. The seats in the coaches are red velvet with the Hohenzollern family crest embroidered on them, and gold tassels swing from the window blinds.

"This coach and the rest of the forward cars are for the prince and his advisors," Corporal Mayer explains. "You and the others will ride back here." We walk through several other cars and I am awed by the rich appointments. The interiors, with inlaid wood ceilings, quilted sofas, and polished side tables, look more like small drawing rooms than like train cars. He shows me the lavatories, which boast gold spigots with hot and cold running water, before taking me back to the sleeping cars. The close compartments aren't nearly as luxurious as the ones set aside for the prince. "My apologies for the cramped quarters. These are usually reserved for servants and train employees."

I give him a reassuring smile. "Well, I'm to be a servant, of sorts. It's appropriate that I should be here. Honestly, our life in the country is simpler than it is in Berlin. This is fine. And please, call me Sophia Thérèse."

He inclines his head. "And you may call me Maxwell, though it might be better if you continued to call me Corporal Mayer in public. The royal family is quite concerned with appearances."

The smile that accompanies his unexpected words is so warm and friendly that I relax, in spite of the fact that I should be on my guard. Thinking of this handsome young man as a friend could be very dangerous.

He continues, "You wouldn't need a sleeper at all, except the prince is stopping in Frankfurt for a meeting with one of his father's generals. That will delay the trip overnight." Setting my trunks next to the bunks, Maxwell gives a short nod. "I'll let you settle in, then."

"Thank you," I say, turning back to the confined quarters that I'll apparently be sharing with the prince's new mistress. The compartment has two narrow beds with a ladder leading to the upper bunk and a single chair that looks so uncomfortable, it's no doubt only used to put on one's shoes. The other side of the tiny room is composed of several shelves and drawers.

Even though the trip is only overnight, I open one of my trunks and hang up my new gray suit. No reason for me to arrive at the palace rumpled and travel worn. I place my nightclothes on the upper bunk, guessing that the older woman would prefer not to climb the ladder to get to her bed.

Even though I know I won't be able to read, I take the book I'd borrowed from Monsieur Elliot's library and my handbag and retrace my steps back to the nearest coach. I nod at a couple of young soldiers sitting in the back, then take a seat at the window. I stare at the book, but can't read the words—I'm waiting for the engine to start, for brakes to unlock, for the movement that will take me into enemy territory.

I swallow, unable to stop the doubts running through my head as my assignment unfolds before me. As Miss Tickford stressed more than once, we're soldiers for the war. We may not wear uniforms, but we pledged to help defeat the enemy as surely as any young man on the front. I am merely a means to an end and the government is using me to achieve its goal. Just like Velvet herself is a means to an end. She isn't important beyond the knowledge she has. My doubt deepens.

Are humans really expendable for the greater good? Is it morally acceptable to blackmail someone to achieve an objective, no matter how noble that objective is?

My thoughts are interrupted by a shadow falling across

my book. I glance up to see Maxwell standing with a lovely woman in a dark blue serge suit. Her burnished auburn hair is dressed in elaborate whorls and her eyes regard me with interest.

"Fräulein Sophia Thérèse, may I introduce Mrs. Elsa Tremaine? Mrs. Tremaine, this is Sophia Thérèse von Schönburg. You will be sharing the same compartment."

She raises her hand as regally as if she were a princess, and I'm unsure whether she wants me to shake her hand or kiss it. In the end, I awkwardly touch her fingers with mine. "Nice to meet you," I murmur.

"It's mutual, darling." Her words have a lilting quality and I can imagine that her singing voice is lovely. She turns to Maxwell and switches to German. For the first time I notice a slender young man standing behind both of them. "Please make sure my trunks are all loaded," she says. "I would hate to arrive in Berlin only to find that my costumes were left sitting on the platform. Arnold, go with the nice soldier and make sure all is well with my things."

Arnold bows his head and follows Maxwell, while Mrs. Tremaine settles herself across from me. She places a white fur muff on her lap. It's only after the muff yawns that I realize it's a dog. I giggle.

"Do you speak English? Please say you speak English. My German is atrocious." She sighs in relief at my nod and turns to the dog on her lap. "This is Penny," Mrs. Tremaine says, bending to rub her face in her pet's fur.

I smile at the dog. "Good morning, Penny."

Mrs. Tremaine raises her head. "You speak wonderful English. You hardly have an accent at all."

I groan mentally at my stupidity and give her a weak smile. "I have a gift for languages. That's one of the reasons the duchess wishes me to teach the children."

Mrs. Tremaine seems to accept it. "So we'll be rooming together? I do hope you don't snore. Penny snores enough as it is."

"Not that I'm aware of."

"Wonderful. So you're traveling to Berlin to be the governess to the prince's children?"

I nod. "An assistant to the governess, actually. The prince's boys are apparently very active."

"I never had children of my own, but they seem like such a trial. Penny is enough for me."

"Are you married?" I ask politely, though from her name I know she must be.

"I was. And, of course, you are not—you're much too young and you wouldn't be considered for a governess position if you were. Have you been to Berlin before?"

"Yes. But I was very young. I'm from a little town outside Cologne." I steer the topic of conversation away from me. "And you?"

Mrs. Tremaine shakes her head. "No. None of my tours brought me to Berlin, unfortunately. I've heard it's quite lovely."

I raise my eyebrows. "So you decided to do a German tour in the middle of a war?"

She waves a hand. "People need music even more during times of trouble, don't you think? Besides, music knows no nationality, so I must ignore it as well. Do you know the governess? What's she like?"

I shake my head. "I've never met her."

The train jerks forward and I startle.

"Here we go," Mrs. Tremaine murmurs so softly I can barely hear her. "May God preserve us."

I'm about to ask her what she means when Maxwell reenters the coach and informs Mrs. Tremaine that the prince wishes to speak with her. With a small smile, Mrs. Tremaine, carrying Penny, takes her leave.

I lean back and watch as the train gathers speed, taking me out of Luxembourg and closer to Germany and Velvet.

Whoever she is.

I wake up early the next morning only to find that Sophia Thérèse's birthmark rubbed off on the pillow overnight. With a glance at Mrs. Tremaine's sleeping figure, I quietly draw the birthmark back on, then add a light dusting of powder to set it.

This birthmark may end up being the biggest challenge of the entire mission.

After making myself presentable, I tuck the Bible under my arm—in case I run into the prince—and head to the servants' coach in search of some tea or perhaps coffee. I'd barely slept and instead spent my time tossing and turning worrying about today. The train had stopped last night in

Frankfurt, and the prince, Mrs. Tremaine, and a half-dozen officers had left to visit with generals, though I have a feeling it was more of a social visit than a military one, judging by the dress Mrs. Tremaine was wearing. Penny stayed behind in a basket, shivering until I took her out and settled her in her mistress's bed.

I must have slept at some point, because Mrs. Tremaine was asleep in her bed when I awoke.

Some spy I am.

Though I suppose my spying won't truly start until I meet Marissa Baum and Lillian Bouchard. I've memorized their data and their faces, of course, but facts and figures can't really give me the information I need. Will I know them when I meet them? Why would either one of them spy for England? What would motivate them to put their lives on the line, much as I am?

A tea cart has been wheeled into the coach. I pour myself a cup and take one of the soft bread rolls stacked next to the pot, before sitting at an empty table.

My brain continues to spin while I eat. Why would an American girl be visiting Germany during a war? As an American citizen, Marissa Baum could easily leave the country. The United States has so far successfully managed to stay out of the conflict, though that could change at any minute. But still . . . with an American passport, why would she choose to stay in Berlin? And how will I get close enough to her to be able to tell if she's Velvet?

It'll be much easier to get to know Lillian Bouchard, since

I'll be working with her. Being so close to the kaiser's family and also half French, she'd be the most obvious choice—but perhaps too obvious? And honestly, how would a governess obtain such sensitive information? Unless it's true that Velvet is conducting an affair with a highly placed general.

I don't even want to contemplate the unthinkable, that Velvet is neither of those two women.

I stare out the window and spot a military convoy traveling down a long road. The motorized vehicles carrying an unimaginable number of troops are followed by legions of men on horseback. I wonder where they're going and how many of them will return. Sadness tightens my throat as I think of all the children who will never see their fathers again.

"Lord, this tea is horrid," Mrs. Tremaine says, settling in next to me. The strong scent of her perfume almost chokes me. "I don't understand why you Germans have such a difficult time making tea, do you?"

I smile. "Not all of us are so poor at it. Where's Penny this morning?"

"Arnold is taking her for her morning walk. Then she'll probably take a long nap, lucky girl."

"I'm sorry, did I wake you?" I ask.

Her musical laugh rings out, causing several of the soldiers' heads to swivel in our direction. "No," she says, ignoring our audience. "I'm not a great sleeper. Plus"—she leans closer to me and lowers her voice—"I'm a bit nervous meeting the royal family. The kaiser has a terrible temper and there's tremendous rivalry and infighting among his grown children, not to mention all those cranky generals."

I raise an eyebrow. The prince must have a loose tongue for her to be so knowledgeable about royal affairs. I wonder if the kaiser knows about his son's penchant for family gossip.

"Then why are you going?" I ask.

"Because I thrive on that stuff, darling. I just wanted to warn you to watch your step. It can be quite frightening for the uninitiated."

Her eyes gleam and her mouth purses with suppressed excitement. I lean away, unsettled by her intensity. England has its own version of such women, women who flourish on court intrigue and gossip. Some so much that they spend their entire lives doing nothing else but attending parties and gossiping. Perhaps Mrs. Tremaine is one of those women. She is, after all, cultivating an affair with the heir apparent to the German throne.

"Who is Arnold?" I ask, changing the subject.

"He's a pupil of mine. I give him free voice lessons and in return he takes care of me. He's quite talented, really. I know I'll lose him eventually, but I enjoy his devotion for now."

My eyes widen as she pulls needles out of the straw bag she seems to carry with her at all times and begins to knit. She sees my surprise and smiles. "It relaxes me." She settles herself more comfortably and accidentally kicks the bag over. A ball of yarn falls out and begins to roll across the car.

"I've got it," I say, jumping up. I bend to retrieve it from under a seat and then roll it back up before returning it to the bag. As I settle the bag upright, I spot a small red book lying in the bottom of the bag. My heart slams into my ribs and I stare up at her.

She takes the bag from me. "Thank you, darling. That could have been a real mess if you hadn't reacted so fast."

I nod before picking up my own small handbag and surreptitiously feeling for my codebook. I want to cry in relief when I locate its hard outline. I sit back down, my heartbeat slowly returning to normal. The book in her bag simply looks like mine. It's not as if small red books are that unusual. For a moment I thought— Well, I don't know what I thought, but the incident serves as a warning to me. I mustn't lose sight of what I'm doing for a moment. To do so is not only foolhardy but downright dangerous.

I think of that later as we reach our destination. Though parts of France and even Luxembourg looked as if spring might not be that far off, Berlin is still locked in the gray, icy grip of winter. Looking at the city now, it's hard to believe that it can be lovely and full of life. Nothing can hide its unique mixture of history and modernity, though. Modern brick buildings sit incongruously next to baroque churches, and while the old streets tend to wander haphazardly here and there, the streets of the newly built sections of the city are ruler straight and meet at perfect ninety-degree angles. The Germans are a strange blend of the industrious and the artistic and their capital city shows this intermingling.

In spite of everything—the nerves, the danger, and the assignment that weighs heavily on my shoulders—a small part of me is oddly excited to be back in the city I'd loved so much. My heart leaps when I see the restaurant where my parents took me to celebrate my eighth birthday. I felt so grown up going out to a late supper. The headwaiter brought out a beautiful *Donauwelle* cake covered with sour cherries and candles just for me.

We'd been so happy here.

Mrs. Tremaine has already said good-bye and that she'd no doubt see me at the palace. I wonder. Somehow I don't think an Australian opera singer will be mingling much with the governesses.

Maxwell turns up to help me with my things. "Thank you," I tell him, even though I know it's part of his job.

He smiles, his eyes crinkling up at the corners. "I'm to make sure you are settled. It seems as if no one knows quite what to do with governesses or ladies-in-waiting. You're not really servants, because of the family tie, and yet you're being paid. It always seems to cause such confusion."

"It's like we're being paid to be family," I say, and he laughs.

"That's it exactly, but on the bright side, you are getting a motorcar to yourself."

Maxwell hands the driver my trunks before helping me climb up into the backseat of the town car. The thin light of the sun casts shadows over the street and Max suddenly feels like the last friend I have in the world.

"Will I see you?"

He must catch the wistfulness in my voice, because he squeezes my hand before letting it go. His eyes, velvet brown, reassure mine. "Undoubtedly, Sophia Thérèse. I'll make sure of it."

He nods to the driver and gives me a snappy salute. I watch him until the motorcar turns the corner and he's gone.

# TWELVE
## WZHOYH

*Target: The victim of surveillance; the subject.*

Sighing, I settle in to watch the buildings go by, wondering how many changes the past seven years have wrought on the city. The streets are all lit with electric lights now. Before, many of the streetlamps were gas. Lights glow from most of the windows as well, making me think that the Germans have been successful in wiring most of the city. Or at least the area between the train station and the Berliner Stadtschloss.

I've seen the City Palace before, of course, but have never been in it. My father had been inside several times, but had no reason to take his little girl there. Built in an unheard-of short amount of time during the Middle Ages, the Stadtschloss has been renovated several times and is the kaiser's chief residence, though the prince and the duchess spend a great deal of their time at the newly modernized Marble Palace in Potsdam.

I'm taken to the servants' entrance, a small, nondescript

door in the back. Several men in livery are standing next to it, smoking, and I can feel their leering as the driver and I go through the door. The driver hands me off to a maid, who silently escorts me to my room, which is somewhere in the back and near the attic. Learning the layout of the Stadtschloss is going to be my first priority.

"Have you worked here long?" I ask the maid, in an attempt to be friendly, but the glance she gives me is less than sociable.

"Two years, miss, and I like my job." The answer is short and to the point, and I know further questions are useless.

This won't be the person to give me a tour.

My room is small and scrupulously clean, but plain in its appointments. Not like servants' quarters—the furniture is too nice for that—but definitely not a luxurious guest suite, either. The bed is covered with a pretty yellow counterpane and I see fresh flowers on the dark wood dresser. I smile. At least someone tried to make it welcoming. There's a key on the dresser next to the flowers, and I let out a sigh of relief. At least I'll be able to secure my door when I leave. Not that the housekeeper doesn't have a set of keys, but at least not everyone will be able to walk right in.

I scan the room, looking for a hidey-hole, as I unpack. Miss Tickford told me to get my papers out of the trunk as quickly as possible, as that's the first place someone would look. Unfortunately, I don't run across any loose floorboards or secret drawers. Not that I really expected to. It just would have made things easier.

I kneel next to the bedstead and run my hand underneath until I find a place between the wooden slats. After making a slit in the bottom of the mattress with the small knife Miss Tickford gave me, I pull out enough cotton batting to hide the folded papers in. Once the papers are safely concealed, I shove the batting back in as best I can.

After I'm done, I sit on the edge of the bed and look around in a kind of stunned disbelief. How did I end up in Germany impersonating a dead woman? As a teacher to the kaiser's grandchildren? Panic flutters in my stomach and I quickly turn to the practical. If I dwell on my situation for too long, I'll be paralyzed by fear and won't accomplish anything.

I make a mental list. One of the first things I have to do, after meeting Lillian and Marissa, is to plan an escape route in case of an emergency. I hope it won't come to that, but it's essential to have a contingency plan. Then I need to make contact with LDB to ensure that communication is properly established. The tension across my shoulders eases as I plan my next steps.

There's a knock on the door and I take a deep breath. It's time to put the plan in motion.

I open the door to a pretty young woman wearing a plain blue suit.

She holds out a hand. "Hello there! I'm Lillian Bouchard. We'll be working together in the schoolroom."

I know from my research that Lillian Bouchard is twenty-three, though she looks much younger in spite of the severe ash-blond knot at the back of her head. There's something different about her and it takes me a moment to notice that her eyes are dissimilar colors—one is spring green while the other is a light blue.

I smile. "You must be responsible for the flowers," I say, switching into French.

Her eyes light up. "I am, and your French is lovely. You have no accent at all, which is unusual for a German. No offense, of course."

I shake my head. "I have a talent for languages." I wonder how many times I'm going to have to say that.

"I can see. That'll come in handy with the children. Their grandfather is insistent that they be fluent in multiple tongues. Would you care for a tour of the schoolroom now? Or are you tired from your journey?"

It doesn't matter how tired I am, I jump at the chance for a tour. "I'd love to see the schoolroom and at the very least this wing of the palace, if you could show me. I'd like to get my bearings."

She nods. "Very wise. The children will lead you on a merry chase if you lose sight of them."

I hang up my coat and follow her out of the room, half listening as she shows me the servants' quarters, which take up almost the entire upper east wing of the palace. While the servants' area is not extravagant, by any means, I'm surprised by just how clean and up-to-date it actually is, considering. Most royal families have installed running water and electricity in the main parts of the house while letting the rooms the staff live in languish from neglect. In the Stadtschloss, even the hallways of the servants' quarters are warm and clean.

"This is the servants' lounge," she says, passing a spacious room with a battered piano, a large rectangular table, and several worn sofas and chairs that look to be hand-me-downs from nicer parts of the palace. I give a tentative smile to several young women playing cards in the corner of the room, only to be eyed coldly in return.

"Don't mind them," Lillian says in French. "They're jealous of our position and education. They'll never be more than maids, while both you and I can move on to other positions or marry well. I don't spend much time here." She gives a typically French sniff and I hide my grin.

We walk on, through several doors and down a narrow stairway, until we reach what I assume is the children's area of the palace. Rich tapestries, depicting panoramic scenes from Roman or Greek myths, hang from the walls. Long red carpets create pathways on the gleaming parquet floors and elaborate chandeliers hang from the ceiling every twenty to thirty feet. The area is completely silent—even our footfalls are muffled by the carpets.

"The children have already been taken to the nursery for the night, so you'll meet them tomorrow," Lillian says.

"I thought the prince's family had moved to the Marble Palace?"

"They have, but the duchess doesn't like to live so far out. The prince rather indulges her. Probably to make up for his other shortcomings."

She casts me a sideways glance and I raise my eyebrows, hoping for some royal gossip, but we've reached the schoolroom and nothing more is said.

"Here is our domain!" She sweeps her arm about an enormous corner room filled with tables, comfortable-looking furniture, and bookshelves. Large multipaned windows occupy two walls, making the room seem even more spacious and airy than it is.

"This is lovely," I tell her truthfully. "Not at all what I expected."

"The duchess has modern views on child rearing and education. We also have several other children here, the offspring of relatives staying at the palace."

"How many children will we be teaching?" I ask.

"Six. The three princes, of course, and three girls—the duchess's nieces and then a Hohenzollern cousin. Not sure how they're related, but they are. The boys and girls are being educated together, at least for now. As I said, the duchess is rather modern."

She takes my arm in a chummy fashion as she switches off the schoolroom light. "I'm glad you're here. They can be a bit of a handful for one person. I've had a maid to help watch them, but of course she can't teach."

"Do you think you can show me the rest of the palace?" I ask. "It's so huge, and I want to make sure I can find my way around." I have the blueprint of the Stadtschloss in my trunk, but looking at a drawing is much different than actually walking through the halls, and I really need to know where Marissa Baum's room is.

Lillian gives me a lovely smile. "Of course. We might as well do it now. Though we have most afternoons free, I'm sure you'll be too tired to do much exploring. What would you like to see?"

I'm trying to think how I might ask to see where the family friends stay in a way that won't raise suspicion when a dim light comes on in one of the rooms down the hall. My companion hesitates ever so slightly before picking up speed.

She stops when we reach the servants' stairwell. "I'm so sorry, I forgot I have some work to do on tomorrow's lessons. We'll have to reschedule our tour. Do you think you could find your way back to your room on your own?" Her voice is casual, but her shoulders are tense.

"Of course. Up two flights of stairs and through those two doors, right?"

She nods, not bothering to hide the relief on her face. "Yes, that's it. I'll come for you at seven in the morning to show you the servants' dining hall."

She opens the door for me and smiles. I give her a jaunty wave and make a show of heading up the stairs until the door shuts. Then, taking a deep breath, I turn back.

Heart in my throat, I tiptoe back down and count to ten before opening up the door a crack. Lillian was acting perfectly normal until the light switched on in that room. If she has a secret assignation with someone, it could mean that she's Velvet.

I see nothing through the crack, and the hall is silent. If I'm discovered, I can always claim to be lost.

Opening the door wider, I slip through and shut it quietly behind me. I pause for a moment, my eyes staring at the dim light down the hallway. I strain to listen for voices, but the only sound I hear is the thudding of my own heart.

A sense of unreality creeps over me as I slink silently down the hall. What am I doing here in the kaiser's palace in the middle of a war?

Looking for Velvet—a woman so important that the British government is willing to risk anything to save her.

Risk *me* to save her.

As I near the room, I hear voices and freeze.

"Do you want to meet with her?" I hear a man ask.

"I don't know." Lillian's voice is laced with pain. "What else did she say?"

"I already told you that you need to make a decision before she leaves. That this may be your last opportunity."

"When is she leaving?"

"She'll be here for another week or so. She doesn't want to stay in Berlin any longer than necessary."

I frown. The man's voice has a familiar tonal quality that I can't quite place.

"Arrange a meeting. Maybe talking with her will help me make up my mind." Lillian's voice is weary and defeated.

A sudden silence warns me that they may be moving toward the door. Panicked, I dart behind a giant potted palm.

"As soon as you make arrangements, let me know," Lillian says.

"Of course," the man says.

The voices are getting farther and farther away, but by the time I get up enough nerve to peep out from behind the potted plant, they're disappearing around the corner. The dark-haired man by Lillian's side is rather slender and, unlike most men I've seen in Germany, isn't in uniform.

I wait another couple of beats before entering the room they'd met in. It's just one of the many hundreds in the palace with grand furnishings that are rarely used and shelves of books that are never opened. The waste of space and money makes me cringe. Nothing looks out of the ordinary and I return to my room without incident.

Once I'm safely inside, I tremble with relief. I've done as much spying as my nerves will allow. And even though I didn't find out exactly what was going on with Lillian's meeting, I didn't get caught, so I consider my first real spy undertaking a success.

Tucking the bag with my codebook under the mattress, I crawl into bed, praying I'll be able to sleep.

Who was the man Lillian was with? Miss Tickford didn't indicate that anyone else knew who Velvet was—on the contrary, the entire reason I'm here is that Velvet's disappeared and no one else knows exactly who she is or how to get in touch with her. But what if Velvet is being led astray by an enemy? Or maybe the man Lillian was talking to is her source? Velvet has to be getting her information from someone. It's not as if they would just allow a woman to waltz into a war council.

I hear footsteps outside my door and I pause, unable to breathe until a door opens and shuts just down the hall.

My breath comes out in a whoosh. I have to relax. Of course there'll be people coming and going all night. Many of the female servants sleep on this corridor.

My mind wanders, as it often does, to my father. I turn to lie on my back again, staring up at the ceiling.

*Is he alive?* I think he is, but I can't know for sure. *Is he a prisoner of war?* Tears form in my eyes and I wipe them away.

Spies mustn't cry.

I awake the next morning to the sound of footsteps hurrying back and forth outside my room. The palace is awakening. I wash quickly in the small water closet in my room and run a comb through my hair. Before dressing in one of the plain suits Miss Tickford bought me, I tuck the codebook into the inside pocket of my jacket, wondering if she'd had the pocket placed there for that very reason.

The mirror in the water closet is small and wavy with age, making it difficult to draw on my birthmark. I look at the finished product. Does it look the same as it did yesterday? It's hard to tell.

By the time I've finished making up my bed, Lillian is calling for me.

"Good morning," she says. "I trust you slept well."

"I did, thank you."

"I'll show you the servants' dining hall, but we'll take

our breakfast to the schoolroom. We should go over the lessons I've planned for the children before they arrive."

After collecting a small breakfast of porridge and sausage, we carry our food back to the schoolroom on trays. I eat hungrily, realizing that I missed dinner the night before.

Lillian is all teacher this morning, in her plain skirt and cherry-red sweater. Her voice is quiet and studious as she explains the routine to me.

"It's not difficult. You'll be teaching the three younger students while I work with the older ones. We'll break at ten to take the children out to the courtyard for some air. Their mother usually joins them there."

A servant comes by to take our trays, giving us a saucy glare. Lillian ignores her until she leaves the room.

"This is another reason why I am glad you arrived. Like the lady's maids, the governess has few friends. It'll be nice to have someone to talk to."

Her voice is wistful but I have no time to comment as our charges file in, each of them casting suspicious looks my way.

Prince Wilhelm has dark hair and his father's blue eyes. His mouth is pinched and his eyes narrow as if, at the tender age of nine, he's already sure that his portion is going to be too small, which is odd because I'm fairly certain his portions have never been too small. His younger brother Prince Louis has similar coloring, but his mouth is softer and I see a bit of mischief in his blue eyes. Mary Elizabeth and Victoria are dressed alike in stiff lace dresses. Both have straight yellow hair, pulled back with giant pink bows; round, dimpled chins; and even rounder blue eyes. Gretel has soft brown hair and chubby cheeks and looks barely old enough to be out of the nursery.

Prince Hubertus looks like his father and stands fiercely tall, glancing to his brothers for approval.

I'm never going to be able to tell them apart.

I take Mary Elizabeth, Prince Hubertus, and little Gretel to one corner of the room while Lillian takes the others to a table under the window.

"I am big enough to be with my brothers," Prince Hubertus says, his bottom lip sticking out.

"Me too!" little Gretel says.

Mary Elizabeth says nothing.

"I'm too big for letters," Prince Hubertus says.

"Me too!" echoes Gretel.

Mary Elizabeth says nothing.

"Why don't I test you on your letters and numbers today, and then, depending on the outcome, I'll talk to Miss Bouchard this afternoon about your progress."

"I want to be with my brothers now."

I smile through clenched teeth. "If you weren't old enough to be with your brothers, you would still be in the nursery, right? But you're in the schoolroom and you have much to learn. Just think. Soon Wilhelm and Louis will be going off to boarding school, and then you will be the eldest."

This seems to appease him, and little Gretel, who obviously adores her cousin, goes along with him.

Mary Elizabeth smiles silently.

We get out their slates and chalk and they copy their letters while I watch. Lillian is reading to the older children in French across the room and for the first time I wonder how on earth I'm going to find out who Velvet is when I'm stuck here in the schoolroom. I study Lillian while she reads, but am not sure what to look for. Obviously, she isn't going to do any spying while teaching the children, and I can't just ask her about it.

Or can I?

Perhaps there's something I can ask, something that might make Velvet come out of her shell without arousing suspicion.

But what?

After the children finish their letters, I hand them pencils and their copybooks.

I hadn't thought of asking if we finish at the same time every afternoon or if the schedule varies. I rack my brain trying to figure out a way to meet Marissa Baum—I have no idea how a teacher is supposed to befriend an American socialite. Maybe if I can figure out which room is hers, I can accidentally run into her? Strike up a conversation? Or maybe I can pretend to be interested in learning more about America and ask to meet her?

Shaking my head, I call Prince Hubertus up to show me his copybook. His sturdy little body leans into mine and he smells like a combination of soap and freshly cut hay. Suddenly he pokes my cheek.

"What's that?"

I duck my head to find him staring at his finger, which now has a bit of red on it.

My heart sinks. "It's a birthmark."

"What's a birthmark?"

I grab his hand and wipe the red off with a handkerchief. Did he smear the mark? Would Lillian notice? "It's a mark you're born with."

"Why don't you just wipe it off?"

"It doesn't come off," I whisper through clenched teeth.

He frowns and holds up his hand. "Then why did it come off on my finger?"

I glance at Lillian, who is engrossed in a botany lesson she's teaching. "It didn't," I whisper fiercely. If Lillian catches wind of this conversation, it could be a disaster.

"It did," he says stoutly. Lillian may not be aware of what's going on, but Mary Elizabeth and little Gretel are watching the interchange with interest.

"I want a birthmark."

"Me too!" chimes in little Gretel.

"Do you like chocolate?" I ask, a little desperately.

A cunning expression comes over Prince Hubertus's face. "Yes."

"Me too!" says little Gretel.

"If you all attend to your lessons and say no more, I'll bring you some chocolates as soon as I can get to a candy shop. Do we have a deal?"

Prince Hubertus tilts his head. "I want two chocolates."

"Fine. Now go sit down," I say with another glance at Lillian.

If Prince Hubertus is any indication of German stubbornness, the war doesn't look so good for Britain. I just pray his grubby little finger didn't smear the mark too noticeably.

After what seems like an interminably long time, Lillian calls for a break. I stand, my limbs cramping from sitting for so long. I resolve right then and there that no matter what happens in my life, I'm never going to be a teacher.

Lillian gives me a worried glance as we get ready to go out. "I'm sorry, I forgot to have you bring your coat. It's a bit chilly on our morning breaks. Here, take my sweater. I'll wear my coat."

She doesn't even glance twice at my birthmark, so it must be all right. I slip into the cherry-red wool sweater she hands me and then help little Gretel put on a blue coat of soft leather with feathers decorating the cuffs and hood. Mary Elizabeth and Prince Hubertus put on their own jackets and then line up with the others. Whatever else Lillian is, she's obviously someone who runs a tight ship. The children seem incredibly well behaved.

You wouldn't know it a few minutes later as they run out into the courtyard with raucous shouts.

I grin at their enthusiasm and Lillian smiles indulgently. "They're penned up too much," she tells me. "It's been a long winter and their fathers are all preoccupied with the war. It doesn't matter as much for the younger ones, but Prince Wilhelm, especially, could use his father's attention."

She glances at me. "Not that I'm judging, you understand," she puts in quickly.

I nod, wanting her to trust me. "Of course." Then I use her words as an opening to talk politics. "My visit to Luxembourg was interesting. There were soldiers. The effects of the war aren't felt much where I live, other than the rationing."

Her eyes are grave as she nods. "I can imagine that was disturbing."

I wait a moment before continuing. "It seemed as if some of the Luxembourgians were quite complacent about the German presence, while others were disgruntled."

I watch her face closely. One of the reasons LDB suspects that Lillian Bouchard may be Velvet is that she's half German and half French and therefore her loyalties may be torn. If she is Velvet, won't she be conflicted about her betrayal of Germany? Or would she? If she's spying for LDB, wouldn't she already have chosen her side?

"I'm sure they are conflicted," she says, her voice harsh. "War is never easy. Especially for those of us with mixed parentage. But if nations don't stand with their allies against aggression, then they might as well not have allies."

I blink. That argument was used by both the British and the Germans at the beginning of the war, and it gives me no insight whatsoever into Lillian's true allegiance.

Her attention is suddenly diverted. "Louis! The stick is for your hoop, not your little brother."

"Stop bullying your siblings and come see your mother,"

a voice calls from the other side of the courtyard.

Three women walk toward us. One of them, dressed in a walking suit of rich peacock blue, is holding her arms out toward the children, a smile lighting up her face. Her brown hair is dressed in a simple chignon and she wears a small hat with matching blue flowers on top.

Another, carrying a sweater and a parasol, is obviously a maid, while the third is much younger and is dressed stylishly in a sporty suit made of soft brown wool. Her reddish-brown hair is cut in a daring bob, like mine, but hers comes to two sleek points on her jawline. Her eyes are a lively brown and freckles dot an impudent nose.

Marissa Baum.

My pulse speeds up with both excitement and nerves. I was getting concerned, trying to figure out how to meet Marissa, and here she is. I follow Lillian's lead into a deep curtsy, remembering that the duchess is a distant cousin who has met me, or Sophia Thérèse, once before.

Lillian introduces us, but the duchess waves the introduction aside.

"I would know my cousin anywhere by those curls, even if the face has changed immensely since she was three."

I smile. The duchess herself is lovely, with lustrous, dark eyes, but I'm more interested in the girl by her side.

"So nice to see you again, Duchess. Thank you for the opportunity to come to Berlin. I'm honored to be teaching your children."

"Not at all. I am sure Lillian appreciates the help. The

boys can be so rambunctious. This is my dear friend, Fräulein Marissa Baum, recently from America. She's related to the Hohenzollerns, though it would take a historian to figure out exactly how."

"And who really cares anyway?" Miss Baum drawls in atrocious German.

Should I curtsy or kiss her hand or . . . ? As if sensing my discomfort, Miss Baum reaches out and shakes my hand.

"How do you do," I say in English, careful to hide my British accent.

"Oh, Lord love you," Miss Baum says, covering up my awkwardness. "I know my German is terrible, though everyone is relentlessly polite about it." She rolls her eyes at the duchess, who merely smiles at her impertinence.

I watch Miss Baum as she speaks. Her gestures are animated and her brown eyes are alert. Actually, I think with a pang, her mannerisms are very similar to my cousin Rose's.

Around us, the children play hoops and ball, and even the girls run about as if they've been cooped up forever. As the others talk, mostly about the children, I glance from Miss Baum to Lillian, wondering which one could actually be Velvet. Miss Baum has more opportunity and freedom to be a spy—Lillian is hampered by her work with the children. On the other hand, as friendly as the duchess and Marissa Baum are, because of America's noncommittal stance toward the war, Miss Baum's heritage would make her somewhat suspect—but then so would Lillian's French parentage. And yet here they both are, practically members of the family.

On first impression, Lillian seems much more mature and serious, while Miss Baum seems far more adventurous, having traveled from America to Germany on a whim.

"What brings you to Germany, Miss Baum?" I ask. I blush, realizing that I've interrupted the duchess.

"Please call me Marissa. All this formality makes me wild. We don't hold to such customs in the States."

"No, Marissa is from the Wild West," the duchess says with a smile.

"I'd hardly call Chicago the West, nor is it wild. It's almost as big as Berlin, though the only palaces we have are on Lake Shore Drive." She grins as if making a joke, then moves on, realizing that none of us understood it. "Sorry, that's where the wealthy people live. Anyhow, I came because I wanted to get to know my German cousins better. I was hoping for a European tour, but when I realized you all were having a war over here, I thought it would be prudent to postpone my trip for a while." Her nose wrinkles as she grins.

My brows rise. "Your parents let you come all the way here alone, during a conflict?"

Her eyes zero in on mine. "How inquisitive you are!" she exclaims. "In America, young women are much freer in their movements, especially when they have oodles of money. And how about you? Your family didn't mind you traveling about willy-nilly by yourself during a war? You look younger than I am."

"I'm actually twenty. How old are you?" I counter, trying to steer the conversation away from myself.

"Twenty? Really? You're older than I am!" She turns to the others. "She looks far younger, doesn't she?"

My stomach knots as everyone looks at my face. Thankfully, Marissa is suddenly distracted by two of the children. "Wilhelm! Louis! Do you want to hear more about the Indians?"

Marissa and the duchess wander off with the children in tow, leaving Lillian and me alone.

"I'm sorry if I offended anyone," I say to Lillian. "I'm not really used to social chatter. Life in my village was very quiet in comparison to the palace."

Lillian shakes her head. "Don't worry. The duchess is actually very modern in spite of her upbringing. Her friendship with Miss Baum attests to that."

"When did Miss Baum arrive?" I ask.

"About five months ago. Everyone was surprised at how quickly she ingratiated herself with the duchess, but I think they're just being mean-spirited. Miss Baum is very nice and fresh and has quite a good mind. She amuses the duchess, who needs all the amusement she can get."

"Why is that?" I ask. I don't want Lillian to think I'm a gossip, but I have no other way to obtain the information I need.

Lillian lowers her voice. "Well, beyond the obvious problems in her marriage, there is a lot of infighting among the kaiser's sons that extends to their wives. As the wife of the heir apparent, Duchess Cecilie is a target. Plus, she's half Russian, and with all the conflict in Russia . . ." Lillian shrugs. "Well, it's no wonder she enjoys Miss Baum. Her conversation is more than just palace intrigue and war talk."

Again, I try to think of something that might out Lillian as Velvet if she is indeed her. "But what will Miss Baum do if the Americans enter the war?"

Lillian looks at me, her blue eyes wide with horror. "Oh, you don't think that'll happen, do you? Why would they? This doesn't concern them!"

I'd forgotten that I, being from England, no doubt had knowledge of things that the Germans wouldn't read in their daily newspapers.

I twitch a shoulder. "Who knows what the Americans will do. Is it time to go back in yet?"

Lillian nods and calls to the children, who clamor about the duchess for their good-bye kisses. When I look at Miss Baum, she is watching the children with a smile. The duchess raises a hand in farewell and I turn away, wondering if Miss Baum could truly be Velvet and how I'm supposed to find out if she is.

Lillian claps her hands for order as the children line up. A chill wind picks up and I shove my hands in the pockets of Lillian's sweater. I find a slip of paper in the bottom of one of the pockets and instinctively clasp it against my palm. It's probably just a note about the children or a lesson, but whatever it is, I need to read it. Maybe it'll provide insight into who she met with last night or what the meeting was about.

When I return her sweater, I keep the note crumpled in my palm, then I slip it in the pocket of my skirt, hoping to get a chance to read it before the school day ends.

I spend the next hour trying to get the children to do simple sums on their slates. All three of my charges are restless, and several times Lillian has to look over at us and call for quiet. My face burns with embarrassment at my own ineptitude and I resist sticking my tongue out at the little heathens. Finally I give up and, in desperation, bring out their pencils and tell them to sketch the small plant in the window. If asked, I'll just say it's both art and nature study.

Turning my back to Lillian, I take the note out of my pocket and open it up.

As soon as I see it, I draw in a breath.

It's in code.

# THIRTEEN
## WKLUWHHQ

*Naked: A spy operating without any kind of backup and very little support.*

"Are you quite all right?" Lillian asks from behind me.

I crumple the note into a ball in my hand and turn my head. "Oh, yes, I'm sorry. I was just yawning."

Her hand comes down on my shoulder and I suppress a shiver. How long has she been standing there?

"I imagine you're still tired from your journey," she says, her voice sympathetic. "We're almost finished for the day. Why don't you go ahead and go back to your room. I'll take the children to their nurse."

"Are you quite certain?" I ask, wanting more than anything to go back to my room to break the code and read the note.

She waves me out, and after bidding the children good-bye, I hurry down the corridor. My heart flutters with anticipation as I race up the servants' staircase, taking the steps two at a time.

I have no doubt that I can break the code. If it's the LDB

code, I have the cipher. If it's not, I'll just figure it out. I'd love nothing more than to find Velvet this quickly and go home. The longer it takes me to complete the assignment, the greater the chance that I'm going to get caught. Simple mathematics.

I burst out the door into the hall and run headlong into someone. "Excuse me," I say in English without thinking.

My heart slams against my ribs and I quickly follow up in German. *"Entschuldigung!"* I say, raising my voice.

"Where are you off to in such a hurry?"

I blink and then smile as I recognize Maxwell. I don't know why I'm so happy to see him. He's a German soldier. If he suspects I'm a British spy, he'll cart me off to prison as quickly as anyone else would. Thankfully, he doesn't seem to have noticed my lapse. "Oh, hello! I just finished my first day of teaching."

"And it looks as if you couldn't get away fast enough. Was it that bad, then?" His sincere and warm brown eyes invite confidence and I find myself lost in his gaze for a moment.

I give myself a mental shake. "Er, no. Of course not. It was lovely. And I got to meet the duchess and Fräulein Baum."

"The duchess? You mean your cousin?" he asks.

I want to bite my tongue off. "Of course. It's just difficult to think of her as such under the circumstances. It's not like we grew up together. I hardly know her. . . ." I let my prattling trail off.

He inclines his head. "Of course," he says graciously,

ignoring my awkwardness. "As it happens, I was looking for you."

"You were?" My voice squeaks upward in surprise and I flush.

"Yes. I wanted to see how your first day went." His brown eyes are serious.

My eyes narrow. Why would he want to know? Is he here as a friend or as a guard? Is there more to his query than simple courtesy? "Did the prince send you, or did you come on your own?"

It's his turn to be surprised. "I came on my own. Why would you think the prince sent me?" Comprehension dawns in his eyes. "Oh, no, don't worry on that account, he's currently distracted by Mrs. Tremaine. Plus, now that you're here and caring for his children, I believe he'll leave you alone. You're much too close to home, so to speak."

"That's a relief," I say.

He gives a surprised laugh. "Funny girl. Many young women would be honored by such attention."

"From what I hear, many girls *are* honored by such attention." I grin.

Smiling, he cocks his head to one side. "Well, don't worry. I don't think you'll need to carry your Bible about anymore."

Maxwell gives me a knowing look and I blush, knowing I've been caught.

Then he clears his throat. "I also came for another reason. I have Thursday afternoon off and was wondering if you would like to go take in some sights after your duties. Berlin is a magnificent city and I thought you might enjoy an outing."

I hesitate. It's not that I wouldn't like to get out of the palace, but should I waste time when I could be trying to find Velvet? On the other hand, Maxwell *could* be a valuable font of information if I work it right. I only feel a small twinge of guilt for using him as I nod. "I'd like that very much."

His smile lights up the planes of his face. "Wonderful. I'll meet you in the servants' lounge about this time Thursday?"

He touches his cap and is about to leave when I place a hand on his sleeve. "Wait."

He turns to me, inquiring.

I clear my throat and give an appealing smile. "Fräulein Lillian gave me a short tour of the palace yesterday, but we were interrupted. I'd love to see a bit more now, if you're free."

My face heats, knowing how forward I must seem, but it's the only way to find out where Miss Baum is staying.

If he's surprised, he hides it well. He checks his pocket watch.

"It's fine if you don't have time," I put in hastily.

He holds up a hand. "No, I have a bit before I must resume my duties. What would you like to see?"

It's on the tip of my tongue to ask where the private family apartments are, but that would be too obvious, so I ask for the grand reception area first.

To my surprise, he takes me through a nondescript door in the servants' quarters. Once inside, he holds the door open with one foot as he lights a lantern that was sitting on a table just inside the door. After it's lit, he lets the door behind him close.

The light casts shadows across his face but I can still see his grin as he leads me down several steps into a dank, dim corridor. "Tunnels!" I say, surprised. "I didn't know the Stadtschloss had secret tunnels." I look around in wonder. This is amazing.

"Most palaces have hidden passageways designed to get the royal family out safely in case of an uprising. The Stadtschloss only has a few actual tunnels, but it has plenty of hidden passageways built in the walls between the formal rooms and the private apartments. It's often much faster to use them than it is to go the regular route. Some of them, such as this one, are occasionally used by servants. Others, like those that lead to the family rooms and guest rooms, haven't been used in years."

My brain is racing with the implications. If I could learn to navigate the secret passages, I would be better able to come and go as I pleased. Plus, these would be a perfect escape route. "How many servants use this one?" I ask as he leads me down the passageway.

"Like I said, this one is used more often than the rest, as it leads from the servants' quarters to the reception areas. And it's nice and large. Most, like that one"—he nods at a heavy wooden door set in rock—"are much narrower and lead to the children's area."

I take careful note of the door. "The nursery or the schoolroom?"

He grins. "Both, actually. I bet you'll be looking for the door tomorrow, won't you? Don't feel bad that you haven't seen it. It's hidden under a small toy box."

Our footsteps seem extraordinarily loud in the empty corridor and the odor of mold mixed with sewage is so strong in places it almost burns my nose. "Not very pleasant," I say.

"No," he agrees. "Most of the maids far prefer to walk the long way, but I figured you were up for an adventure."

I glow at his words, but being me, want to know more. "Why would you think that?"

He grins. "Any young woman as pretty as you would have to love adventure to leave her home and travel across the country during a war."

I blink. *He thinks I'm pretty?*

"Either that, or have an ulterior motive." He raises an eyebrow. "Do you have an ulterior motive, Sophia Thérèse?"

My heart pounds. "I don't know what you mean," I choke out.

He laughs. "I was teasing. No one as nice as you could have an ulterior motive."

*If only he knew.*

"How about you?" I counter. "How do you know your way around the tunnels so well?"

It's his turn to look discomfited. "My father was a friend of Kaiser Wilhelm's. We stayed often when I was a child. Of course, once I discovered that there was a labyrinth beneath the palace, I couldn't stop until I had explored it all."

I hear the smile in his voice.

I wish he weren't so nice. It makes using him for my own ends much harder.

He points at another door, which has an X scratched into the wood. "That tunnel is barely passable. It leads outside the palace to the Lustgarten across the street. I don't think it's been used in years."

I'd been to the garden as a child but I don't remember any secret doors. Of course, that's probably because they were hidden. "Where does it end?"

"I think the old opening was under a clump of bushes surrounding the statue of Zeus. I couldn't follow it all the way; the passage became far too narrow."

We reach another set of stairs, which takes us to a narrow hallway. The air is lighter and fresher and I take a deep breath. He then leads me to a door so small I have to duck to go through it. Once I can stand upright again, I look about in confusion. We're in a tiny, oddly shaped room with a steeply slanted ceiling. "I thought you were taking me to the grand reception room?"

"I am." His voice is so close to my ear that I jump, bumping my head on the low ceiling.

He gives a soft laugh. I turn my head to find his eyes inches from mine and glowing from the light of the lantern. "I wanted you to see this first."

I look around and spot several small cushions, a few

worn-out stuffed animals, and several books piled in one corner. "What is this place?"

"The hideout for generations of children who wish to spy on their elders. Look." He bends and kneels in front of what looks like an illustration from a nursery book that had been tacked to the wall. He moves it sideways and a sudden light shines through. He waves his hand and I bend to look through the hole. It's not very big, about the size of a coin, but I can see part of an ornate room decorated in gold and blue.

"We're under the staircase of the reception room. Come on."

He blows out the lantern and carefully opens another small door. When we emerge, I find myself under the staircase of a reception room so ornate it makes the one in Luxembourg seem almost shabby. I turn back to see him carefully shutting the door behind us. The door is so well hidden that if you weren't looking for it, you might not even know where it was.

"Does the kaiser know it's here?" I wonder aloud.

"Undoubtedly. I'm sure your young charges do, as well. It's almost a rite of passage to show it to the next generation. Now, would you like to see the Grand Hall?"

He holds out his arm and I take it. The Grand Hall leads from the outside to the reception room and is designed to intimidate, with giant tapestries depicting scenes from the Bible and mythology.

I'm giggling over a particularly horrid rendition of Diana

the Huntress when the sound of footsteps reaches me. A tall, reedy man rounds the corner. The relief crossing his face when he spots Maxwell changes quickly to hesitation when his eyes move to me.

My instincts scream and I freeze even before I see the small black pistol in his hand. Something shoves me, hard, and the next thing I know, I'm sprawling on the floor and Maxwell has his gun against the man's head. The man drops the pistol he was holding and it clatters against the polished marble. Without thinking, I scramble to snatch it up.

"Give me the gun, Sophia Thérèse," Maxwell says, his voice tight. "Slowly."

He puts out his hand without ever taking his eyes off the man, who, all reptilian intensity, is staring at Maxwell. I place the gun in Maxwell's palm without question.

"Do you remember how you got here?"

I nod and then, realizing that he isn't looking at me, croak out a yes.

"I want you to go back to your room immediately. Tell no one about this."

I hesitate, not wanting to leave him with someone who is clearly dangerous, with or without the gun. Sweat beads on Maxwell's forehead as if he and the assailant are locked in an invisible duel.

"Go!" he commands.

I lift my skirts and run back down the Grand Hall and into the majestic reception room. My hands are trembling so badly that it takes me two tries before I can get the door open. I shut it behind me just as I hear a gun go off. I hesitate in the darkness, my hand on the lantern. *Should I go back out? What if Maxwell is hurt?* I shake my head. No. I have my own business to think of. The last thing I need is to be involved in any sort of shooting incident. Apparently, Maxwell felt the same, because he definitely sent me off in a hurry.

I race through the corridors, my pulse pounding. Thankfully, the way back to the servants' quarters is well marked and I'm soon in my own little room.

I lean back against the door, my legs trembling.

*Who was that man? Why did he have a gun?*

I lock the door behind me and then go to the small water closet and splash water on my face. My eyes look huge and my pale skin is even paler than usual. I turn away, my nerves jangling like coins in a tin cup.

Then I remember the note I took from Lillian's sweater.

Even though the last thing I want at the moment is more intrigue, I have a job to do. I take another deep breath and pull the codebook out of the inside pocket of my fitted jacket and sit at the small desk underneath the one tiny window in my room. With fingers that are still trembling, I unfold the note. I'm prepared for a challenge. It takes me a moment to realize what I'm seeing, and when I do, my heart dips in disappointment. This is barely a code at all. Each number represents its corresponding alphabetic letter. Little Gretel could have deciphered this. If state secrets are being passed to Velvet, wouldn't the code be more sophisticated?

One would hope.

Sighing, I quickly decipher it.

*Meet me by the fountain tomorrow night at ten.*

I frown. Obviously, this is meant for Lillian. But who wrote it? I look at the note again, but there's no way of knowing if she received this today or yesterday, or even a week ago. It could have been in her pocket for days, for all I know. No. I'm betting that she received it this morning. She came to fetch me wearing the red sweater.

I wonder if this has something to do with the mysterious visit with the young man.

But what fountain? Sighing, I slump in the chair. Did I really think it was going to be simple? If figuring out who Velvet is was easy, the people at La Dame Blanche would have done it already and she'd be safely out of Germany.

I rub my temples, trying to think it through logically. The information Velvet had been passing along has to do with troop movements. So wouldn't the person giving her the information have something to do with the German army? A strategist, perhaps? But now she has information regarding some kind of new weapon. Where could she obtain that sort of intelligence?

There has to be a way I can find out.

I need to search Marissa's and Lillian's rooms, but I hesitate to do so until I'm certain I have the time to do so safely. Besides, I need to have a clearer idea of which direction I should be going in. Right now, given the note, Lillian seems most likely, but I need more information. Who would have their finger on the pulse of all the gossip in the palace? It comes to me in a flash.

The servants, of course. The ones who hate me because I'm a governess. I stand and smooth out my gray serge skirt. As a governess and someone related to the duchess, I can elect to have my meals brought to my room, but I think perhaps it's time for me to make friends.

Problem is, none of them wish to make friends with me.

Supper is served buffet style. The fare is simple: stew, biscuits, sausages, and the like. Lillian is nowhere to be seen, which doesn't surprise me, given the mutual antipathy between her and the maids. She no doubt takes her supper in her room. That actually serves my purpose quite well.

Several girls are eating at a small table while a number of footmen and other male servants are eating at the big table. I help myself to a cup of tea and a plate of stew and biscuits from the sideboard. I hesitate a moment before joining the women.

A ginger-haired girl with snapping brown eyes gives me the once-over as I sit. I smile at her but she ignores me.

"Look who decided to slum it," she says to the others, as if I'm not there.

"Imagine, the likes of her eating supper with the likes of us," a girl with a snubbed nose says.

The other one darts a look at me out of the corner of her eye and bites her lip as if unsure of what to do.

Taking a deep breath, I play along. "Perhaps she's just

tired from spending the day with a dictator and six spoiled monsters and is in need of some decent conversation." I take a sip of my tea, watching them out of the corner of my eye. The reaction to my words is tangible. One girl gasps and then looks to see if the men overheard me. The ginger-haired girl grins.

"Rough day, I take it. I was wondering what it would be like to work with her unroyal highness. She gives herself such airs, but unlike you, she has no tie to the royal family."

My brows arch. The rumor mill is skilled. "How do you know about my connection to the duchess?"

The ginger-haired girl snorts. "Lovely Lillian let it slip to everyone within earshot. I'm Mathilde, by the way, and this is Deirdre, and Johanna." The other girls nod shyly, but there is nothing shy about Mathilde.

"So what are you doing here with us?" she asks.

It's my turn to snort. "I'm on staff—no matter what my connections are." I steer the conversation away from myself. "How long has Lillian worked here?"

"She's been here for a little over a year, but you'd think she owned the place," Mathilde says. "Took right over and looks down her nose at everyone. She has no friends here at all."

The other girls let Mathilde do all the talking, but they punctuate her words with nods.

"None?" I ask, thinking about the note I'd secreted back in my room.

Mathilde shakes her head. "None that I know of."

I take a sip of tea, trying to figure out how to discover what the staff knows about Marissa Baum. Fortunately, Mathilde gives me the opportunity with her next words.

"I think she's trying to use the children to ingratiate herself with the duchess. It might have worked except that Miss Baum showed up."

"What happened after that?" I ask.

"Ever since then it's been nothing but Miss Baum for the duchess. Put the lovely Lillian's nose quite out of joint, I'm sure."

"I met Miss Baum today," I say.

Mathilde sniffs. "She's quite nice, but no manners whatsoever. But then, what can you expect from an American? She and the duchess go out all hours. The empress quite hates it. Thinks it's improper."

I hide a grin. If you want gossip and information, always go to the staff. They know far, far more than anyone thinks they do and are usually quite willing to share their knowledge. "What do they do when they go out? Does Miss Baum have any particular young men she likes?"

Mathilde shakes her head. "No. She prefers old army types. Quite the scandal."

My eyebrows arch. This is exactly the type of information I was hoping for. "What sort of old men?" I ask, but just then a young woman in an upstairs-maid uniform bursts into the room.

She pauses in the doorway, her hand dramatically clutching her chest. "Did you hear? Oh, it's horrible!"

Everyone halts what they are doing and listens with varying degrees of interest. Only Mathilde shrugs her shoulders. "Hear what?"

"There's been a man shot dead in the Grand Hall!"

I freeze as the room suddenly erupts in horror. Several servants rush over to the maid, who is still grasping her chest. Mathilde leaps up and helps the overwrought woman to the divan.

I listen, my heart thudding, as she relates her story to her captive audience.

"I was going through the Grand Hall—you know how I dust the portraits every Tuesday evening, yes?" Several people nod, and she continues. "Well, I just saw a crowd of people all looking down at something and talking. There were guards everywhere and some had their guns drawn. Then I saw what they were looking at." At this point her eyes widen so much they look like marbles. "It was the body of a man!"

"No! In the Grand Hall? Who was it?" someone asks.

"Listen and I'll tell you!" the woman says, cross at having her moment interrupted. Everyone leans closer to catch her words. I'm so still, I feel my heart pulsing in my throat.

"An assassin!"

"No!"

The woman's head bobs. "That's what the guards were saying—and I saw him myself in a pool of blood."

"But who was it?" Mathilde asks.

"Well, I don't know! It's not as if he left his calling card in the bowl at the door! They don't know who he was after. That handsome young guard shot him. Quite the hero."

I look down at my stew, my stomach churning. An image of the moment I left them replays in my mind. Maxwell with his gun to the man's head and the man so quiet and still, as if daring Max to do it.

Apparently, Max did.

Quietly, I get up and slip out of the room unnoticed. I remember the tour through the tunnels Maxwell had given me and how ready to smile he was, so different from his official guard persona. Who knew that only moments after, he would be forced to kill someone?

Horror fills my chest, even though, logically, I understand that Max is a guard for the royal family. He wouldn't and shouldn't even hesitate if he thought the family was in danger.

But there was no family in the hall, and what's more, there was a look of recognition in the man's eyes as soon as he saw Maxwell. He knew who Max was, I know he did.

I shake my head. I can't get sidetracked. I must remain focused on finding Velvet.

But I can't help praying that Max is all right.

# FOURTEEN
## IRXUWHHQ

*Hunting Pack: A surveillance team of agents stalking a target from one place to another.*

The schoolroom routine is almost the same the next morning, except we don't go out to the courtyard for a break. I wonder if it's because of the assassin, but Lillian doesn't say and I don't ask. I do notice that there is now a guard stationed in front of the schoolroom door.

In spite of the undercurrent of tension, I can't help but notice what a wonderful teacher Lillian is. Leaving the little ones to their writing, I move closer to where Lillian and the older ones are discussing science.

I smile when she glances over at me. "It's a rare classroom that teaches chemistry this young," I tell her.

"Trust me, chemistry is going to rule the world someday. It's a bit of a passion of mine." She turns back to the children. "Finish reading the rest of the chapter and then I'll quiz you on it."

A governess who's passionate about chemistry? She seems more the literary type, but perhaps I've read her wrong.

Still, I file her words away. Perhaps they mean something or perhaps not. I can't take anything for granted.

Lillian doesn't seem in the mood to chat when we finish school, so I excuse myself and make my way back to my room. I've only been here for a few days, but I'm no closer to finding out who Velvet is than when I arrived. My heart sinks. I could be here for weeks.

All I can do is pray that Captain Parker is keeping his end of the bargain and investigating my father's disappearance. If I pull this off, MI6 is going to owe me, and all I want is information on my father's whereabouts so I can go get him.

If he's still alive.

By the time I reach my room I'm out of sorts and ready for a rest before supper. It isn't until I put my hand on the knob that I realize my door is ajar.

I freeze. Had I left it open this morning? No. I'm always careful to lock it because of the false documents and the palace schematics. Then I hear the scrape of a drawer opening.

My heart leaps into my throat and for a moment I'm tempted to call for help. I discard the idea immediately. I can't draw attention to myself. Nor can I go away and let someone fish out any of my secrets.

I make sure I'm alone before stepping closer to the door. Pulling it open just enough to peer through the crack, I suck in a horrified breath.

My room has been ransacked.

From where I'm positioned, I can see drawers hanging open and clothing strewn all over the floor. The covers of my bed are rumpled and askew. I can't see anyone inside, but know I have to confront whoever is there even though I have no weapon.

Surprise—Monsieur Elliot said my best weapon is surprise, so I take a deep breath and slip into the room.

My eyes dart around, but I see no one. The lid to the jewelry box is open and my heart lurches. Have I been discovered?

Suddenly a stocky, blond-haired man steps out of the bathroom, his eyes flying open when he sees me standing in front of the door. Without thinking, I launch myself forward, tackling him at the waist. He falls heavily, pinning me on the floor before scrambling to his feet. I turn quickly, arms raised in a defensive position, but he's more interested in escaping than in fighting and is out the door in a flash.

Leaping to my feet, I race to the door but only catch a glimpse of him as he rounds the corner. I consider following, but the sound of voices coming from the other direction makes up my mind. Stepping quickly back into my room, I quietly shut the door. The last thing I need is for someone to see the mess and ask questions.

Trembling, I cover my mouth with my hand as I survey my room. Could someone know something? But how? I run the last couple of days through my mind. Had I unintentionally given myself away? The only real close calls were when Prince Hubertus rubbed off some of my birthmark with his finger and when I accidentally said "excuse me" to Maxwell in English instead of German.

I dismiss the Hubertus incident from my mind and concentrate on Maxwell. He *is* a family guard, no matter how nice he is. It's his job to be mistrustful. Maybe he suspected something, even though he didn't seem to notice at the time.

Had he been a little too friendly on our tour through the tunnels? Asked too many questions? No. Nothing in his behavior seemed out of the ordinary. Besides, if he suspected something, wouldn't the guards be here looking through my things instead of an unknown man who ran the moment he could?

Hurrying over to the small jewelry box Miss Tickford gave me, I dump the contents out onto the desk and remove the false bottom. The little packets of sleeping powder and poison spill onto the desk. I note that several pieces of jewelry are missing and take a deep, shaky breath. Not espionage. A simple robbery.

For a moment I consider alerting the guards, but I decide against it. That last thing I want is to call attention to myself in any way.

I straighten up my quarters, practically jumping out of my skin every time someone walks past my door. All I want to do is crawl under my covers and sleep, and then I realize that if someone came into my room it means that someone has a key. Besides, I can't go to bed even if I could sleep. My job isn't finished yet. I have to find out who Lillian is meeting.

I know I won't be able to eat anything, so I sit on the edge of my bed and wait. I remember seeing a fountain in the courtyard where the children play, but there are also fountains in the Lustgarten, across from the palace. Somehow I think that one would be a more likely meeting spot. It's more private and removed from prying palace eyes.

I wait until twenty-five minutes to ten and then slip into my coat. Opening the door slowly, I make certain there is no one out and about before hurrying down the hall. I wish I knew if Max's tunnel to the Lustgarten was passable. Though on second thought, I'm not sure I want to go through the tunnels at night.

According to Lillian, the housekeepers are not as strict about female curfews as they used to be, but I'd just as soon not have to explain what I'm doing wandering about so late at night.

Voices waft out from the servants' lounge as I hurry past. I'm fairly sure I know the way out, but it takes me two tries before I find the servants' door onto the street.

A husky guard raises an eyebrow as I appear and I give him what I hope is a saucy grin. "I'll be back in just a bit. I do hope that's all right."

He grins. "I've been known to look the other way now and again . . . for a price."

I nod. I'd expected as much. "I'll pay your price on my way back in."

"Smart girl. Now don't keep your young man waiting."

I smile again and hurry down the street, pulling my hood as far over my head as it will go. My blond curls are a dead giveaway and I'm hoping to find Lillian, see who she's meeting, and make it back to my room without detection.

There are few people out on the street this late and I'm fairly certain that most of those I pass are up to no good, if their rough appearance is any indication.

The Lustgarten is a testament to Germany's love of the orderly. It's divided up into six grass sections, with concrete walks between the sections. Different statues, including the one of Zeus, surround the garden. There are two fountains, one on either entrance to the garden, and I have no clue as to which one is their meeting place.

I don't have a lot of options for places to hide, so I choose the equestrian statue of Friedrich Wilhelm III, former king of Prussia. The base of the statue is tiered like a wedding cake, and around the first tier is a circle of life-size stone figures of people important to the Prussian state. I look around to make sure I'm alone and climb up to join them. Ducking behind a monk, I crouch down and peer out over the grass. From this position, I'll be able to keep an eye on both fountains until I know which one is the meeting spot. It's not ideal, but with any luck they'll pass close by. If not, I suppose I'll be reduced to following them, which I'd prefer not to do. I'm simply not confident enough in my surveillance abilities.

A bright half-moon shines across the parade ground and glints off the fountain at the exit of the garden. My breath hitches when I spot a woman hurrying across the grass. She's wearing a cape and I can't see her face, but her height is the same as Lillian's.

The woman circles the fountain impatiently, her head swiveling this way and that. She pushes the hood of her cloak back and the moonlight glints off of Lillian's blond hair.

I breathe a sigh of relief in spite of the cramping in my legs. I'm so intent on Lillian that I nearly miss the person passing five feet from my position.

My heart leaps in my chest and I still, not even daring to breathe.

It's a woman. I hear her skirts swish as she passes, but a wide-brimmed picture hat obscures her face. The scent of something floral wafts up toward me. I frown as I recognize the scent. I try to remember where I've smelled it before, but am distracted as Lillian turns and hurries to meet her.

The two stand for several minutes. I can hear the rise and fall of their voices, but they're too far away for me to hear what they're saying. Maybe if I jumped down from the base of the statue I would be able to hear better?

I carefully make my way past several other stone figures so I'm further out of the two women's line of vision. Holding my breath, I ease my way down and drop the last three feet to the ground. I land on a small rock and my foot rolls out from underneath me. A sharp pain slices through my ankle as I fall heavily to the ground and bite back a cry.

Then a dog barks.

My head whips sideways, but they don't see me. Ignoring the pain in my ankle, I swiftly move to the opposite side of the statue, my heart beating wildly.

I stand, frozen, waiting to be discovered, but after a moment of silence the rise and fall of voices continues. I creep back to where I was.

As I peer out at the women, my suspicion is confirmed when I see a small white dog poking about on the grass at their feet.

Penny.

Why would Lillian and Mrs. Tremaine be meeting in secret in the dead of night? How would a French-German governess know an Australian opera singer?

Is this the proof I need that Lillian is Velvet? It's not like I can waltz up to them and ask.

Since I can't get any closer, I decide not to push my luck. Staying out of sight, I hurry back toward the palace. I slow my steps as I near the guard, not wanting to look as if I'm running from someone. He tips his cap and holds out his palm.

I roll my eyes as I hand him a few coins.

He smiles. "I hope it was worth it."

"Me too," I say as he holds the door open for me.

"This has been an unusually lucrative night for me."

I pause on the threshold. "What do you mean?"

He shrugs. "Just a lot of coming and going."

"Really?" I keep my voice casual. "You've been busy, then. Who's been coming and going?"

He puts his palm back out and my eyes narrow as I dig out another coin.

He takes the money and shrugs. "The other governess,

for one, and one of the prince's private guards went out right after you did. Oddly enough, that friend of the duchess, Fräulein Baum, decided she needed to take the back way out, too."

"And they all paid you?" I ask, my mind spinning. I put my hand on the doorjamb to steady myself. Could someone suspect me?

"All except the guard. I don't take gifts from the guards."

"Smart man," I murmur before heading up to my room. The last thing I want is for one of them to come back and catch me coming into the palace. Right now my room seems like the only safe place in the entire world.

Then I remember the man going through my things and it doesn't seem so safe anymore. Maybe that's for the best. Maybe I'll be sharper if I don't feel safe anywhere. I'm a spy. Safety of any kind is just an illusion.

Once I return to my room, I get ready for bed, my thoughts floating about in my mind like tattered bits of paper. I know why Lillian is out and about, but what about Marissa and the guard? Could it have been Maxwell?

After tilting the chair against my door for added protection, I crawl into bed, remembering that I'm going sightseeing with Maxwell tomorrow after school is done for the day. Maybe I can find a way to ask him what he did tonight without being obvious. Because the last thing I want is to make one of the prince's private guards suspicious of me.

★ ★ ★

If anything, the schoolroom is even more tense than it had been the day before, which makes me think that the authorities still don't know who the assassin is. I wonder if Maxwell will still be able to take me sightseeing.

Lillian is tired and pensive, and she uncharacteristically snaps at the children several times.

The note is tucked in the pocket of my own sweater. I'd planned on slipping it back in her pocket, but Lillian kept hers on all morning. So I pretended to pick it up on our way back into the schoolroom after break. "Excuse me, I think you just dropped this." I hold the note out to her and she snatches it out of my hand, her face mottling.

"Where did that come from? I was looking for it." She looks at me and then shakes her head. "Never mind. Thank you."

I watch her closely. Could she really be Velvet? So far the evidence is all circumstantial—the secretive conversation with the young man, the coded note that she doesn't want anyone to see, her interest in chemistry, and her meeting with an Australian foreigner in the middle of the night. But none of that makes her Velvet. I remember that Miss Tickford told me there might be other plots in the palace and I needed to be careful not to stumble upon one. Kaiser Wilhelm has his enemies and has been called on more than once to abdicate the throne. Even though Prince Wilhelm is considered a playboy, there are many Germans who would rather see a womanizer on the throne than a blowhard like his father. The tension between them and their different takes on politics is well known. And as Lillian told me, there's infighting among the royal siblings. Perhaps she is involved in one of those plots? It would make sense that Mrs. Tremaine would like to see her lover on the throne. She could be trying to enlist Lillian's help.

I need to update LDB. Perhaps they can give me some guidance on what my next move should be.

Before I get ready for my outing with Maxwell that afternoon, I take out my LDB codebook and compose a short note.

*Have possible evidence that L is Velvet. How should I proceed?*

Even though I'm just going with Maxwell to obtain more information and drop off the note, I take special care with my appearance. Looking over my limited wardrobe, I choose a stylish gray gabardine walking suit with pleats in the front of the skirt and tortoiseshell buttons on the cuffs of the jacket. I brush my hair until my curls encircle my head like a halo and pin on a walking hat with a taffeta brim and a plaid crown. Looking at myself in the mirror, I can't help but smile at how smart I look.

"Well, hello there, Sophia Thérèse," I say to my reflection. "How nice to see you."

I tuck the note in the inside pocket of my coat and head toward the servants' lounge, where I'm to meet Maxwell.

Thankful that the gossips seem to be otherwise occupied, I take a seat at the table to wait.

Several minutes later, Maxwell comes in looking harried and rumpled, his cap askew.

"I'm sorry I'm late," he apologizes. "My duties kept me longer than I'd expected." His eyes look bruised, as if he hasn't slept since the incident in the ballroom.

Sympathy pangs in my chest. "I can imagine. We can reschedule if you need to," I say, even though I desperately need to get out of the palace.

He shakes his head. "No. I really need the outing. Things have been a bit crazy. . . ." His voice trails off and he looks at me, the expression on his face unaccountably sad. "Are you sure you still want to go? I mean, I'll understand if you changed your mind after what happened."

He doesn't say it, but I know we're both thinking about the man and the gun.

"I haven't," I reassure him. "I've been looking forward to it."

The relief on his face bruises my heart and I take the arm he holds out. I hate that I'm using him, but what is spying but using people? In the past few days I've used Lillian, Mathilde and the other maids, and now Maxwell, who has been nothing but nice to me. I fidget a bit, guilt gnawing at my insides.

It's all a bit morally confusing, really.

"Is everything all right?" I ask.

He sort of nods and shakes his head at the same time.

"We still don't know who the man was. I'm glad you made it back to your room safely. I was worried."

My breath catches. He killed a man coming to assassinate a member of the royal family and he's still been worried about me? "I was fine. I was more concerned about you. Does anyone know who his target was?"

He shakes his head and then takes a deep breath. "It's clear and bright outside, even though it's pretty cold. Let's just try to enjoy ourselves and forget about all that. I've done nothing but think about it since it happened and I could use the reprieve."

His dark eyes are pleading, and I think of all I've been through the past few weeks. I could use a break, too. Even if it's short-lived. I turn to him with a smile. "That's a wonderful idea."

He squeezes my arm. "How was your day?"

"Good. They let us go out for a bit, earlier. It's fun to watch the children interact, but it's difficult to relax while making sure they don't hurt one another or themselves."

As we walk through the palace, I realize that I never got a full tour of the inside. "Do you think you could show me around the palace a bit before we go out? I've seen more of the tunnels than I've seen of the actual living quarters."

His eyebrows arch upward and he nods. "I suppose I could. What would you like to see?"

I hesitate, then plow ahead boldly. "I'd like to see where the family lives. I'm curious about my cousin's life," I explain.

To my surprise he just nods. "Of course. I can't take you

through the whole wing, but I can show you part of it."

I guess that will have to do. He's quite a knowledgeable guide as he gives me a quick tour. The family apartments are as opulent as you would expect. They are also empty.

"Fräulein Baum and the duchess Cecilie are out shopping and the prince is with his father," Maxwell says when I remark on how quiet it is.

"Does Fräulein Baum live in the family apartments?" I ask.

Maxwell shakes his head. "No one except family stays there. She's in the east wing. The duchess made sure she has the corner suite, though."

"Does it overlook the Lustgarten?" I ask, trying to orient myself.

"Yes. It has a lovely view. Are you ready to go now?"

Smiling, I nod. I've gotten what I needed.

I sniff the cold, clear air once we're outside, and something inside me unwinds. I hadn't realized how oppressed I felt inside the palace walls until we step out into the street. Last night doesn't really count. Again, I'm reminded of childhood outings with my mother, of my father teaching me to ride, my governess taking me to the art museum. Memories that have nothing to do with Velvet, La Dame Blanche, or even this horrid war that seems to have no end. A lump rises in my throat and I blink back tears before resolutely turning to Maxwell.

"Where are we going?" I ask.

"I thought we could stop for a ginger beer and bratwurst

and see some of the sights, if that suits you?"

I nod and then remember the note in my pocket. I chew my lip. Dropping off and picking up secret messages with a German guard on my arm is not a good idea. But then again, I'm not sure when I'll get another chance. I give myself a mental shake. It shouldn't be that difficult. "Could we stop by the Hess Bakery on the Nürnberger Straße? I remember having some wonderful gingerbread there as a child and would love to see if they still have it."

His eyes light up. "Have it? I could live on it!"

"Oh, good!"

It seems as if all of Berlin wishes to enjoy the sunshine, no matter what the actual temperature, and men, women, and children fill the sidewalks. A child passes by with his nanny; he's leading a small puppy with a giant blue bow. Young women walk arm in arm, their skirts swishing as they pass.

If it weren't for the numerous coats with black armbands, you could almost forget that, several hundred miles away, men from both sides of the conflict lay dying, far from the people who loved them.

Taking a deep breath, I scan the area behind me, recalling what Miss Tickford had told me concerning surveillance. The fact that I'm out on a lovely day with a handsome young man can't take away the fact that I'm in constant danger and must be on my guard.

After we have a quick bite at a nearby tavern, he takes me past the Berliner Dom, a Protestant church built to rival St. Peter's Basilica in Rome. The church is on the other side of the palace, and we walk across the Lustgarten to reach it. It reminds me that I still need to find out whether it was Max who went out last night, and I rack my brains trying to figure out a way to do it subtly.

"So what did you do last night?" I ask.

So much for subtlety.

His brows knit together as if he's trying to remember. "Oh, I attended a ball with the prince, and then went home. What did you do?"

He's lying. I can tell by the way his arm stiffens against mine and by the overly casual tone of his voice. Whatever he was doing, it isn't something he wants me to know about. What could it be? Could he have been spending time with another girl? Not that that's any of my business.

I toss my head. *Tit for tat*, I think. "I went to bed early," I lie in return. "The children exhaust me."

"I can imagine. Would you like to see the inside of the church?"

I shake my head, wondering if he knows I'm lying just like I know he's lying. The feeling of being exposed increases and I want to go to the bakery and then back to the palace. The walls that had seemed so close just an hour ago now seem more protective than stifling.

We walk to the Nürnberger Straße, which isn't that far from the palace. No wonder La Dame Blanche chose the bakery for a drop site. The red-and-white awning has been replaced with a solid blue one, but other than that, the *Bäckerei* looks just as I remember. My eyes scan the storefront and there it is—a small blue card in the front window, left by one of the assistant bakers, who is an LDB operative.

I have a message.

My heart hammers in my chest as Maxwell gallantly holds the door open for me, and for a moment my confidence falters. Why did I think I could do this right in front of Maxwell? What if something goes wrong?

Then I press my lips together. Not for nothing did I receive medals for my academic prowess and earn more badges in the Girl Guides than anyone else. I sail confidently into the bakery and nod at the woman at the counter. The card would only be put out if the operative was here to hand off my message, and I wonder if the little round-faced woman expectantly smiling at us secretly works for LDB.

Taking a deep breath, I say the key words. "I haven't been here since I was a child," I exclaim loudly. Maxwell gives me an odd look.

Perhaps my delivery needs a bit of work.

A man steps up to the counter. "I'll get this, Olga," he says. "Why don't you check on the strudel?"

She shrugs and goes through a swinging door into the back kitchen. The man facing us has a shock of black hair, and long sideburns frame his face like fuzzy caterpillars. His black eyes dart from me to Maxwell as if assessing the situation. *Friend or foe?* the look seems to ask.

Thinking fast, I turn to Maxwell. "Thank you so much for escorting me here," I say. "I'm not sure I could have found my way back without you." I give the man at the counter a friendly smile and repeat, "I haven't been here since I was a child. Could I have some gingerbread?"

Maxwell nods. "I would like one as well, please."

This isn't so hard.

Turning, I take the folded note out of my pocket. Should I try to pass it when he hands me the gingerbread? Making a quick decision, I bend as if I'm retrieving something. "Excuse me," I say to the man, who has turned toward the pastry case. "Did you drop this?"

My chest tightens as he turns back toward me. "Thank you," he says, taking the paper.

I smile. One down, one to go. I don't dare look at Maxwell.

The man turns to get our gingerbread. Each small rectangular slab is encircled with a band of gold foil, signifying that it's been made from a recipe handed down from the Middle Ages. As he gets our treats, I note that while he grabs the first one from the front and hands it to Maxwell, the one he chooses for me is from the back. His hand trembles as he gives it to me and I accidentally knock it out of his hand as I take it. The bag skitters across the floor and I watch, aghast, as Maxwell retrieves it.

"I'm so sorry," the man squeaks, obviously as horrified as I am.

"No, it was my fault," I tell him, reaching out to snatch the bag from Maxwell. He holds it away from me.

"You don't want that one. It's been on the floor," Maxwell says, handing the bag back to the man.

The baker takes it automatically and holds it away from him as if it were about to burst into flames. He gives me a stricken look, as if waiting for me to do something.

"Is there a problem?" Maxwell asks, his voice pleasant.

My pulse hammers in my throat. I grab the bag from the man, who is still frozen with horror. "Oh, don't be silly. The gingerbread itself didn't touch the floor. It's fine." I grip the bag in my hand so tightly that my knuckles turn white. I force myself to relax as Maxwell hands the man a few coins.

Maxwell opens his immediately after exiting the bakery. "Aren't you going to eat yours?" he asks.

I reach my hand into the bag and break off a small corner. The message will probably be on the foil band around the cake. The last thing I want to do is pull it out where Maxwell can see it. My nerves can't handle much more.

The gingerbread must be good, the way Maxwell is eating it, but I'm so edgy, it feels as if I'm chewing on sand.

"Would you mind if we go back to the palace?" I ask Maxwell. "I think I'm still weary from the trip." The lie slips out of my mouth with oily ease and I wonder at myself. Dishonesty seems to come quite easily to me.

"Not at all," he says, his brows knotting with concern. "I should have taken that into consideration."

"No, it's been fun, but I *am* tired."

"We're not far from the palace. Would you like me to get a motorcar to take us back?"

I shake my head, feeling more than a little foolish. "No. Let's enjoy the last of the evening."

"Are you sure?"

"Positive."

Maxwell grins, and his brown eyes are so warm and velvety that I have to look away.

Reaching out, he tweaks one of my curls. "I like you, Sophia Thérèse."

He holds out his arm and I take it silently, unable to form a single coherent response.

Maxwell talks easily as we stroll, telling me about summers spent on his grandparents' farm outside of Munich.

"My mother said she wanted me to experience the healthy farm life, but I think she just wanted the break. I was a bit of a troublemaker."

I laugh. "I can't see it."

He gives me a rueful smile. "I was," he insists. "Nothing bad, really. Just mischievous and full of energy. She was right, though. Farm life was good for me. I was too exhausted from helping my grandfather and exploring the woods to have a chance to get into trouble."

"Were you close to your grandparents?"

He nods. "I think I was closer to them than I was to my parents. How about you?"

"My mother and I aren't as close as I would like, but I was very close to my father."

He frowns. "I thought your parents died when you were very young?"

A wave of cold washes over me. I'd given him my history, not Sophia Thérèse's.

I frantically try to fix it. "They did. It's still so hard for me to accept that they're gone. I just meant I wasn't as close to my mother as I was my father. I regret that now. My aunt was wonderful, of course, but it wasn't the same after she remarried."

He says nothing more about it and I wonder what he's thinking. How could I be so stupid? What is it about Maxwell that makes me so perilously comfortable?

Whatever it is, it has to stop.

"I'm very lucky to have had not only my parents but my grandparents, growing up," he says. "For a child it's just heaven to spend every summer milking cows, making hay, and fishing with your grandpa."

He stares off into the distance for a moment, and when he continues, his voice is suddenly hard. "I just want you to know that it's *that* Germany that I would fight for. If someone attacks us, I will fight to the death for my grandfather's land."

I stare up at him as we walk, but he isn't looking at me. His thin mouth is straight and firm and his jaw resolute. "So please don't take it the wrong way when I tell you that this debacle we are calling a war should have never happened."

I gasp at his words, which would get him in serious trouble if overheard. His trust touches me. "Why are you telling me this?"

He finally looks at me, and his smile is bittersweet.

"Because you're an educated woman. I'm sure you have opinions on the war. I just wanted you to know that not even the soldiers are certain they're doing the right thing."

I squeeze his arm. "I think war is like that," I say softly.

He nods without looking at me and seems preoccupied when he drops me back off at my room. He says nothing about wanting to go for another outing with me but I don't take it personally, considering. We both have work to do. And getting involved with a German guard, no matter how handsome or tragically conflicted, isn't a good idea.

After shedding my coat, I pull the foil band off the gingerbread and set it on my dresser. Knowing the gingerbread note is from La Dame Blanche, I pick it up first. Taking the codebook out of the inner pocket of my jacket, I easily decode it.

*Proceed with caution. Steer clear of songbirds.*
*They have their own agenda.*

The pencil falls from my fingers as I stare at the message. What does this mean?

I remember Mrs. Tremaine talking with Lillian last night. Is Mrs. Tremaine the songbird who has her own agenda? It doesn't make sense, but then nothing really has since the moment I walked into Captain Parker's office.

I think of Maxwell and wonder again if he was the guard who went out last night, and if so, what he was doing. My face heats as I remember my stupid blunder, and I run the conversation through my mind. Something about the incident bothers me. I suck in a breath when I realize what it is. *I thought your parents died when you were very young?* he'd said. Why would one of the prince's guards know so much about the assistant governess's background? Does he suspect me of spying? Of not being who I say I am? I remember how I felt when he told me how much he liked me.

Is that true or is it just a ruse?

Whatever it is, one thing is for certain—I need to be very careful around Corporal Maxwell Mayer.

# FIFTEEN
## ILIWHHQ

*Flaps and Seals: The tradecraft involved in making secret
openings or compartments for envelopes and pouches.*

"*Ringel, Ringel, Reihe, sind wir Kinder dreie . . .*"
Frowning seriously, I listen to Mary Elizabeth
sound out the words to "Ring Around the Rosie." I clap my
hands when she finishes. "*Wunderbar!*"

The smile she gives me lights up her face and I find myself
sinking into the comforting role of teacher. After a bit of
a rocky start, I now look forward to these simple sessions.
The children have warmed to me, especially the little ones,
and there are times when I'm so immersed in what I'm doing
that I forget that I'm not really Sophia Thérèse, assistant
governess, but Samantha Donaldson, spy.

Sometimes it's just easier to be Sophia Thérèse.

When we break to go outside, Lillian helps the little ones
on with their coats while I go to get mine.

"Will you get my coat as well?" she asks. "I can't seem to
get warm today."

"Of course." I open the small wardrobe and pull out my

coat as well as hers. One side of her coat feels oddly heavy, and I frown. Glancing back over my shoulder to make sure she is still engrossed in helping the children, I lift the flap on the pocket and peer inside.

Nestled within is the small, dark shape of a lady's pistol.

My heart slams against my ribs. The gun is so unexpected in this warm child-space, and I was so absorbed in my role of Sophia Thérèse, that the shock of the weapon is a cruel splash of reality.

"No, not that one," Lillian calls quickly. "It's too heavy. The other one, please."

I swallow hard, hang the coat with its deadly little secret back up, and get her the dark blue one hanging next to it.

I'm quiet out in the courtyard, only half watching the children while my mind spins. If Lillian really is just a mild-mannered governess, why does she have a gun in her pocket? Why would she be arranging secret meetings with an Australian opera singer whom she couldn't possibly know? And if Lillian really is Velvet, how does Mrs. Tremaine fit into everything?

I'm jumpy and out of sorts when we get back to the schoolroom. I can't stop thinking of the gun in the wardrobe, just inches from where little Gretel is working so diligently on her slate, her lips pressed together in concentration.

"Are you all right?" Lillian asks.

"I'm just tired," I tell her.

"Why don't you leave early," she says. "Teaching can be exhausting when you're not used to it."

"Really?" I ask, not bothering to hide the relief in my voice.

She laughs. "Of course. Off with you."

I wave to the children and step into the hallway, pausing when I see Marissa Baum and Duchess Cecilie coming toward me.

I give a deep curtsy. "Fräulein Baum, Duchess."

"Hello, Cousin. We were just coming to visit the children. Are they still inside?"

I nod. "Yes, they're just finishing up their lessons."

Duchess Cecilie smiles and enters the schoolroom.

"It was nice seeing you again, Fräulein Sophia Thérèse," Marissa says before following the duchess.

I wait until the door is shut before hurrying down the hall, my heart beating wildly. This may be my only chance to search Marissa's room. Even though circumstances are pointing toward Lillian, I still need to investigate Marissa, if only to rule her out. If she is Velvet, surely there will be some sort of clue in her private quarters. I walk with purpose, keeping my pace steady, even though I want to break into a jog. Whenever I meet someone, I nod pleasantly, trying to look both casual and busy, as if I belong in this part of the palace. There are more guards in this part of the house, no doubt due to the assassination attempt. I'm hoping I won't run into Maxwell.

I come to the room I believe is Marissa's, from Maxwell's description, and close my eyes as I try the door.

Locked.

Sighing, I pull out the hairpin that I use to keep my curls out of my eyes. I look around; the corridor is still empty. Then I stick the pin in the lock. Miss Tickford showed me how to do this in France and even had me practice on Monsieur Elliot's office door. I got fairly proficient at it, but was nowhere as adept as she was.

I hear heavy footsteps coming down the hall and a hot flush of desperation sweeps over me. With one last effort, I twist the pin and the knob at the same time. The knob turns so suddenly that I almost fall into the room. Shutting the door behind me, I wait, heart thudding in my ears, until the footsteps pass by outside.

I take a quick visual inventory of the room. From the cunning little hats and kid gloves lying about, I know I've found Marissa's quarters. The suite consists of a fresh, pretty boudoir decorated in rose and soft greens with a bedchamber just beyond it. Trying to keep my moral reservations at bay, I work quickly but carefully, riffling through her cupboards and drawers, feeling guilty when I remember how I felt when someone did the same to me.

Nothing. I stand in the middle of the room, thinking hard. If I were Marissa, where would I keep incriminating documents? I go into the bedroom area and riffle through the trunks at the end of her bed. There's nothing in them, but I didn't really expect there to be. Too obvious.

How much time has elapsed since I saw Marissa and the duchess in front of the schoolroom? Marissa will be coming to dress for supper soon.

I spot another stack of hats on the shining vanity table next to her bed, and I frown.

Most people keep their hats in hatboxes. I drop to my knees and pull up her bedcovers. Sure enough, there's a large hatbox under the bed. I pull it out and open it. Empty. My breath whooshes out in disappointment. I move to replace the lid and then frown.

Why is the inside of the lid so lumpy? I run my hand over it and feel the hard outline of an envelope underneath. *Ha!* The paper has been glued over it. Working carefully so as not to rip the paper, I loosen it with my fingernail and gently peel it off. The envelope underneath falls into my lap.

I slip the envelope into the waist of my skirt and pull my sweater over it. Then I shove the hatbox back under the bed. At this point, I have no idea how I'm to get the envelope back into Marissa's room, but right now I just want to get out of here.

Pressing my ear against the wood of the door, I listen for any sounds outside in the corridor. I open the door slowly and slip out, praying that I can get out of this part of the house before I'm caught.

No such luck. I'm halfway down the stairs when I hear my name. I turn, trying to think up a good excuse for being in this part of the palace. Marissa is coming toward me, an inquisitive look in her dark eyes. "Were you looking for me?" she asks.

I smile, hoping I'm not as pale as I feel. "Only if you can tell me which way the servants' quarters are. I'm so bad at directions. My aunt always said I could get lost in my own home."

She links her arm in mine. "I'll show you. It took me a bit to get used to the size of the place, too."

"I feel so silly," I say breathlessly.

She raises an eyebrow and I realize I'm putting it on a bit much.

"I was actually going to send a note to you," she says.

"You were?"

"The duchess and I would love to have you join us for supper and a performance by the opera singer Elsa Tremaine. Your cousin wishes to thank you for coming to help with the children."

As oblivious to royal etiquette as I am, I know enough to realize this isn't a request—it's a command. "I'd love to," I tell her.

"Wonderful." She hesitates and I wait. We're almost to the servants' quarters and I hope she finishes up soon. I don't want the maids to see me arm in arm with her. They'd think I was too snooty for words, and I may yet need their help.

"Your cousin also wanted you to know that if you didn't bring an evening gown with you, she would be more than happy to lend you one."

I shake my head. "I did bring one. But please extend my appreciation for her offer. Which dining room will the supper be in?"

"I'm not sure," she says. "I'll send someone to escort you."

Wonderful. I stop and disengage my arm from hers. The envelope I stole from her feels as if it's branding my waist. "I can find my way from here. Thank you so much. I'll see you at supper?"

She nods, then turns away, and I sigh in relief.

After returning to my room and locking the door, I take the envelope out from under my waistband and pull out the contents. There are several pieces of paper inside. The first two look to be travel documents. I scan down and draw in a breath. The papers are for a Maryann Donovan. Is Marissa really Maryann, or are these fake? Could this be proof that she's Velvet?

The third paper is just doodles of circles, or at least that's what it looks like. *Hab* is scrawled across the bottom and followed by a squiggly line, as if the word was written quickly and left unfinished. I frown. What is this? It looks like a sketch done by a child.

Unless the entire drawing is some sort of sophisticated code. I turn the picture and look at it from all angles. I guess it does look rather like a solar system. The middle circle, the one that has *Cl-35* written in the center, could be the sun. Then I shake my head. No. There aren't enough planets for it to be the solar system.

The beginning of a headache throbs in my temples and I sigh again. Tonight promises to be a very long night.

After washing up in my tiny bathroom, I slip into the antique blue charmeuse gown, grateful that Miss Tickford thought to pack it. Had it been up to me, I'd have worn the sensible gray suit that I wore with the children all the time. Luckily, Miss Tickford knew I'd need more clothes than that if I was to look the part.

A knock sounds at the door and I give myself one more glance in the mirror to make sure the birthmark is properly drawn. Sometimes I don't even recognize myself. I take a deep breath, again feeling the strange sensation of being two people at the same time.

A very sulky Mathilde is waiting for me. "Apparently, I'm to escort you to the Anna Amalia Dining Room."

"Yes," I growl, following her rapid footsteps. "I've been summoned. The only bright note is that Lillian's nose is going to be put out of joint."

I send a silent apology to Lillian.

Mathilde actually giggles at this. "Well, let me know if you like Elsa Tremaine's singing. Though I suspect it's not her singing the prince is enamored with." She glances out of the corner of her eye to see my response.

I shrug. "Who knows what people see in other people? Take Marissa Baum, for example. What do you think the duchess sees in her?"

"I think she just likes to irritate her mother-in-law. You be careful of that one."

"The empress?" I ask, surprised.

"No. Fräulein Baum. There're some funny rumors going on about her," Mathilde says.

"Like what?" I ask.

"That she's a witch."

I scoff. "There's no such thing as witches."

"Maybe, but one of the footmen says she's been seen walking the Mendelssohn Hall at midnight, and everyone knows it's haunted. The royals won't even go there."

"I'd be more inclined to think that she's meeting a secret lover than that she's practicing witchcraft."

Mathilde hushes me then, as more people are milling about the hallway. She points. "It's right in there, Fräulein. Just follow the other snooty aristocrats."

I fall into line behind a stout woman whose hat is almost as big as a wagon wheel. She's talking to a tall, thin woman in pink.

"I'm so glad the empress invited us this evening. My poor cook is having to ration sugar. You can't buy any extra for love or money. Not that I'd try to get more than my fair share," she puts in hastily. "But I do wish this dreadful war would end so things can go back as they were. I like a bit of cake with my tea."

The other woman clucks, and then they fall silent as they enter the dining room. I understand their awe. The domed ceiling is painted in the classical style and I recognize the story of St. John the Baptist. Poor taste, if you ask me, to have a painting of his head on a platter in a place where people are supposed to be eating. The walls are covered with gold-embossed leather, and giant stone lions decorate a fireplace large enough to stand in. If this is an intimate family dinner, I have to wonder what a state dinner would be like.

The long, ornately carved table seats at least forty.

I walk next to the empty seats, looking for my name on the place cards. Once I locate it, I take a seat, wishing I were anyplace but here in this stuffy, perfume-scented, overly lavish room with all these pampered people whose main problem in life is missing their cake at tea.

The headache that dogged me all afternoon is now pounding at my temples as if a roomful of drummers have taken up residence in my brain. I stifle a yawn and glance at the clock hanging above the mantel. It's eight o'clock. Hopefully, I'll be able to get to bed before midnight.

Marissa slips into the chair next to me. She's stunning in a steel-blue silk gown with creamy lace sleeves and a plunging décolletage. "Just in the nick of time," she says.

"What?"

She nods toward the door. There's a stir at the end of the table and a woman with silver-white hair arranged in an elaborate pile on top of her head enters the room on the arm of an imposing man with a giant moustache. Everyone stands as the empress and the kaiser walk through the room to take their places at the head of the table. My stomach tightens. I'd be killed on the spot if any of these people knew who I really was.

They are followed by the duchess and the crown prince.

The duchess stops on her way past my chair and lays her hand on my shoulder. "Thank you so much for joining us, Cousin."

Everyone around us looks at me with renewed interest

and I flush. "I'm honored to be invited, Duchess Cecilie."

"I was sorry not to get to talk to you more this afternoon, but Lillian said you were tired. I hope you used your time off to get a bit of rest?"

Cold washes over me as I remember searching through Marissa's things. Did someone tell her they saw me in the family wing of the palace? I search her face, but her expression tells me nothing.

"I did, thank you."

I'm relieved when she moves on and all eyes turn away.

The prince and the duchess stop at the head of the table to pay their respects to the kaiser and the empress. I watch, along with the rest of the guests, the frigid formality of their greeting.

"I thought you'd be long gone to your duties at the front," the kaiser says stiffly.

"I had some important matters to attend to here," the prince says, equally stiff.

"And yet you have time to throw a lavish party for an Australian songstress?" Even the kaiser's moustache looks disapproving.

The prince gives a grim smile. "You know as well as I do, Father, that I'm not really needed until the spring offensive."

"And maybe not even then." Kaiser Wilhelm gives his son a scathing look and waves him away.

The prince inclines his head and leads his wife to their seats.

I glance over at Marissa.

She catches my eye and shoots me a wry smile. "Well, isn't this fun?"

"Does that happen often?" I ask, nodding to where the kaiser and the empress sit.

"Much too often," she says, her voice low. "But then I suppose conflict happens in the best of families."

"I suppose it does," I murmur, trying to think of a subtle way to get more information. But before I can, she changes the subject.

"I'm glad it's just an informal little dinner," she says. "A person could starve at a formal one."

I smile back. "Or freeze."

She giggles. "That too, Fräulein von Schönburg."

"Please call me Sophia Thérèse."

"And you may call me Marissa."

We smile at each other and I find myself responding to her friendliness. Her eyes are so open and frank that I have to look away. No matter how pleasant she is, we're not friends. After all, she doesn't know my real name and now I'm not even sure if I know hers.

"So how are you finding life at the palace? Very different from your real life, I imagine."

I catch my breath, wondering what she's implying. A waiter in red livery sets our first course in front of us. It's a cream soup that smells strongly of beer. I pick up my soup-spoon, then put it down when I find it trembling in my fingers.

"What do you mean by 'real life'?" I ask.

"Oh, back in . . ." She pauses. "Where are you from again? Cecilie mentioned it, but I forget."

Her deliberately casual tone catches my attention. Why is she so interested? Or is it just me being suspicious? "Cologne," I say shortly. "I was raised in a little town outside Cologne."

"Have you ever visited Berlin before?" she asks.

"Yes, as a child. You said this is your first time here, but your parents are from Germany?"

"My grandparents."

We're speaking in English and I lower my voice. "And what are you going to do if America enters the war? Chances are, the Americans won't be on Germany's side."

She shoots me a look out of the corner of her eye. "And what would you know about that, Sophia Thérèse?"

I raise the soupspoon to my lips. "I try to keep myself informed."

"Most women do not. And if you do, you must be aware that there are people who are working to get America to come in on the side of the Germans. There are many rich, influential Germans in America. But as far as I can tell, most average Americans are isolationists."

"And which side are you on, Fräulein Baum?" I ask, lowering my voice even further. As we speak, my eyes rove the room. I notice that Maxwell has entered and is standing behind the prince on the far side of the room. His eyes swivel toward me and I can see the smile in them even if the expression on his face doesn't change. I duck my head, warmth fluttering in my chest.

"I told you to call me Marissa. And I am on the side of whoever throws the best party."

The words are lilting and gay, but I already know she's not as she appears to be. How could she be when she's hiding false travel papers in a hatbox?

"And whose side are *you* really on, Sophia Thérèse? You seem too serious a girl to bother with parties."

*Careful, Sam. Don't give away too much.*

I sit back with my hands in my lap as the waiter takes away my bowl. "I'm on the side of right," I tell her pleasantly. "Isn't that what everyone likes to think?"

She leans toward me and whispers, "I'm rather jaded. I think the side of right changes depending on circumstances and mood."

My lips curve upward as I try for nonchalance. "Well, we're among Germany's finest tonight. Right is obvious."

"One would think," she says, and then begins a conversation with the person on her left.

I turn to the person next to me, a bald older man with a pair of wire spectacles perched on the end of his nose. "The soup is good, don't you think?"

"It is indeed, Fräulein. So you are the duchess's cousin?"

He seems nice, and we talk about nothing in particular for several minutes until I find out that he's a chemist. "I love science!" I exclaim. "I'm better at math, but am interested in science and chemistry as well."

"Ah, then you must meet my wife. She is a chemist, too. Quite talented."

"I would like to very much," I tell him truthfully. "Is she with you this evening?"

For some reason, he looks uncomfortable. "No. She wasn't feeling well this evening, but we're so glad young women are taking an interest in the sciences. It was my pleasure to give Fräulein Baum and the duchess a tour of my laboratory just the other day, though I think the duchess was just being kind to her young friend. It's easy to see that Fräulein Baum was the one who really had the scientific interest." He glances across me at Marissa as if waiting for confirmation, but she's having an animated discussion with her neighbor and doesn't notice.

So Marissa, the girl who feigns interest in only fun and frolic, is interested in science? I say no more and the conversation moves on without me. Something flits into my mind and I frown. Marissa isn't the only one in the palace who is interested in chemistry. Didn't Lillian say she was passionate about chemistry? Is this merely a coincidence?

The dinner seems to go on for hours, and Marissa doesn't address me again until it is time to go watch Mrs. Tremaine perform.

"You're in for a real treat. Elsa Tremaine is incredibly talented."

"I'm looking forward to it."

The chemist with the spectacles bows slightly. "It was very nice to meet you, Fräulein . . ." He pauses at my name and I jump in.

"Fräulein von Schönburg."

He takes my hand. "And my name is Fritz Haber."

"It was nice to meet you as well, Herr Haber."

"And good to see you again, Fräulein Marissa. Any time you would like another tour, just send a note to the institute." The look he gives her is pointed, but she just smiles sweetly and murmurs her gratitude.

He wanders off, and Marissa and I follow the rest of the crowd to the palace's private theater. The seats are plush red velvet and enormous crystal chandeliers hang from a ceiling decorated with the Hohenzollern family crest. Like a public playhouse, the theater has boxes above the regular seats, and Marissa and I are escorted to a royal box where the duchess and the prince are. The duchess nods at me, her face a frozen mask, and I wonder what's wrong. Then I remember about the prince and Mrs. Tremaine and realize that the duchess is being forced to watch the performance of a woman rumored to be her husband's latest paramour. The poor duchess.

At the entrance sits a table covered with chocolate truffles and other sweets for the royal family to enjoy while watching the performance. With a quick glance around, I sweep a handful into my reticule.

Marissa raises an eyebrow.

"I have a debt of honor to pay," I explain.

She gives a nod and doesn't question me further as we take our seats.

There look to be about one hundred people in attendance. Is this truly what the palace calls an intimate performance? I watch the people below us taking their seats. The rich colors of the gowns the women are wearing rival those of the tapestries hanging from the walls. The men, in uniform or white tie, gather in smoky knots, puffing on cigars. Again I'm struck by how odd it is to be amid such obscene luxury while men are dying in trenches on the front.

I turn to Marissa. "I didn't know you were interested in science."

She smiles, seemingly unfazed by my question. "There are many things you don't know about me, Sophia Thérèse."

I smile in assent and continue to watch the people below us.

There are so many vivid and dazzling women that I hardly know which way to look. My lips quirk upward when I spot one woman who looks like a zebra crossed with a partridge in her black-and-white-striped gown and the ostrich feathers that bob above her head. I'm just about to point her out to Marissa when my eyes are drawn to the less imposing woman by her side. She's wearing demure gray silk with a small matching hat sitting atop her dark, upswept hair. There's something strangely familiar about her. Frowning, I lean forward, hoping she'll turn my way. Could it be someone I knew as a child? My parents had many friends in Berlin and were quite social. Of course, being so young, I didn't join them often, but I was invited on special occasions. When I took the assignment, I hadn't even considered running into someone I knew.

A bell rings out, giving people a five-minute warning. The woman and her companion move down toward the stage and I wait, curious to see the woman's profile. When she turns and raises her eyes to the boxes, I suck in my breath, everything in my world turning topsy-turvy. My hands grip the sides of my seat and for a moment I feel as if I'm going to faint.

Miss Tickford.

Our eyes meet for a fraction of a second before hers slide away without recognition. My knuckles whiten and it takes everything I have to remain upright.

I sit, stunned, as the giant electric chandeliers above us dim. A hush falls over the audience as the orchestra plays the opening notes. Then the velvet curtains part and Elsa Tremaine's powerful soprano joins the instruments. All around me, rapt faces stare at the lovely woman who lights up the stage with the glow of a thousand candles. Her exquisite voice washes around me almost unheard, drowned out by the tumultuous noise of my own thoughts.

*What is Miss Tickford doing here? Did she think I couldn't complete the assignment? If so, why send me here at all?* I sit, trembling, as each new thought spins round and round in my head. Every aria seems to last an eternity and I'm nearly wild with impatience by the time the lights come on, indicating that it's time for intermission. My eyes zero down on the place where Miss Tickford was, but the seat next to the zebra-partridge is now empty.

"Excuse me," I whisper to Marissa. I slip out of my seat and past the duchess and the prince. If anyone says anything about my sudden disappearance, I'll tell them that I didn't feel well and returned to my room.

As soon as I reach the stairs leading down to the main part of the theater, I pick up my skirts and break into a run. By the time I'm at the bottom, people are out of their seats and socializing. I slow, hoping not to draw too much attention to myself, while slipping in and out of the crowd. Perhaps she's gone to the restroom. I dart out of the theater and into the hall, where there are fewer people. I turn this way and that but can't see the slim woman in the gray dress.

"Excuse me," I say to a soldier standing guard outside the theater entrance. "Can you tell me where I might find a restroom?"

He points down the hallway. "Take a left at the end of the hall."

I move away and then ask, "Did a woman in a gray dress just come through here?"

He looks at me as if I'm crazy and I wave a hand at him. "Never mind."

Hurrying down the hallway, I stop dead when I see a line of women waiting for the restroom. No wonder the guard looked at me the way he did.

I turn away, disappointment tightening my neck and shoulders. If Miss Tickford doesn't want to be found, I'm not going to find her. The question is, Did she want me to see her or was that just a coincidence? Didn't she think I'd be successful enough at portraying Sophia Thérèse that I'd be invited to dinner and a private performance after so little time in the palace? Or was she sure that a governess's assistant wouldn't be invited to dine and attend a private performance with the royals, no matter the familial connection?

But what is she doing here in Berlin?

"You don't enjoy opera, Sophia Thérèse?"

I whirl around to find Maxwell, handsome in his dress uniform, standing behind me.

He sounds so kind and solicitous that a lump comes to my throat. "I have a terrible headache and just want to go back to my room."

I must sound as pathetic as I feel, because sympathy comes over his features.

"Let me escort you," he says. "I won't be needed again until the performance is finished."

"That would be wonderful," I tell him. "I thought I was going to have to go outside and come back in through the servants' entrance."

"That's a very clever idea, actually. You didn't seem to be having a very good time at dinner," he says, taking my arm.

I smile, glad for his company. Seeing Miss Tickford was such a shock that walking arm in arm with a German guard seems strangely natural. "You barely glanced in my direction," I tease.

"Of course I did. How could I resist, with that hair?" He smiles down at me and I blush.

"I hope the others didn't notice that I wasn't enjoying myself. I'd hate for my cousin to think I'm ungrateful."

"Don't worry. No one could tell. They don't know you as well as I do."

"Oh, you think you know me, do you?" I say this lightly, ignoring the tremors of unease in my stomach. I feel more like myself when I'm with Maxwell than I do with anyone else in the palace. I have to stop thinking of him as a friend.

*Caution, Sam.*

"I know there is much more to you than meets the eye."

His voice is solemn and I stop walking to look at him. His eyes meet mine and I can scarcely breathe. "That could be said about anyone," I finally say, and continue walking.

"Yes, but I think it's particularly true in your case. I heard you were in the family wing of the palace this afternoon."

My stomach clenches and I almost falter. Does he suspect me of something? Is he fishing for information? Heart beating in my throat, I make a rash decision. I look at him from under my lashes and give what I hope is a flirtatious smile. "Actually, I was looking for you."

It's his turn to be surprised. "You were?"

"Yes, I wanted to thank you again for the outing. I really enjoyed it."

"I'm glad," he says. "We must do it again sometime."

Does he believe me? It's difficult to tell. "I'd like that."

"I'm sorry dinner wasn't what you expected. You did look to be having an interesting conversation with the gentleman next to you, though."

I frown. "Herr Haber? Yes. I've always loved science."

"He's a chemist of some sort, isn't he?" he asks.

"Yes," I say, wondering what it is he wants to know.

We reach my door and I turn to thank him. "I don't know what I would have done if you hadn't come along," I say.

"Then it was a good thing I did, isn't it?" He looks down at me and a wistful expression crosses his face. "You know what I wish, Sophia Thérèse?"

His mesmerizing dark eyes stare into mine and my breath catches. My gaze drops to his mouth before I jerk my eyes back up to meet his. "What's that?"

"I wish there wasn't a war going on. That I had met you in that little town outside Cologne . . . what did you say the name of it was?"

My mind goes completely blank. I stare at him as I frantically shuffle through German names. Why can't I remember?

The sound of whistling breaks the spell and I look away to see Mathilde coming toward us. "You're not supposed to have male visitors in this part of the house, Fräulein," she warns as she passes.

I close my eyes for a moment in relief. "Good night," I say, hastily unlocking the door.

"Good night, Sophia Thérèse," Maxwell says, his forehead furrowed as if he's trying to figure something out. "Pleasant dreams."

I shut the door. I'm caught between relief that our conversation was interrupted, and regret. I know exactly how Max feels. I wish I could have met him in my real life, too.

# SIXTEEN
## VLAWHHQ

*Dirty Tricks: Undercover sabotage that can run the
gamut from disruptive pranks to assassination.*

I don't know whether it's the late night or the nightmares
I have, but I awake tired and out of sorts. The strain of
being Sophia Thérèse is wearing on me, and yet sometimes I
feel as if I've always been a wellborn German girl. Samantha
Donaldson, along with her life, is becoming more and more
remote.

I feel as if I'm losing who I really am.

Plus, I can't get over the uneasy sensation that I'm
missing something important. Like I'm on the edge of a discovery and yet I can't quite grasp the last piece. As I near
the schoolroom, the rise and fall of heated voices reaches me
and I pause just outside the door.

"You know this is the last chance you'll get," I hear Mrs.
Tremaine say.

*Last chance to do what?*

"I can't do as you want. I'm risking everything as it is. If
anyone found out . . ." Lillian sounds on the verge of tears.

"As you wish. I think you're being unwise."

"Perhaps, but I think you're deceiving yourself." Lillian's voice drops and I have to lean closer to the door to hear her words. "Remember Napoleon's words, a throne is only 'a bit of wood gilded and covered in velvet.'"

The word *velvet* reverberates in my ears. Is that a clue?

I hear voices down the hall and quickly step into the room to avoid getting caught eavesdropping.

"Good morning," I say.

The effect of my greeting is like a shot going off. Both women startle.

"Good morning," Lillian says quickly. "Mrs. Tremaine just offered to give the children singing lessons, but I told her it wasn't appropriate." This last part is directed at Mrs. Tremaine, who just shrugs.

"You know where to find me if you change your mind." Mrs. Tremaine gives Lillian a hard stare. "And I truly think it in your best interest to change your mind."

Mrs. Tremaine sweeps out of the room, so angry that she gives me only a frigid nod. To my surprise, Lillian says nothing about the incident. The morning passes slowly. When we break for some air, I take out the chocolates I'd procured the night before and hand them out to all the children.

"Where did you get the chocolates?" the duchess asks when she and Marissa join us.

"Frau Sophia Thérèse gave them to us." Prince Wilhelm licks melted chocolate from his fingers.

"You spoil them, Cousin," the duchess says.

"I don't do it often," I assure her.

"She only gave them to us because I promised not to tell the secret about her burbmark," Prince Hubertus says.

I freeze as the duchess turns to me with an inquiring look on her face.

Lillian hushes him. "It's called a birthmark, Hubertus, and I told you we weren't to speak of that."

Marissa's eyes narrow.

*Think fast.*

"The secret is that it's shaped like a crescent moon," I tell them all. "I told him that was my little secret. And it's all right if the children talk about it. It's plain as day, after all."

"And quite lovely," the duchess says. "Now, Hubertus, you promised to show me how you can walk the garden wall."

I stand still as the duchess follows the children to the low wall surrounding the winter garden. I'm praying that no one can see the trembling that has seized my entire body. Lillian and Marissa kindly change the subject and my heart finally returns to normal.

That was entirely too close.

As I watch Marissa and Lillian talking, I'm wondering if Lillian is indeed Velvet. Why else would a mild-mannered governess have a gun? But if she is, then what is Marissa doing with someone else's travel papers? Could she have them as just a safety net? A way to get out of the country?

I see several men walking across the courtyard and recognize one of them as Prince Wilhelm. Lillian notices him as well. "He may want to see the children doing their lessons," she says to me. "He occasionally checks in on their progress."

One of the guards flanking the prince is Maxwell, who acknowledges my presence with an almost imperceptible nod.

The tension is almost palpable when we reach the prince and the duchess.

"I don't have time to go with you to Potsdam," Prince Wilhelm says to her. "I'm working on some critical negotiations. In case you haven't noticed, there's a war going on." The prince sounds weary and his face is drawn.

"Oh, really?" the duchess asks, her voice deceptively sweet. "I thought you were too distracted by your singing lessons to worry about the war."

He shakes his head, disgusted. "You know nothing. The only thing you have to worry about is where you're going to get your silk now that trade with China has been interrupted." He turns to Lillian, whose eyes are downcast. "Fräulein, I would very much like to return to the schoolroom with you to see how the children are doing with their lessons."

"Of course," Lillian says.

She and I herd the children into the schoolroom while the duchess departs in a huff, with Marissa on her heels. The prince joins the older children as they write out their math problems on the chalkboard while the little ones watch. Prince Hubertus looks longingly at his father and I hope for his sake that the prince remembers him, as well as the older ones.

"How are you settling in, Sophia Thérèse?" Maxwell asks, his voice pitched low enough so only I can hear.

"I'm doing well, thank you."

"Are you craving more of that delicious gingerbread yet?"

The question comes out of the blue, and chills run down my spine. Frantically, I try to figure out if his words have a double meaning. Does he suspect that the bakery is a drop spot, or is he simply asking if I'd like to go on another outing with him? I glance at him from the corner of my eye, but he's staring straight ahead, his jaw tight. My eyes widen. *He's angry with me. Why?* I take a deep breath. "Sadly, it didn't taste as good as it did when I was young."

"Things seldom do, Fräulein," he says before moving to stand closer to the prince.

I stare after him, baffled. *What did I do?*

Getting the children to settle back down into the routine of lessons is almost impossible after the prince leaves. Finally Lillian throws up her hands. "I give up; go ahead and take out your art supplies or your books. You can even play some games, if you like."

The children give a raucous cry and the boys break out their marbles while the girls get out the watercolors.

"Does this always happen after their father visits?" I ask, helping her put away the schoolbooks.

"Yes. Thankfully, it doesn't occur very often." She smiles, her pretty eyes tired. "Would you like me to order up some tea after we're finished for the day? I feel as if we haven't had a chance to talk much in the past few days and I was looking forward to getting to know you."

The wistfulness in her voice tugs at my heart and I place a hand on her arm. "That would be lovely." I hesitate and then ask, "Are you all right, Lillian?"

Her mouth tightens and tears spring up in her eyes. "I just really love my position here. My own governess was such an inspiration in my life that while other young women were planning their debut parties, I made plans to teach. When I obtained this position, I couldn't believe my good fortune. And then the war began. . . ."

She shakes her head and, with a glance at the children, lowers her voice. "It isn't easy, knowing my family in France might be in danger. That's all. Some days it's harder than others. And if given the choice to return home or stay here, I'm not sure what I'd do. . . ." Her voice trails off as she watches the children play. Then, with a quick glance at me, she gives a little laugh and waves her hand. "I'd stay here, of course. The children need me. I don't know why I'm so maudlin today. I must be tired."

I think of my father and mother and nod. "Wars tend to tear families apart," I tell her softly.

"Indeed they do. And there's no reason to mention this conversation. I wouldn't want to give anyone the wrong idea." She gives me a sideways glance, her fair skin reddening.

"Of course not."

She squeezes my shoulder. "I'm so glad you came. I've needed someone to talk to for a long time." Her voice lightens. "Not to mention that the boys are just too active for one woman!"

She claps her hands. "Put your things away. Fräulein Sophia Thérèse will take you out to play in the Lustgarten."

She leans toward me. "Let's see if we can wear them out before finishing up their French lessons."

She shoos me off, and the children follow me dutifully out of the palace and over to the Lustgarten. As we leave the building, another guard joins us, and I tense. Maxwell is the only guard I'm comfortable with, though after his odd behavior this afternoon, that might change. After all, I'm a British spy taking care of the royal children. There wouldn't even be a trial if I were discovered—I'd be executed immediately.

Once we reach the garden, the children scamper off and I amble after them, trying to put my whirling thoughts into some semblance of order. What if I just asked Lillian if she's Velvet? I straighten, mulling over the idea. If she is Velvet, I'd know by her reaction. If not, I could make something up. Maybe tell her that one of the children told me that her middle name was Velvet.

Relief washes over me. That's what I'll do. If she is Velvet, she'll tell me what Mrs. Tremaine's involvement is. We can escape the country and I can get the information Captain Parker has concerning my father.

It could all be over soon.

I turn back to the children, who are playing a game of tag around the statue of Friedrich Wilhelm. Taking a seat on a bench nearby, I will myself to relax. The breeze is cool but intermittent enough that the sun has a chance to warm me before it blows again. I want to forget about Velvet, Miss Tickford, and everything else for just five blessed minutes. The muscles in my neck ache from days of nonstop tension.

It feels as if I'm on a carousel that never stops.

My relaxation deepens as the children run amok all around me. It's easy to forget that under their royal accoutrements—the imported linens and silk, the velvet and the gold braid—they're just children like any other children and occasionally need to be allowed to behave as such. And it is rather amusing watching the guards try to keep an eye on all of them.

So why are my instincts suddenly pinging, as if something's wrong? I almost feel eyes grazing along the back of my neck. Shivers race up my spine as I stretch, using the movement to look all around the park. The Lustgarten is strangely empty for such a lovely day, no doubt due to so many men off fighting. The feeling doesn't leave me, however, and when a dark cloud obscures the sun and the wind picks up, I use it as an excuse to call the children in.

"Come along, children. Line up, it's time to go in."

As I gather my things, someone bumps into me so hard, I almost fall over the bench I'd been sitting on. After righting myself, I turn to see a man in a black suit and bowler walking swiftly away. It happened so quickly that it's hard to believe it happened at all.

If not for the bit of paper he's left in my hand.

"Are you all right, Fräulein?" a guard asks.

I nod, my hand curling around the paper.

The children line up obediently and follow me to the palace with the guards bringing up the rear. My step quickens. I hurry inside, my heart racing. I need to get to my room and read the note. A feeling of foreboding presses down on me and the back of my neck prickles. LDB isn't supposed to contact me except in the usual manner. Something is very wrong. The children giggle behind me as I accelerate my pace, wanting nothing more than to get to the safety and security of the schoolroom. As we hasten through the Grand Hall, I see Maxwell, ahead of me, hurrying away from the staircase. His hat is askew; I wonder if he just came from the tunnel. I'm about to call for him when I remember the guards bringing up the rear. Instead, I turn to the children. "I'll race you to the schoolroom!"

I have the unfair advantage of being in front, but Prince Wilhelm is hot on my heels as we run. The other children fall a little further behind as I race up the stairs, two steps at a time. I reach the door moments before he does and we burst into the schoolroom laughing, knowing that Lillian is going to turn to us with a smile, asking us what all the commotion is about.

Only she doesn't, because she's lying on the floor in a pool of blood.

# SEVENTEEN
## VHYHQWHHQ

*The Take: Information gathered by an agent or agents during an undercover operation.*

I freeze, then whirl about, looking for a possible intruder. Prince Wilhelm's eyes are wide as he stares at his teacher, still and quiet on the Noah's Ark rug. The stomping of the younger children nearing the schoolroom grows louder and I bend to look the transfixed boy in the face.

"Wilhelm! Look at me. Fräulein Lillian is very ill. We mustn't let the little ones see or they'll have nightmares." He nods, but his eyes keep going back to where Lillian is lying. I grab his shoulder and give him a little shake. "You must take them all back to the nursery. Can you do that for me? Tell them they will get treats if they obey. You have to be in charge."

His small shoulders square as he turns and heads back out into the hallway. I hear his voice ordering the children away.

"Guard!" I call, rushing to Lillian's side. I kneel next to her and pick up her hand. It's lifeless and cold, and my heart sinks. She's so pale I can see delicate blue veins tracing her eyelids. Her shining blond hair is matted with blood on one side of her head and my stomach heaves as I spot a neat round hole in her temple. Several feet away, I see a small-caliber gun. For a flash of a moment I remember the gun I found in Lillian's pocket, and my stomach heaves. Dropping her hand, I scramble backward, whimpering as the guard hurries past me. He skids to a stop and looks away, cursing under his breath.

The next few minutes are a blur as the guards sound the alarm. Someone leads me to a chair and shoves a glass of water in my hand. Clutching the glass, I sit and watch as guards come in and out of the room, creating disorder where this morning there had been only peace and orderliness.

Someone thoughtfully covers Lillian's body with a blanket. No matter how hard I try to keep from looking, my eyes keep darting in her direction.

How could this have happened? Just an hour before, we'd been discussing her calling as a teacher, and now she is dead. My throat swells. We will never have that tea and chat.

As chaos reigns all around me, I'm suddenly stricken with a horrifying thought.

*If Lillian was Velvet and she is now dead, what does that mean?*

My blood runs cold as I consider the ramifications. If Velvet is dead, how will we know what new weapon the Germans have? Did someone kill Lillian for that information? If so, who? I swallow hard, knowing that the spring offensive is just around the corner. What could this mean for the men in the trenches?

"Sophia Thérèse! Are you all right?"

Maxwell's voice reaches me from across the room and, for a moment, I almost run to him. Then I remember how upset he had seemed with me earlier and my grip tightens on my water glass.

I meet his gaze and his eyes show only concern. Remembering how many other officers and soldiers are in the room, I nod formally. "Yes, Corporal Mayer. I am fine, though considerably shaken. I don't understand how this could have happened."

He reaches out and squeezes my shoulder. "Neither do I."

"We were hoping you could tell us." A burly police officer has joined Max. "I am Captain Friedrich and I need to ask you a few questions," he says. "Can you tell me your whereabouts the last hour or so?"

"I was with the children in the Lustgarten. Lillian told me to take them for an outing. We were gone only a little while."

The captain nods as if I am confirming a story he already knows. Heard it from the children's guard, no doubt.

"Did Fräulein Bouchard seem upset today?"

I'm about to shake my head, then I stop, remembering. "A bit," I answer. "She told me she was worried about her family in France."

Max and Captain Friedrich exchange glances.

"Has Fräulein Bouchard ever seemed deranged or unstable?" the captain asks.

"Of course not!"

"What is going on, Captain Friedrich?" The crown prince

muscles his way into the crowded schoolroom and then stops dead when he spots the body on the floor. His face pales.

The captain steps forward. "Fräulein von Schönburg took the children to the Lustgarten for some exercise, and when they returned, they found your governess on the floor."

The prince winces and glances my way. "How much did the children see?"

"Prince Wilhelm saw everything," I tell him. "But together we kept the little ones out of the room."

He nods, a muscle in his jaw jumping.

I wrap my arms about myself, suddenly cold.

"Someone get a blanket," Max says. "The Fräulein has had a terrible shock."

"It's a sad episode, Prince Wilhelm, but the children were never in any danger," the captain says. "At least your governess had the tact to wait until the children were gone before ending her life."

Shock jolts through my body and my head jerks up. "Lillian didn't kill herself! She wouldn't! She was murdered!"

The room falls silent and the captain clears his throat. "And how would you know that, Fräulein? Who would want to kill a governess?"

Beside me, Maxwell stiffens, and everyone stills, waiting for my reply. I open my mouth, but nothing comes out. How can I explain to them without giving myself away?

There's a moment of silence before Max puts his hand on my shoulder. "I think Fräulein von Schönburg is just dazed by the events of the afternoon. She and Fräulein Bouchard were no doubt good friends."

I nod, still speechless. I'd almost made a terrible tactical blunder. I glance at Lillian's shrouded body. But who could blame me?

The captain and the prince continue to question me, though I don't have a lot to add. Max moves from my side and I watch him as I give my answers. He circles the schoolroom, peering under tables and behind bookshelves, finally reaching the alcove where the toy box is kept. Is he merely investigating a crime scene? None of the other guards are poking about so obviously. They're all standing in the middle of the room talking.

Maxwell bends over the box and I wonder what he's looking at, when the prince suddenly calls to him.

Max startles.

"Could you please escort Fräulein von Schönburg to her quarters?"

"Of course." Maxwell hurries back and helps me to my feet.

Surprisingly, the prince stops me with a hand on my arm. "Thank you for your quick thinking with the children. I'll speak to Wilhelm before he goes to sleep tonight."

I bow my head. As we're walking, I see Maxwell's eyes dart back to the small alcove. I follow his gaze and notice that the rug on the shining wooden floor is not in its place and neither is the toy box that sits on the rug. I spot the almost undetectable outline of a square cut in the wood.

The trapdoor.

Shocked, I glance back at Max, but his face reveals nothing as we leave the room.

My mind races. Max said the tunnels went to the schoolroom, but I haven't thought about the conversation since and never looked for the trapdoor. I would have spotted it earlier except that the rug and the toy box were always sitting on top of it, no doubt to keep inquisitive children from tumbling down into the tunnels.

But everything had been moved, which could only mean that someone had used it recently.

Perhaps even this afternoon while I was in the park with the children.

I look at Max's face again. Why hadn't he pointed it out to the captain? My brain, swift and logical, comes to the only conclusion possible.

Because Maxwell was the one who had gone down it. Hadn't I seen him earlier hurrying out of the Grand Hall? My stomach lurches.

Could Maxwell have killed Lillian?

Even as my heart rejects the possibility, my mind turns the idea over and over, examining it from all angles. Maxwell had been called a hero after the incident with the assassin, but perhaps that's not the way it was at all. By the time we reach my door, I'm shaking.

He pauses, placing a gentle finger under my chin and tilting it upward so he can see my face. The dark eyes searching mine are filled with sadness.

"I am sorry about your friend, Sophia Thérèse." He takes

my hand and kisses the tips of my fingers so tenderly that tears spring to my eyes. "I suggest you rest. You've been through a lot."

I nod and he leaves. Shutting and locking the door behind me, I collapse onto the chair and cover my face with my hands. I can't get the image of Lillian lying on the floor out of my mind. Could Maxwell really have killed her? I remember the look in his eyes just moments ago and I feel that he isn't capable, but then I remember how he and the assassin had faced off in the reception room and how angry he'd been with me earlier.

My heart constricts and I realize that I don't know Maxwell Mayer at all. No matter how much I wish things were different, we didn't meet in my real life.

I pace the room, my thoughts whirling about in my head like ribbons round the maypole.

If Lillian *was* Velvet, La Dame Blanche and the Allies just lost what may have been their most important asset. What if Lillian was killed because she was discovered? How long before someone discovers me? Panic swirls in my stomach.

No. If Abwehr did discover that Lillian was an undercover agent, they wouldn't just kill her, would they? Wouldn't she be worth more alive than dead?

I plop down on my bed and rub my temples. I have to do something. Even if Lillian was Velvet, she didn't deserve to die. And if she wasn't . . . But who would want her dead if she wasn't Velvet? Who would want to kill a governess? I close my eyes, thinking. Mathilde hated her, but not enough to kill her. Not with a gun. As far as I know, everyone else adored her.

Mathilde did tell me that Lillian's nose was out of joint because she and the duchess were close until Marissa showed up. Could there have been bad blood between Lillian and Marissa? If so, I never noticed. The only one I've ever seen arguing with Lillian is . . . Suddenly an image of Mrs. Tremaine's face flashes before my eyes. Mrs. Tremaine knows something. I'm sure of it.

Throwing caution to the wind, I leap up and hurry to the servants' lounge. If there's one person who knows where Mrs. Tremaine is staying, it'll be Mathilde.

I find her, along with several other servants, all knotted together in the middle of the room. Her face is streaked with tears. "Oh, isn't it horrible?" she wails when she sees me. "That poor woman. How could this happen?"

Mathilde seems to have forgotten her dislike of Lillian in the midst of all the drama. I shove away my aversion. "Can I speak to you alone?" I ask.

"Of course." She flashes the others a smug look over her shoulder. "This must be so difficult for you," she says, following me from the room.

"I need your help," I tell her before she can go into how sorry she is about that poor teacher.

"What do you need?"

"I need you to show me to Mrs. Tremaine's room."

Mathilde raises an eyebrow.

"Mathilde, it's important." I'll offer her a bribe if I have to. I need to see Mrs. Tremaine before I lose my nerve.

She doesn't hesitate. "Follow me."

Mathilde takes me to the west side of the palace, far away from the family quarters. I wonder if that was the prince's doing—as if keeping his lover far away from his wife would fool anyone.

"Thank you, Mathilde," I say. "I owe you."

"That you do," she says cheerfully.

I wait until she leaves before I face the door, my heart pounding. Now that I'm here, it doesn't seem like such a good idea. I know Miss Tickford certainly wouldn't think so, but then Miss Tickford isn't here. Or rather she's in Berlin somewhere, but she certainly hasn't been that helpful so far. For all intents and purposes, I'm on my own.

How can I confront Mrs. Tremaine without giving myself away?

Very carefully, that's how.

I rap sharply on the door and Arnold opens it almost immediately.

"Who is it?" Mrs. Tremaine calls from the other side of the room. "Tell whoever it is that I'm very tired and to go away."

I muscle my way past Arnold and then stop short, almost gasping at the opulence. The room looks somewhat as you would expect heaven to—all white and gold. If there had been a harp in the corner, I would not have been surprised. Heavy velvet draperies hang at the windows, snow-color lambskin rugs dot the floors, and the furniture has been finished in gold leaf so brilliant it almost makes me blink.

Mrs. Tremaine is lying on a divan across the room with a washcloth pressed to her forehead. Penny barks.

"Well, you don't listen very well," Mrs. Tremaine says, sitting up. In spite of the dark circles marring her face and her auburn hair a mess, she's still languidly beautiful. "I really wasn't expecting company."

She smooths her venetian-blue tea gown trimmed with Valenciennes lace and waves toward a tea cart next to the divan. "I was just going to have some tea. Now that you're here, you might as well join me. Arnold, please get Miss von Schönburg a cup."

"I'm fine, thank you, Arnold."

"Oh, please, you've interrupted my rest, the least you can do is have tea with me." Her lilting voice belies the fatigue I see in her blue eyes.

"Of course." I sit on the stiff Louis XVI chair across from her and reach for the cup of tea Arnold hands me. Taking a sip, I peer at Mrs. Tremaine over the rim of my cup. Is she really who she presents herself to be? When we first met, I thought her an Australian version of the French *femme fatale*—a seductress only interested in dalliances with rich men, and in gossip and court machinations. But after discovering that she and Lillian were involved in some sort of intrigue, I began to doubt my original assessment. Could this vain coquette be a spy? If so, who is she working for? It certainly can't be Germany.

Whatever she and Lillian were arguing about this

morning made Mrs. Tremaine angry—but angry enough to sneak back hours later and kill her in cold blood?

"So what is the purpose of your visit, Sophia Thérèse?" Mrs. Tremaine asks.

I bite my lip, thinking hard. How can I get her to tell me what I need without giving myself away? "I'm concerned about the argument you and Lillian were having this morning," I finally say.

If Mrs. Tremaine is surprised, she doesn't show it. "And why would that concern you?"

I swallow. "Well, the children . . ."

"What do they have to do with anything?" She shrugs a petulant shoulder. "They weren't even there."

"They might have come in, and I think it's highly inappropriate, considering the circumstances. . . ." I let my voice trail off and give a delicate shrug. I don't say *considering that you're sleeping with their father*, but my meaning is clear. I give her a withering look, hoping to provoke her.

It works.

She glares at me. "If you must know, Lillian was going to do something for me and then backed out of it. I was angry. That's all." Her eyes slide away from mine and I know she's hiding something. The sudden tension in her shoulders and the pinched look about her mouth confirm my suspicion. Then her gaze returns to me and unease slithers up my spine as her eyes narrow. "And how dare you waltz into my boudoir and pass moral judgment on me. You don't know anything about me."

She leans forward as if she's going to spring across the low table separating us and attack me.

The hair on the back of my neck prickles. Why didn't I think to bring a weapon? Especially since I came here to confront her. If Mrs. Tremaine did kill Lillian, what's to stop her from attacking me? The only person here to witness it is Arnold, and he's devoted to her. I glance at him, my eyes widening. Of course! Arnold must be the one I saw talking to Lillian the first night I came to the palace. I grip my teacup and plow on. "What was she going to do for you?"

She brings herself back under control and leans back on the divan. "I fail to see why that's any of your business."

*It's time to bluff, Sam.*

I take a deep breath and will my voice to remain firm. "You can tell me or you can explain it to the guards."

Mrs. Tremaine stills and her blue eyes regard me like those of a cat watching a mouse. A hushed silence descends upon the room and even Arnold seems to have stopped breathing. "And all this time I thought you were a silly debutante. Why would the guards be interested in my argument with Lillian?"

I raise an eyebrow. "They're going to be interested in anyone who spoke to Lillian just before her death."

The teacup in her hand crashes to the floor and her eyes widen. The horror on her face is so real that I know it isn't a ruse.

"You didn't know," I whisper.

She shakes her head. "No. When?"

"Today. I found her in the schoolroom."

Her hand covers her mouth and tears fill her eyes. "That poor girl. What am I going to tell her family?"

I stare at her, my pulse racing. "Her family? You know her family?"

Penny leaps into Mrs. Tremaine's lap and tries to lick the tears now rolling down her mistress's face.

"I met them in France before coming here. They asked me to try to get Lillian to return home. They were so afraid for her."

My mind scrambles to put the pieces together. "Is that why you're here? For Lillian?"

She nods. "But not just for Lillian. There are several others I was to make contact with. Lillian was just the easiest to get to because of the circumstances."

"Who sent you?" I ask.

"Their families. How . . . how did she die?"

I hesitate, and then tell her the truth. "A gunshot to the head. The guards think it was suicide."

Mrs. Tremaine goes white as a sheet and Arnold rushes to her side. "It is my fault, then," she whispers.

I carefully set my own cup down and take a deep breath. My mother would be proud of my composure. "How is it your fault?"

"She was going to leave last night," Mrs. Tickford whispers. "I paid someone to get her out of the country, but she backed out at the last moment. I'd given her a gun for the journey."

Her eyes meet mine.

"So it's my fault. I should have left well enough alone. I thought she would jump at the chance, but she loved the children so much. Apparently, she was more conflicted than I ever suspected."

Mrs. Tremaine breaks down in tears and Arnold looks up at me. "I knew this would happen," he says. "She's far better suited to gossip than to being a war hero."

Mrs. Tremaine sobs against his shoulder. "I just wanted to help," she says. "I thought it would be amusing!"

Arnold pats her back. "Don't worry. We won't be here long."

"I would wait," I tell him, and I stand. "It'll be less suspicious if you hold off until things calm down a bit."

He nods, and I leave an inconsolable Mrs. Tremaine in Penny and Arnold's care.


By the time I reach my room, I feel as if I'm going to be sick.

*So Lillian did kill herself.*

My chest constricts and I feel as if I can't breathe. Moving over to the window above my bed, I push it open to let in some fresh air.

It doesn't seem possible that Lillian could do such a thing. She seemed sad, yes, but desolate enough to turn the gun on herself? Especially knowing that I would return with the children and they would see?

Something isn't right, but no matter how much I think about it, I can't come up with the solution. The window looks out onto a side street where deliveries are made and the servants' door is located. As I idly watch people coming and going, I'm wondering what the prince and the duchess are going to do with me now that their children's governess is dead. I don't have the qualifications to be a head teacher.

My mind moves on to Miss Tickford and I remember how I felt when I saw her in the theater. What is she doing here? Why hasn't she contacted me?

I suddenly remember the note in the pocket of my coat and the man who delivered it. Is it from Miss Tickford? With everything that has happened since, I'd completely forgotten it.

As I'm turning to get the note out of my coat pocket, I notice Marissa Baum's neat bob coming out the servants' door.

The sight of her is like an explosion in my mind and I can't believe I didn't think of it sooner.

*If Lillian wasn't Velvet, then Marissa most certainly is.*

Snatching up my coat, I race down the stairs, hoping to catch her. I nod at the guard on my way by. Curfew isn't until dark, so he'll probably wait until then to ask for bribes.

I spot Marissa rounding the corner and I cut across the street, slowing when I near the intersection. Peering around the side of the building, I hurry after her. She has crossed the street and is moving west toward the setting sun, making it more difficult for me to track her. Her pace slows as we move into the shopping district, and I stay across the street and several stores behind her so she won't see my reflection in the display windows.

I scan the people around me, but see nothing unusual. I'm so busy watching the pedestrians that I almost miss seeing Marissa slip into a millinery shop. I watch for a moment and then hurry across the street. I stay outside the window, hiding behind a display of cartwheel hats with flowers dripping from their brims. For a moment, I don't see anything, and then I make out Marissa at the counter, talking with a woman dressed in black. The woman nods and points through a door to what looks like the workshop.

Marissa's slipping out the back way.

My heart skitters in my throat as I hurry down the street and around the corner, hoping to find the back alley before Marissa gets away. Marissa either knows I'm trailing her or is taking special precautions to be discreet. In either case, if you take this behavior along with the false travel papers, it's clear that she's far, far more than just a rich American debutante who came to Germany on a lark.

Towering heaps of garbage dot the narrow alleyway and the smell of rotting refuse assaults my nose. The sun is just setting as I pick my way carefully around the piles. Hearing the low murmur of a woman's voice, I frantically dart into a deep doorway.

The voice is joined by a male voice. I carefully peer around the corner of the doorway, only to find a stack of barrels obscuring my view. Heart in my throat, I tiptoe out of the doorway and then pause, listening. The woman speaks again and I take in a deep breath.

It's Marissa.

I can't hear well enough to discern what she's saying but

I know it's her. It's hard to disguise the American twang mangling German pronunciation.

If only I could see who she's with. I take another cautious step toward the edge of the stack of barrels. As I do, I accidentally kick a piece of metal pipe on the ground. I freeze, my heart shooting up into my throat as the pipe clatters across the ground. There's a sudden silence and I hold my breath, wondering if I'm suddenly going to see a hand coming round the barrels to grab me by the throat. I clench my fists, knowing I would fight if I had to.

After a moment, the conversation resumes, and I breathe a sigh of relief. Then I stiffen again as Marissa's voice takes on an obvious pleading quality. I frown, wishing I could make out exactly what she's saying.

I'm stepping a bit closer to the edge of the stack of barrels when I hear her say, "But do you think the prince will really do it? Couldn't he be tried for treason if it's discovered?"

I stand frozen, waiting for a reply.

The prince? Is she talking about Prince Wilhelm?

*My God!*

I hear the quiet murmur of a man's voice and then Marissa says, "You spoke to the prince. I know he's appalled by the general's tactics and can't believe the kaiser agrees, but then, Haber is persuasive."

The man whispers something and, heart pounding, I lean forward, straining to hear more clearly.

"It'll change the entire war," Marissa says. "All those men in the trenches will be smoked out like rabbits out of a warren."

The man answers, still in a whisper, but loud enough for me to hear. His words send chills down my back. "No. It'll change the world for all time. A weapon such as this—"

A door opens down the street and music spills out into the alley. There's a sudden, silent flurry of movement from where Marissa and the man are standing, and I crouch low behind the barrels. Shadows pass close by and then melt away into the twilight. The door slams again and I wait, terrified, in the darkness.

After several minutes of deep silence I'm sure that I'm alone. I want to close my eyes and have everything disappear. But it won't. I'll still be stuck in a Berlin back alley listening to people talk about war and treason and betrayal.

Lillian will still be dead.

It's clear now that Marissa is a spy. But is she Velvet? Something is missing, some elemental piece to the puzzle. Miss Tickford said that Velvet's handler had passed on messages that Velvet was working on something that had to do with weaponry.

As I make my way back to the palace, I replay the conversation in my head over and over. *All those men will be smoked out of the trenches like rabbits out of a warren.* That definitely doesn't sound like U-boats. Could it have something to do with airplanes? What am I missing?

*Thirty-five.*

My father's voice whispers the number as clearly as if he were standing right next to me.

Thirty-five? What does that mean? The paper I found in Marissa's bedroom contained a picture with circles and one of them had *Cl-35* in the middle of it.

Suddenly it feels as if fireworks are exploding in my head. I stop and the noise of the street fades. My pulse races as a circle or square with *Cl-35,5*—not *35*—flashes before my eyes. Marissa had written it wrong.

It's from the periodic table of elements. *Chlorine.*

Herr Haber is a chemist. It must have been his name that was going to be written across the bottom of the paper. Then I remember that Marissa visited his laboratory.

My mind is racing and I feel as if I can't breathe. *If this is true . . .*

Somehow I make my way back to the palace on legs that feel as if they're made of rubber.

"You know you're supposed to be back by sunset. There's a curfew," the guard growls.

Part of me wants to mutter an expletive, but the first rule of spying is not to be memorable and I have a feeling that he'd remember the governess who told him to bugger off.

Back in my room, I tilt the chair under the doorknob and hurry to take the envelope from under my mattress, where I secreted it.

I stare at the picture, unable to believe I didn't pick up on it earlier. Horror rises up in my throat.

That's what Velvet has been working on. She discovered that the new weapon the Germans are developing is made from chlorine.

# PART IV

*Master*

# EIGHTEEN
## HLJKWHHQ

*Cobbler: Someone who puts together false passports, travel documents, and birth certificates for fellow spies.*

When I wake up the next morning it takes a moment for the awful truth to wash over me.

Lillian is dead.

Marissa is Velvet.

The Germans are developing a weapon that will be able to kill hundreds of men at once.

I must get a message to Miss Tickford. While I'm still unsure as to why she's here in Berlin, that's secondary to letting LDB know about the Germans' plan. No wonder Marissa said that it would smoke men out of the trenches like rabbits out of a warren. If the Germans have discovered a way to utilize and disperse a noxious gas like chlorine on a mass scale, it will change the entire course of the war. No longer will men simply be stuck in trenches, unable to gain any ground. Now they will be stuck in trenches and choking to death on deadly fumes.

I dress for the day. I have to get to the bakery. Taking

out the LDB codebook, I quickly write, *Urgent. Velvet found.* I pause, wondering if I should include something about the chlorine gas. Finally I add, *Arma inventa.* Latin for "Weapon discovered."

There's a knock on the door and I quickly hide the note under my pillow before answering. A servant hands me a message.

"Thank you," I say.

She bobs her head and is gone.

I unfold it and read.

*Prince Wilhelm and the duchess have taken their children to Potsdam. They thought it best to suspend the children's lessons temporarily. You will be called on when they decide to resume them.*

It isn't signed and I can only surmise that it was written by the prince's secretary. I haven't even thought about what I'll be doing at the palace now that Lillian is dead. But then, now that I've found Velvet, I no longer have to stay.

I slip on my coat, anxious to be off to the bakery. I'll plan my next move, whatever that is, after I return. It isn't until I put my hand in my pocket that I remember the note that I'd been passed. I freeze for a moment, stunned that it had slipped my mind. What kind of spy was I anyway? I pull it out of my pocket and stare at it, unease fluttering in my stomach. La Dame Blanche set up the drop spot believing it to be safer for me than trying to do brush passes. Why wouldn't they just go through the regular channels?

Perhaps the regular channels have been compromised.

Alarm washes over me. I might have been walking into a trap if I'd gone to the bakery.

Removing my coat, I pull out the LDB codebook and then unfold the note, with my pencil at the ready.

Except it's not written in LDB code.

I stare at the slip of paper, puzzled. Something about it looks familiar. I tap the pencil against the wood, thinking. It almost looks like . . . The room suddenly spins and I grip the edge of the desk to keep from slumping to the floor. I close my eyes and wait for the dizziness to pass.

Then I open them again and stare at the numbers. I'm right. I know I'm right.

It's my father's code.

My hand covers my mouth. Could the man who bumped into me be my father? Who else would know this code? But no. That would mean that my father isn't imprisoned, and I know the only way he would stay away from my mother and me for so long would be against his will.

Wouldn't it?

I frown at the handwriting. Is it my father's? It's hard to tell.

My hand trembling, I reach down and pick up the pencil that I dropped to the floor. The code itself is simple once you know the formula. We'd made it up when I was nine.

Instead of shifting three spaces forward on the alphabet, you shifted three back on the first letter, two forward on the second letter, one back on the third, and then you started all over again. Elementary, really, but I'd been so proud of it.

The message is short and to the point, so it only takes me a minute to decipher it. When done I stare at it, shock spreading throughout my body.

*Go home.*

Cold sweeps over me and I shiver. The temperature in my room seems to have dropped ten degrees.

Standing, I take the quilt from my bed and wrap it around my shoulders. Then I pace the room, my mind racing. My father would want me to go home because he knows I'm in danger. But if he's free, he would come home with me, wouldn't he?

So he must have sent the note to me under duress, unless there's a reason he can't come home.

I freeze.

What if Father is doing the exact same thing I am? His German is impeccable and he's a lot smarter than I am. Perhaps he's an agent, too? Is that the information Captain Parker has for me?

Then I remember the note in my pocket waiting to be delivered to LDB. Torn, I stare at my father's message. I want nothing more than to rush out and try to find him.

I've been waiting for something like this for so long.

Then an image of countless troops choking to death on a poisonous gas flashes through my mind and my duty is clear.

I put my coat back on, wondering if my father ever had to face a situation like this. Family or country.

Somehow I think he must have.

My legs are still shaking as I hurry out of the palace. My heart aches for poor Lillian and I am desperate to find my father, but my first priority is to get the note to the bakery.

I hurry down the street, my mind spinning. If Father is an agent, who is he working for? If it were LDB, wouldn't Captain Parker or Miss Tickford have told me?

Or would they?

Maybe they wanted me to be a part of LDB so badly that they would have told me anything to get me to join. But why?

I enter the bakery, but the operative is nowhere to be seen. Heart in my throat, I buy a cookie and leave, too spooked to try to see if anyone has taken his place. Maybe he was on a break. Maybe he's taken the day off. There are many reasons he might have been gone, but somehow the streets feel less safe than they did just a few moments ago.

I pass a little café where my father had taken me once when I was a child. He put me on the counter stool and ordered me a hot chocolate, while he had a pint of beer. I don't remember exactly what I said, but he threw back his head and laughed and called me his little genius. Then we walked home, my small hand in his big one. I remember how safe I felt.

I halt so quickly that the person behind me almost bumps into me.

*"Dummkopf!"* he mutters as he passes by, but I ignore him.

That image of my father and me spins around in my brain. When it stops, it grows crisp and clear in my mind.

We'd been walking *home*.

I know where to find my father.

Turning quickly, I head down into the U-Bahn and hop on the train going toward the Königsplatz, where the Reichstag building is. If Father knows I'm here—and the note clearly indicates that he does because he would never share our code with anyone—there's no reason for him to think that I don't know that *he's* here. He'll know that I'm looking for him. So if he wants me to find him, he'll make himself available. He'll go to a place that we both knew and loved.

That's what he meant when he wrote *Go home*.

We'd loved the Bellevue neighborhood. Because it was near the government buildings, our neighbors were families from all over the world. Even the bustling shops had an international feel.

A wispy cloud of nostalgia settles over me as I enter the part of our district where we had spent so much time. The homes still show pride of ownership, though many of the foreign families left after the war started.

And then I'm in front of the house I'd been so happy in.

Built more for function than form, it is not a remarkable house, but I loved it. The narrow brick building rises four stories into the air and each floor boasts two multipaned windows. Steps ascend from the street to the first floor, while a small path leads around the snowball bush to the servants' door in the back. The stoop is clean, and I wonder if Frau Engel still scrubs it twice a week.

We lived in the house for seven years, longer than we'd lived anywhere else as a family, and a lump rises in my throat as I look at it. *Enough*, I tell myself, turning away. Since we no longer rent the house, if my father is here, he will be in the gardens across the street.

The park is as large as four city blocks and follows the curve of the Spree River. Stately linden trees guard the entrance to the park, which seems oddly wild and overgrown—not at all the manicured park of my memories. Then it dawns on me—of course Berlin's parks would be neglected. All the able-bodied young gardeners are off fighting the war.

There are a few women in nanny uniforms giving their young charges an airing, but for the most part the park is strangely empty of people. I remember it as a lively place, but perhaps my memory is playing tricks on me. Of course, that was before the war.

The path by the river is punctuated by willows, but I veer away from the water toward the epicenter of the park—a large oval pond surrounded by acorns and birch trees. My father and I used to build boats to float on the water, each trying to design the swiftest craft.

Memories, as painful as a hangnail, fill my mind and I turn away from the pond. Taking a deep breath and pushing the images away, I scan the tree line. He has to be here. I know it as surely as I know the color of my hair. The connection my father and I have always had comes into sharp focus. *Go home* meant to come here. I know it did.

"Samantha."

A shudder runs through my body at the sound of my father's voice and I close my eyes against the assault of emotions rushing through me. I yearn to throw myself into his arms, but my hurt and doubt are so strong that I'm frozen in place.

"Samantha," he says again, stepping in front of me. I tilt my head to search his face and notice that he's let the trim little beard he always wore grow into a tangle of whiskers shot through with white. There are lines in his face that weren't there before. Lines that say much about the grief and worry he must have experienced during the time we were apart.

He opens his arms wide and my paralysis is broken as I throw myself at him. He pulls me close and relief courses through my body. He's alive. He is here and he's alive. All the complications—La Dame Blanche, Velvet, even being in an enemy country in the middle of the most violent war the world has ever seen—mean nothing next to the fact that my father is alive.

"I missed you so much," I finally say, my voice muffled against his shoulder.

"Oh, Sam. What are you doing here?" His voice is tired and I pull away to look at him again.

He's much thinner than I remember and his cheeks are gaunt, but his greenish-gray eyes are still warm.

Without waiting for an answer to his first question, he asks the next one, so I know it's been weighing on his mind. "How is your mother?"

"Fine," I say. "Heartbroken, but fine."

He bows his head and I feel a twinge of pain for having hurt him. But it's the truth. I move on to the question uppermost in my own mind. "But what are you doing here? Why have you stayed away for so long?"

He hears the anguish in my voice and pain etches his face. He pulls away. "We should walk. I don't like to stay in one place for too long and we're exposed here."

I nod and fall into step beside him without letting go of his arm.

I never want to let go of him again.

"First," he says, "I need to know what you're doing here and who you're working for. When I first learned of your arrival, you could have knocked me over with a feather. Especially when I discovered you were living in the Stadtschloss and caring for the kaiser's grandchildren."

"How did you know?" I ask.

He gives me a grim smile. "I know all the comings and goings in the palace. When I first heard of a new governess, I didn't think anything of it. It wasn't until I saw you walking into the bakeshop arm in arm with a German guard that I knew it was you. Why couldn't you just stay home where it was safe and take care of your mother?"

I bristle at the reproach in his voice. "I was recruited for La Dame Blanche. I actually told the captain no at first, but he promised me that if I helped them, he would give me information about you. It was the first time I knew for sure that you were alive. I couldn't say no." I glance at him, so many questions spinning in my head, I'm not even sure what to ask first.

"Who told you they had information on me?"

His voice is sharp and I stop walking.

"Captain Parker—the assistant to the head of Military Intelligence. He's the one who sent me to find Velvet."

"Velvet?" He sounds confused. Of course, he knows nothing about what I'm actually doing here in Berlin.

I lower my voice. "Velvet is an undercover operative who has been feeding the British information on some new sort of weaponry. I was recruited to extract her before the Abwehr became aware of her presence."

He pauses and turns to me, frowning. "Why on earth would they recruit a child to extract a valuable agent?"

Resentment flashes through me. "I'm not a child and I happen to be very talented."

His face softens. "I'm sorry, Sam. You know I think you're brilliant, but you're also untrained."

His words align so exactly with my own insecurities that I turn my head and swallow. "I think they wanted someone who knew Berlin and spoke several languages. I also look very much like the duchess's cousin from Cologne. Apparently, *they* had faith that I'd be able to complete the assignment."

My jab isn't lost on him and he changes the subject. "Who is Velvet?" he asks. "There are just two operatives in the palace that I know of, and only one of them is loosely connected to LDB and unknown to all but a few highly placed officials."

*Two?* "Who are they?" I ask.

He shakes his head. "Samantha, there are people who would slit throats for that information. I'm hardly going to give it to my daughter. Now, who is this Velvet?"

I hesitate, thinking of Marissa. "At first, I wasn't sure who Velvet actually was," I finally admit. "But now I'm fairly certain I know who she is."

My father's bushy eyebrows fly up on his forehead. "Pardon? They sent you in to extract an operative and didn't tell you who it was? Of all the irresponsible . . . No. This can't be right."

"Her handler disappeared," I put in quickly. "No one within LDB except her handler knew who she was."

He shakes his head. "No. That isn't how it's done. Samantha, listen to me." His voice is urgent and low. "Something feels very strange about this whole thing. We must get you out of Berlin. Go to Marissa Baum. She'll help you. She is the duchess Cecilie's friend."

His grip on my arm tightens as he propels me out of the park. I jerk away, impatient. "Yes, I know. But you have to come with me. I discovered what kind of weapon the Germans are developing. We have to tell LDB and MI6."

He grabs my arm again and marches me across the grass. "You know? Good God, Sam, do you have any idea how much danger you've put yourself in?"

"No, Herr Donaldson," a voice says from behind us. "It is *you* who have put your daughter in danger."

# NINETEEN
## QLQHWHHQ

*A Wilderness of Mirrors: When an operation becomes so complicated and confusing that it's no longer possible to tell the difference between truth and untruth.*

I whirl around and see Miss Tickford holding a gun. She's flanked by two armed men in black coats.

Father lunges for the men. "Samantha, run!"

One of the men hits Father behind the head with a gun and I watch, horrified, as he crumples to the ground. "Father!"

Miss Tickford catches me in her arms before I can reach him. "I am so sorry, little one, that you had to find out this way."

I struggle against her, but she's stronger than she looks. Then, remembering Monsieur Elliot's advice, I force myself to relax. I may not know exactly what's going on, but nothing is more important than the fact that my father is hurt.

Her grip lessens and I twist sideways, slamming the palm of my hand into her face. Miss Tickford cries out as blood gushes from her nose. Monsieur Elliot was right—surprise does work.

I turn to run back to my father but slam straight into the

hard chest of one of the men.

He twists me around to where Miss Tickford is glaring at me. "And here I thought I sent you in too soon. Well done, but right now I need you to *think*!" She takes a handkerchief out of her purse and holds it to her nose. "We've already attracted too much attention. Do you want to get us all thrown in prison? We need to get to safety before the authorities are alerted to an altercation. Your father will be fine. Now, walk."

She takes my arm and this time I know I won't be able to free myself. I go with her, twisting my head to see the two men lifting my father between them. "What is going on?" I demand. "What are you doing with my father?"

"Remember your training," she whispers fiercely. "We cannot cause a scene. I'll tell you once we reach the motorcars."

I start to pull away and her hand tightens. She turns her lovely green eyes to me. "Samantha, you must trust me. This is for your father's own good."

I subside, questions whirling about in my head. *What is she doing? How could hitting my father in the head be for his own good? Who are those men?*

There are two automobiles parked at the entrance. Miss Tickford leads me into one, while the two men put my father in the other. "Where are we going?" I ask. Panicking, I crane my neck, trying to see out of the narrow back window.

"Someplace safe," she says. "Don't worry. You'll be able to see your father soon enough, but for right now, you must listen well. Your father's life depends on your cooperation."

My head jerks back. "What are you talking about?"

"Your father is a double agent," she says, looking into my eyes, over the handkerchief that is now dotted with blood. "He is a traitor."

I start shaking my head. "No, he would never do that. You're wrong."

She holds up her hand. "Of course he wouldn't do it."

I stop. "But you just said . . ."

"He's been misled. He was taken by Germans in the Arabian Peninsula just like the reports said, and was imprisoned for months. The Germans knew there was someone on the inside feeding the British information on their specialized weapon program. They wanted your father to find out who it was. They allowed him to escape and then be recruited by Germans posing as French operatives before he could reach home. That's who he thinks he's working for—the French."

"I don't understand. Why would they recruit him? He's an ambassador."

She shakes her head. "No, Samantha, he's always been a spy. This is why he hasn't returned home. He believes that his work here is crucial."

I frown. She's talking in circles and I'm on the verge of tears. So much has happened in the last twenty-four hours—it's as if my brain has simply stopped taking in new information.

Miss Tickford puts her arm around me. "I know it's confusing, but you need to understand that your father has worked for MI6 for a long time. We were building a network even before the war, even back when you lived here as a child. Your father has much inside information on our operations. He has inadvertently handed several spies over to the Germans."

Horror crawls along my skin. "What do you mean?"

"Lillian Bouchard."

I clap my hand over my mouth to keep from being sick. "But Lillian is dead," I whisper.

"Yes. I believe it happened accidentally when the Abwehr tried to apprehend her. But she wouldn't be dead if your father hadn't given her up."

My eyes fill with tears and my stomach somersaults.

"I'm so sorry, little one, but I need you to be brave and do exactly what I tell you. It's the only way to save your father's life and to get Velvet safely out of the country. It might be a little difficult once we get back to England, but I can attest to your father's innocence. We may be able to save his life, if not his freedom."

Panic swirls in my stomach. This is a nightmare that I can't wake up from. I nod. I want nothing more than to leave Germany and never return.

Her eyes soften and she pats my arm. "Good girl. Now I have news that can't wait. I know who Velvet is."

I blink, trying to follow the abrupt change of topic. "I do, too." I tell her. "I just discovered it was Marissa. How did you figure it out?"

"Never mind. But circumstances necessitate quick action

on our part. She's in grave danger."

An image of Lillian's body floats before my eyes. *Aren't we all?*

I remember how Father said that I should go to Marissa for help, but he didn't know her LDB code name. Does that strengthen Miss Tickford's argument that my father is a traitor, or does it mean that Marissa is inadvertently working for the Germans as well?

I grow quiet, thinking hard. First Miss Tickford claimed that Velvet may have turned. Then my father is a double agent. My heart is thudding in my chest and my breathing quickens. Who can I trust?

She leans close, her eyes filled with sympathy. "You've done a wonderful job, Samantha. I know how devastating and confusing this must all be for you. Trust me, once this is over, you can go home. Don't you want that?"

I nod.

She pats my leg. "Good girl. Velvet's intelligence has saved countless lives. Now we must get information on the weapon. Have you discovered where the formula is? Once we have that, we can get all three of you to safety."

I shake my head. "No," I lie. "Now, what do you want me to do?" Time enough to discuss the chlorine once Marissa and my father are safe.

"Velvet will be understandably jumpy right now. The easiest way to get her out of the palace is to do it without her knowledge. I'm afraid she will think we're with the Abwehr if we approach her."

I frown. "Excuse me?"

"You must go see her alone. Take her some tea. Use the packet I gave you, the one that will put her to sleep. You remember which one that is, yes?"

I nod.

"Good. Once she's asleep, you'll pull her blinds down to signal our operatives. They'll pose as a doctor and his assistant. That way we have a perfect cover story if anyone asks questions."

Panic runs through my veins and all I want to do is make sure my father is all right. "I want to see my father," I tell her.

"Of course you do. You can see him as soon as we get Velvet out of the palace. I fear that the Abwehr are very near to discovering who she is. We must get the information on those weapons. So many lives hang in the balance, Samantha. If those weapons fall into the wrong hands . . ." Her voice trails off.

Something strikes me and I pull away. "You recruited me because of my father, didn't you? You knew if he discovered that I was in Berlin, he would come out of hiding." Everything falls into place and I stare at her, stunned. They didn't want me because I was so talented or smart, they wanted me because of my father. "My God," I breathe. "You had me followed the whole time."

"Of course we did, but we needed to get Velvet and the weapons as well. As much as we wanted your father, we wouldn't have asked you if we hadn't thought you capable of doing it. You are a real member of LDB, Samantha. That hasn't changed. You are honor bound to serve the war effort no matter what that might mean."

I lapse into silence. Something isn't right. I search Miss Tickford's eyes but see only earnest concern.

"Trust me, Samantha. What you do next has ramifications that stretch further than anything you can imagine."

I shiver and then nod just as the motorcar pulls up to the palace.

"As soon as we obtain Velvet, we'll take you to your father."

I slip into the palace and back to my room. My instincts are screaming at me, but I can't see any other way to get to my father. I'd been so sure that it would all get sorted out once I found him, but instead everything is more of a mess than ever.

Taking out my jewelry box, I run my fingers along the sides until I trigger the mechanism that opens the false bottom. I take out the packets with trembling fingers.

I slip the packets into the pocket of my skirt, wishing I'd never taken the assignment, never traveled to France and Luxembourg, and especially never come to Berlin.

But then I would never have met Maxwell or found my father.

Maxwell. I think of him again hurrying away from the tunnels all disheveled just before I discovered Lillian's body. Cold rushes over me. What if he is more than just a guard? What if he's a member of the Abwehr? I run all of our conversations through my mind. How could the young man who had told me stories about life on his grandfather's farm be a cold-hearted spy? Could he kill one governess one moment and then kiss the fingers of another hours later?

Could he really be that person?

But then, who am I to judge? I'm about to slip a young woman a sleeping powder in order to get my father back. People will do the unthinkable under pressure.

I quickly pack my satchel with everything I may need, including the envelope with Marissa's travel papers. Chances are, I won't be returning to the room. *Good-bye, Sophia Thérèse,* I think as I leave.

I slow as I get to the family wing. It would be disastrous if Maxwell were to discover me right now. What I'm about to do feels wrong, and that wrongness increases with each step. By the time I reach her door, I have half a mind to run back to my room and hide under the bed.

But I'm in Berlin. There's no place to hide.

I firm my resolve and give a short knock.

There's a moment's silence before she calls, "Who is it?"

"It's Sophia Thérèse," I say.

Another long pause. My chest tightens as I wait. What if she doesn't let me in? What if she says she's tired or busy or . . .

She opens the door.

I stare. If anything, she looks even more drained than she looked the last time, and there's a frantic edge to her that I've never seen.

"You're just the person I wanted to see," she says. "Come in."

Stepping into her boudoir, I notice that there are small personal items strewn over her bed and all over the sofa of her sitting room. "Are you going somewhere?"

She looks around as if surprised by the chaos. "Well, yes, actually. That's why I wanted to see you. I wanted to say good-bye and to tell you how sorry I was to hear about the governess. She seemed such a caring person."

My chest tightens. "She was, and thank you. I feel sorry for the children. They loved her very much."

"Indeed. I could tell."

A silence falls. Then I lick my lips and continue. "So where are you going?"

She shrugs, but I get the feeling that she isn't nearly as nonchalant as she pretends to be. "Mummy and Daddy gave me an ultimatum. They want me to come home, or at the very least go somewhere neutral, like Switzerland."

We stare at each other for a long moment before she averts her gaze.

"What does the duchess think of you leaving?" I ask. "You two have become such good friends."

Marissa strides over to her vanity and sits. "I'm going to leave a note. After everything that's happened, I don't think she'll be too upset."

I glance around at her belongings tossed everywhere. It looks much like my room did when it was ransacked. Had someone gone through her things?

"Will you be ready by morning?"

Marissa stares in the mirror, running a comb methodically through her short hair. "A maid is going to finish packing up my trunks and will send them on once I'm settled."

I look around.

"I sent her off on an errand," she says quickly. "Would you like something to drink? I can ring for tea." She looks around at the mess. "Or better yet, why don't we have a cocktail? They're all the rage in America."

I think of the packet of powder in my pocket. "That would be lovely."

She hurries to the sideboard against the wall. "Have a seat. This will only take a moment."

I sit on the edge of a wingback chair. Her movements seem stiff and unnatural, and when she hands me the drink, the ice is clinking from the trembling of her hand. "Are you all right?" I ask.

"Of course," she trills in a voice that is far, far from all right. "Now, I've prattled on and on about myself, but you came to see me. What did you want?"

My mind blanks. I raise the glass to my lips to buy myself some time. The strong scent of alcohol reaches my nostrils and I lower the glass. "I wanted to ask you about America."

Her eyes shoot open. "America?"

"Yes. I was wondering what it was like. I might want to move there, you see."

A knock sounds on the door and we both startle.

She gives me a faint smile. "One moment, please."

As soon as she moves away from the table, I grab the packets from my pocket and open the correct one. I glance over my shoulder, but she's halfway out the door and I can't see who she's talking to. My hands shake so badly as I pour the contents of the packet into her drink that I spill some of it on the table. I snatch up the drink and wipe the spilled powder into it, and then stir it quickly with my finger.

I set it down just as the door shuts. Wiping my fingers off, I clasp my hands in my lap to stop the trembling.

She takes a seat.

"Is everything all right?" I ask politely, trying not to stare at her drink.

"Of course. That was just the driver confirming my travel plans. It wasn't easy to obtain train tickets on such short notice, as I'm sure you can imagine."

I nod.

"So what did you want to know about America?"

My eyes track her movements as she picks up her cocktail and takes a small swallow. She grimaces.

My heart slams against my ribs.

"I think I put too much bitters in this. How is yours?"

I quickly take a gulp of my drink and then cough as the alcohol hits my throat. "It's fine," I say.

"Oh, good. Where were we?"

I take a deep breath. "We were discussing America." My next sip warms my stomach in an ever-widening circle like a pebble dropped into a lake. I set the glass down. The last thing I need is to be tipsy when the agents get here to cart her off. I frown as my sense of unease increases.

"Can I tell you a secret?" Marissa asks suddenly.

Is her speech slurring a bit? Are her eyes just a bit drowsy?

"Of course. You're leaving tomorrow, so you can tell me anything you like."

"I don't think I like Germany as much as I thought I would."

I blink. "But I thought you were having the time of your life?"

"No, I like the duchess well enough, but there's far too much intrigue going on around here, if you know what I mean." She waggles her finger at me and squints. "Funny. I haven't even finished my drink yet and I already feel blotto."

Her words are definitely slurred.

"Perhaps you would feel better if you lie down?" I suggest.

"But you wanted to talk about America. You know America is going to enter the war sooner or later, right?" She puts her finger to her lips. "But that's a secret. Wait. I already told you a secret, right? I have so many secrets."

I swallow. That makes two of us.

# TWENTY
## WZHQWB

*SERE: An acronym for Survival, Evasion, Resistance,
and Escape: techniques for when an operation goes wrong.*

I help Marissa to her feet. The powder is working very fast and I don't want her to fall before I can get her to the bed. Why didn't I think about asking Miss Tickford what the effects were?

"I should lie down. I feel horrible."

I put my arm about her and she leans on me heavily. "Are you sick to your stomach?" *Did I give her the wrong powder?* Remorse runs through me.

"No. It just hurts. I'm sure I'll be fine." I help her sit on the bed and then swing her feet over the edge. "What was I saying? Oh, yes. Secrets. I shouldn't tell you any more secrets. I don't know why I trust you. You shouldn't trust anyone. I had a friend tell me that once."

I'm about to answer her when she suddenly clutches at her stomach. "It hurts," she moans.

*Don't trust anyone.* Does that mean my father? Miss Tickford? Maxwell? Who am I supposed to trust? I walk over to the window, indecision dogging every step. I wrap my arms around myself, thinking. All I have to do is give the signal and Miss Tickford's agents will be here to take Marissa and me to my father.

Or will they?

Miss Tickford says my father betrayed his country. That he was tricked into giving the enemy information. So if Marissa is Velvet and is getting information from the Germans and giving it to my father, and my father is giving it back to the Germans . . . why wouldn't the Germans have already taken Velvet out of the equation? Miss Tickford told me that my father has unknowingly given up other spies . . . but wouldn't he have noticed a pattern of spies disappearing and figured it out by now? Of course he would have.

My mind goes from solution to solution, as if I'm solving the most complicated code in the world without the key. Perhaps I am.

If the Germans did suspect someone of leaking information, they wouldn't need the information, and they certainly wouldn't need their own chemical weapon formula, they would need all the people in the chain who were passing it along. My heart stops.

They would need my father and they would need Marissa Baum.

And I just gave up both of them.

Why hadn't I seen it before? I was upset about my father, but that didn't excuse my complete disregard of the truth. Why had it taken me so long?

Because if this were true, it would mean that Miss Tickford is lying and has been lying since the very beginning. Which would mean my father isn't the traitor. Miss Tickford is. As soon as it comes into my head, I know it's true. Miss Tickford mentioned the formula three times today when she told me that LDB didn't know what kind of weapon the Germans were developing.

My stomach churns in horror.

Miss Tickford is a traitor.

And so am I.

I back away from the window. Marissa moans and I break out in a cold sweat.

I just gave her Miss Tickford's powder. What if it's not even a sleeping concoction? For all I know, I may have just given her arsenic.

Rushing to my bag, I take out the small vial of syrup of ipecac. I unscrew the lid and smell it, remembering the scent from childhood illnesses. Marissa is dead white, droplets of sweat decorating her forehead. I pat her cheeks. "Marissa, wake up. You need to drink this."

Her eyes open and I can see she's trying to focus on me. "What? Wah?"

Her eyes flutter shut and I shake her a bit more forcibly. Slipping my arm behind her neck, I lean her forward. "You've been poisoned. You need to drink this. It'll make you feel better."

"Makesh shense," she slurs. "Feel awful. Who poishened me?"

I don't think now is the right time to tell her it was me, so I put the vial to her lips. "Never mind that. Drink."

Her eyes focus on me. "Not supposed to trust anyone."

I wave the vial in front of her face. "This will make you feel better." I don't mention that it will first make her much, much sicker.

She finally nods. "Can't make me feel worsh."

That's still to be determined, but I say nothing as I pour the contents of the vial into her mouth. I have no idea what a single dose is, but I can't afford to give her too little. For all I know, it won't work and I'll have killed a war hero.

She grimaces and gags once or twice. I toss the vial on her night table and rush out to the sitting room. The door is locked, but I pull her chair in front of it anyway. The last thing I want is for Miss Tickford's men to burst in on us while Marissa is incapacitated. I find a washbasin in the water closet and bring it to Marissa. Her eyes are shut and her skin is, if possible, even whiter. How much time had elapsed between my giving her the powder and giving her the ipecac? Five minutes? Fifteen minutes? Will she be able to expel enough of the poison to keep it from working?

"I'm going to be sick," she says, and I help her sit up over the basin.

I breathe a sigh of relief and hold her hair back as she throws up. I only pray that it works and she feels better fast. We have to get out of here. I wonder how long Miss Tickford's men are going to wait before they come up to get her, signal or no signal.

When she's through, I take the basin back to the water closet and wet a cloth. I'm so angry that my hands shake as I wipe Marissa's forehead, though I'm not sure who I'm more angry with, myself or Miss Tickford. I allowed my feelings for Miss Tickford to cloud my judgment, or as my father would put it, I allowed Miss Tickford to distract me while she made the moves to win the game. I let her determine every step, even when my own instincts were screaming otherwise.

Marissa's breathing is more normal now and I hope that the worst is over. At some point, I'm going to have to get her dressed and out of here—but where to go? Would the man at the bakery know of a safe place for us? I certainly can't go to the safe house Miss Tickford told me to go to if things went awry.

How am I going to get my father away from Miss Tickford? Does Marissa know someone who could help us?

The room is so silent, I can hear the clock ticking over the mantel in the sitting room. I pray that Marissa is sleeping peacefully. Opening her wardrobe, I pull out a wool coat and a pair of walking boots.

Then I sit and wait. If she doesn't recover enough to walk, we have no hope of escaping anyway, so I wait as long as I dare before gently shaking her shoulder.

"Marissa, wake up. We need to get out of here."

Her eyes flutter open and her eyes seem clearer.

"How do you feel?" I ask.

"Horrible. Alive. Who poisoned me?"

I clear my throat. "Me."

Her eyes fly open. "And then you saved me?"

"It's a long story. But yes." Taking a deep breath, I hold out my hand. "My name is Samantha Donaldson, and we are in big trouble."

Marissa takes my hand, but hers is so weak she can't even shake. She accepts my words without question. "And how do we get out of trouble?"

If I'd had any doubts about her, they would have been swept away with her calm acceptance of the situation. "As soon as you're able to walk, we need to get out of the palace. After that, I'm open to suggestions. Would you like a glass of water?"

She nods and I fetch her one from the sideboard where she'd made our drinks.

"Who are you with?" she asks.

For a moment I hesitate, and then I give a mental shrug. If we're to survive and rescue my father, we need to lay all our cards out on the table. "La Dame Blanche. At least I think so."

Her forehead wrinkles. "What do you mean, you think so?"

I sit on the edge of the bed and pluck at the bedspread with nervous fingers. "I was recruited to get to my father and you. I think my handler is a traitor and working for the Germans." I shake my head. "Or maybe she's working for herself, I don't know. I was trained with LDB agents, but who knows what actually has happened."

"Why would they want your father?" Marissa asks, taking another sip of water. I'm gratified that color is returning to her cheeks.

I almost tell her and then decide she needs to give me more information about what she is doing in Berlin. "You first," I tell her. "Who do you work for?"

She hesitates and then apparently comes to the same conclusion that I have. If we're to get out of this alive, we need to rely on each other. "I work for a joint coalition between Britain and the United States. The Americans are mostly interested in the sabotage on American soil. The Germans have blown up munitions factories, as well as factories making goods that we're shipping to the Allies. The Germans believe that if they can keep us occupied by troubles back home, we won't enter the war."

I digest that. "I had no idea that the Abwehr was active in the States."

She nods. "Yes, but of course there are many German sympathizers and pacifists who want us to stay out of the war completely. They say the British are performing the acts of sabotage and blaming the Germans to get us into the war."

I rub my temples. "We wouldn't do that."

"I know. That's why our government sent me . . . to find out who it is." She leans back against the pillow and sighs. "God, I could sleep for a week."

"What about the formula?" I ask. "When did you first learn about the chemical weapon?"

She frowns. "What are you talking about?"

"You don't have the formula? But I found the paper with the chemical symbol for chlorine on it."

"That was you?" she squeaks, her eyes wide.

I nod, somewhat shamefaced.

"I wondered. You seemed so innocent, with all that hair and your big blue eyes. No, I don't have the entire formula. My friend has that."

"Who's your friend?"

She shakes her head. "I'm sorry. I just can't."

I nod. I understand completely. "How on earth did your friend get the formula?"

Her cheeks redden. "Let's just say I kept Herr Haber occupied while my friend snuck the formula out the back door of the lab."

My mouth forms a little O of surprise. That explains Herr Haber's behavior at the dinner party. "We should go," I tell her regretfully. "Do you think you can walk now?"

Marissa takes a deep breath and nods. "Let me get cleaned up and I'll change. If you could just help me to the bathroom."

I assist her out of bed. Her skin pales with the movement, but by the time she comes out of the bathroom she's looking somewhat stronger.

I pack a bag for her as she points here and there. Finally she takes a pistol from under her bed and hands it to me. I add it to the bag.

She looks at me, curiosity written on her face. "How old are you really?"

"Uh, seventeen?"

Marissa grins. "I'm only a year older than you. How odd is it that we both ended up undercover in Berlin at the same time?"

I give her a wry smile. "There are a lot of odd things about this war."

She nods. "Agreed." She sighs, sitting heavily on a side chair and closing her eyes.

"Are you going to be able to make it?" I ask. I'm not sure what I'll do if she says no. I can't possibly leave her here.

Her mouth twists. "At some point the Abwehr, or the people who trained you, will be here to arrest me. So I really don't have much of a choice, do I?"

I shake my head. I wonder what choices led Maxwell to this place and time. Perhaps we've all run out of choices.

The thought of Max gives me an idea.

"I know where we can go!" I exclaim. "And a way out."

"I do hope it's not very far away. I'm not sure how far I can make it."

I give her a grim smile. Wouldn't it be too ironic if a German guard unintentionally gave two spies the means to escape? "It's closer than you could ever imagine."

Getting Marissa down to the children's hiding place under the stairs without detection is much easier than I expected. Everyone is asleep, and if the servants who are awake at this time of night think it strange that we are up and about, they don't say anything about it.

I settle her back on the cushions and tell her to stay put.

"I'm not going anywhere," she says. "I feel horrible."

Not knowing how long we will be stuck in hiding, I make a risky run to the servants' lounge to get food and water.

Most everything is gone, and not wanting to disturb a cook, I just take what I can find—two soft bread rolls, a jar of peaches, and another jar filled with water. Surely enough to last us through the day. We'll sneak out this evening after Marissa has had time to rest.

The clock is striking two in the morning by the time I reach the hidey-hole again, and my eyes are gritty with exhaustion. Marissa is already asleep when I come in. I set the provisions on a small bookcase and join her on the cushions. Then I blow out the lantern, trying not to think about the last time I was here. Was that a week ago? Two? The last month has run together into a stream of tension and fear.

I don't think I'm going to sleep, but the next thing I know, I'm waking up. Marissa is sitting up next to me. Relighting the lantern, I turn to see if she looks any better.

"I was hoping this was all a dream."

"No dream." I tilt my head to one side. "At least you don't look like you're about to die anymore."

"Did you really poison me?" she asks, rubbing her eyes.

"It was an accident," I tell her.

"Well, that's some consolation. I think it's about nine a.m. I heard the clock. How are we going to get out of the palace?"

"I have a plan."

She yawns. "I certainly hope so."

"We can't leave until tonight, though. I think it would be better if we remained in hiding."

"Indubitably. May I sleep some more? I feel like I was just poisoned or something."

I smile. "Might as well."

I blow out the lantern again and stare up into the darkness, trying to figure out how I'm going to get us out of here. We can't use any of the main doors, because by now Miss Tickford must suspect that I've betrayed her, since I haven't handed Marissa over to her yet.

I fall asleep and wake up feeling just as confused and unsure as before. The fact that Miss Tickford has my father in her possession is an ever-present gnawing in my stomach. I can't let her make the next move. I have to do something surprising, something she won't expect.

Of course, first I have to get out of the palace without her seeing me. Maxwell said that he thought the tunnel led to the Lustgarten but wasn't sure.

I'm not sure I remember which door it was—we passed so many.

In that half-sleeping state where the mind wanders free, I realize that I haven't heard my father whispering in my head in quite some time. The last time was when I realized the symbol on the paper was for chlorine. I'd heard his whispering for so long that I find myself missing it, even though I now know that my father is alive. I swallow as an idea comes to me.

*Maybe it wasn't my father advising me at all.*

*Maybe it was me.*

Maybe I'd always known what to do but simply didn't trust my own instincts. And look what a mess of things that made.

But then, my instincts can be wrong sometimes. I instinctively trusted Maxwell even though, logically, I knew I shouldn't. I remember how conflicted he'd seemed about the war. Does he feel conflicted about his part in it? I wonder how many Germans feel the same way. I think of my German governess, Frau Engel, who kept our house; and the dozens of other Germans I knew as a child. They're good, kind people. Surely not all of them could think that this war is a good idea or that chemical weapons are defensible.

I blink as the thought hits me. No. Most, like Lillian, have family ties that cross borders. The thought of a weapon that could kill hundreds of men at one time and in such a manner is horrifying.

*They don't know.*

I sit up, careful not to disturb Marissa. That's what I'll do. I'll let them know. I'll let everyone know. Then if the Germans allow it to happen, it will be on their own conscience.

Fierce with purpose, I light the lantern and then move over to where I'd stashed my satchel. I take out the LDB codebook and tear out some of the blank pages in the back. Working quickly, I rip each page into smaller and smaller strips until I have a dozen ready to write on. I don't know how many pigeons there are, but twelve should do it. I know that three of them at least will go to various British and LDB operatives around the city. The rest will go to whoever it is that the pigeons are trained to carry messages to, Germans who may or may not know about the chlorine weapon being developed.

Now to write the message.

*Germany has a poisonous gas weapon that will choke hundreds of men at once.*

I have no room to add *if the wind is right*, but I want to. If the wind is wrong, the gas could blow to the nearest town and indiscriminately kill women and children. Or it could even blow back in their faces and kill their own men.

What are they thinking?

I finish writing the messages and take out my sweater. Unraveling some yarn, I break it into smaller pieces. I only have three little tubes, so the rest of the messages will have to be attached to the birds' legs with yarn. It's not ideal, but it's the best I can do.

Now I just have to make my way up to the roof through a palace filled with overly vigilant guards. Has anyone noticed my absence? A few of the servants may wonder why I haven't been to meals, but perhaps they think I'm too upset over Lillian to eat. I'm fairly certain no one will notice or care if they see me wandering about.

Except for Maxwell. And anyone connected to Miss Tickford.

I smooth my hair down and blow out the lantern before I leave. I don't know how much oil is left in it and we have to be able to make our way out of the tunnels. It's the only way to get out of the house without picking up a tail.

But right now, I've got a mission to accomplish.

I walk swiftly through the Grand Hall to the door leading to the servants' stairway. My heart leaps when I see a couple of guards heading in my direction, but neither one is Maxwell and they don't give me a second look.

I race up the stairs, trying to remember from the blueprint Miss Tickford gave me exactly which way I should go. There are several ways to access the roof, but the palace is so massive that only one will take me directly to the pigeon roost. I enter one of the many attics and hurry across a cramped, dusty room stacked with several hundred years' worth of discarded furniture.

The sun is just starting to set when I reach the rooftop. It will be time for Marissa and me to leave soon.

A chill wind is biting at my face as I make my way over to the small pigeon house. The birds coo noisily when I arrive. "Sorry to disturb you," I tell them, opening the small gate. "But you have work to do."

Slipping my arm inside, I snap my fingers three times. One of the birds jumps onto my wrist. "And we have a volunteer. What a nice, brave bird."

The pigeon, a handsome gray-and-white gentleman, sits perfectly still while I attach one of the tubes to his leg. When I finish, I release him, watching as he circles the palace and then flies off in an easterly direction. It may not work—I have no idea if these are LDB birds or Miss Tickford's own pigeons—but I have to try. At least I'll have the knowledge that I didn't sit idly by without attempting to stop a weapon of such serious consequences.

I finish sending the LDB birds off and then work on the others. I don't know where they'll fly to, but hopefully my message will be carried far and wide. It takes me longer to attach the message securely to their legs with the yarn.

I've just finished up the last pigeon when I hear the unmistakable sound of a pistol cocking behind me. I freeze, holding the bird in my arms.

"Turn around, Sophia Thérèse."

I turn around slowly. Max's eyes are wary. We stare at each other for a long moment before he finally breaks the silence. "Who do you work for?"

I clear my throat. "Currently, I work for the prince and the duchess—"

He shakes his head. "Oh, stop. We both know better." He points the gun at my cheek. "Your birthmark is gone."

I touch my cheek, feeling a strange loss. It must have rubbed off as I slept. "It's no longer needed, is it?"

"Too bad," he says. "It was cute. I thought you would have been long gone by now."

"Why is that?"

"I know you're not who you say you are. I just thought with everything that had happened it would have been prudent for you to leave."

My heart is knocking against my ribs so hard that I'm surprised he doesn't hear it. "Unfortunately, circumstances impeded my hasty departure, but trust me, I'm working on it. How did you figure it out?"

He gives me a sad smile. "Little things. You said 'excuse me' in English. Your odd behavior at the bakery. Then I spotted you sneaking out of Marissa Baum's room. I really wanted you to be just a smart, pretty governess from outside Cologne. You have no idea how disappointed I was when I started putting it together. You should have left earlier."

"How did you know I was up here?"

"I have friends in the guards who have been keeping an eye on you. One of them told me they saw you going upstairs to the attics. It didn't take long for me to figure it out." His voice is regretful and I stare at him, surprised. "You should have left the moment Lillian was killed."

"So it wasn't suicide." I look away to gain control of the tears stinging my eyes.

He shakes his head.

"Did you kill her?" I ask softly. I stare into his brown eyes, wondering if I could spot a lie.

He recoils in horror. "Of course not!"

I believe him, and my entire body sighs with relief.

Hurt comes over his face. "Did you really believe that?"

I swallow. "I didn't think so, but who knows what's true and what's not?"

"I saw you notice the trapdoor. I'd been in the schoolroom earlier and needed a hasty escape. It had nothing to do with Lillian."

"What *did* it have to do with?" I ask.

"I was trying to find out if you were a spy or not."

I stay silent. Was that why he was so angry with me the morning before Lillian was murdered?

He nods toward the pigeon in my arms. "Are you calling for help?"

"In a way." I suddenly toss the pigeon in the air. The surprised bird flaps its wings uncertainly for a moment and Maxwell points his gun upward.

"No!" I cry out and he slowly turns the gun back toward me.

"Who do you work for?" he asks again, his voice harsh.

"Who do *you* work for?" I counter. "Are you just a guard or are you Abwehr?"

"What do you know of the Abwehr? What do you know of anything?" Pain lacerates his voice and I know with certainty that whoever Maxwell Mayer is, he wants to be on this roof under these circumstances even less than I do.

"We're in an interesting predicament," I say to him.

"Indeed." His voice is once again under control. "How do you suggest we get out of it?"

I step closer to him—so close that I can see him swallow. The pistol is inches from my chest. I search his face. "You're going to put your gun down and let me leave. Then I just disappear."

Tears clog my throat as we stare at each other steadily. I know he's thinking about the words he'd said to me in the hallway—how he wished we'd met under different circumstances.

"And why would I do that, Sophia Thérèse, or whoever you are?"

"Because we're friends," I say simply.

For a moment I don't think he's going to do it, and then, inch by inch, the pistol drops. My breath comes out in a small sob. "Thank you," I whisper before hurrying to the door. I turn the knob and then pause, looking back at him. He's staring out over the twinkling lights of the city, his shoulders tense.

"Maxwell?" I say softly.

He turns to me and I almost cry again at the isolation in his eyes.

"My real name is Samantha."

He nods and I wrench open the door and run.

# TWENTY-ONE
## WZHQWB-RQH

*Friend: An agent who shares pertinent information with another agent.*

Marissa's still sleeping when I return, so I gently shake her awake. "How do you feel? Are you hungry?" I ask.

"Better. Starved." She smiles, looking more like her old self than she has since I poisoned her.

We eat the peaches and bread with our hands and then drink the water that's left.

"Here." I hand her the lantern and gather our things.

"Where are we going?" she asks nervously.

I bend and open the small door that leads down into the tunnels. The dank smells of mold and sewage hit us and Marissa sighs.

"Down."

"I was afraid you were going to say that."

We walk down the stairs, the odor of sewage getting stronger.

"What is this place?" she asks, her voice daunted.

"An ancient escape route for the royals in case of an uprising. We need to find our way out."

She stops. "You don't know the way out?"

"Well, not exactly. I do know that the door we are looking for has an X on it and it leads to another tunnel, not a room."

"So what if we open a door and find Kaiser Wilhelm taking a bath?"

I shrug. "Beg his pardon and go back the way we came."

Luckily, we find the door that opens to a small tunnel without incident and pick our way through the darkness. This is no nice, neat tunnel with paving on the ground. It looks much like I imagine a mine would, with ancient timbers keeping the roof from caving in on our heads.

I shudder as spiderwebs heavy with dust and grime cling to my face. The odor of mildew and sewage burns my nostrils and makes my eyes water.

I scramble over a pile of rocks, praying the timber above my head doesn't give way. Maxwell is right. A grown man could never make it through this tunnel. Two smallish girls can barely make it in some spots. When we reach the end, I hold my breath. How horrible would it be if we had to go back the way we came?

The door is about three feet high and two feet wide and made of rough-cut lumber. It opens easily, almost as if it were recently oiled. It's as if someone knew we'd need a way out. Just as Maxwell told me, it comes out under a clump of bushes. It's dark outside, and I give a relieved sigh. Marissa and I both crawl out from under the shrubbery and pick up our bags.

"Now what?" Marissa asks. "We need to find someplace to rest and clean up. I'm fairly certain those are spiderwebs in your hair."

I shudder. "Thanks for telling me. Come on. Let's get away from this area before we start looking for an inn."

She nods, but only makes it a few blocks from the palace before she starts leaning on me.

"I'm sorry," she says. "Crawling through the tunnels took more out of me than I thought."

Guilt gnaws at me and I slip an arm around her for more support. "Don't worry about it. We're a team."

It feels good to say that and mean it. Like me, Marissa's a girl stuck in a dangerous situation far away from home. The only difference is that she chose to be here and I was coerced into being here.

Well, that and the fact that *she* didn't poison *me*.

Berlin at night looks less like an efficient modern city than like a noxious maze of concrete, brick, and stone. Light from the windows spills out over the streets, creating long, eerie shadows. We're both wearing hats pulled down over our hair, but the people who inhabit the night still look at us like we're prey. We pass a tavern and my stomach clenches as the doors open and a couple of soldiers stagger out. Thankfully, they turn the other way and don't give us a single look.

We have to get off the street.

We only make it a few more blocks before Marissa

stumbles. "I'm going to have to rest soon. I'm so sorry."

"We can't stop out here," I tell her desperately. "If the authorities question us, we're done for. Let's go down there."

We duck into a narrow alleyway. I almost run into a trash container and then find a wooden crate for Marissa to sit on. I have to find us someplace safe to stay. We can't just wander about until morning. The police are only one of the worries on the street at night.

I squat down in front of her. Her breathing is shallow and I know I'm going to have to get her somewhere safe soon. "I'm going to go find us a place to stay for the night. Will you be all right here?"

She nods and I open her bag and rummage through it until I find her gun. "Here, keep this for emergencies."

"What about you?" she asks.

I give her a grim smile and show her mine. "I've got one, too."

She smiles again. "I'm glad you're on my side."

I don't tell her that I'm not sure I could shoot a person even if I had to.

I hurry out of the alley and pause at the street. We're definitely in a slum of Berlin and it doesn't take long for me to find what I'm looking for—a dilapidated inn with a tired keeper who isn't too picky about her guests. I pay for a room, get the key, and then hurry back to Marissa, wondering what I'd do if she isn't there.

Thankfully, she is, with her eyes shut and the pistol loose in her hands.

I call her name and she jumps, dropping the gun. She gives a self-deprecating chuckle. "Glad it didn't go off."

That makes two of us.

We make our slow, painful way the three blocks to the inn. The stairs are narrow, and I half carry her, half pull her to the third floor. The stairwell smells of mold, trash, and some unidentifiable decayed thing. The room is tiny and dust coats the bedstead and the small dresser, but the bed is large and the sheets seem to be clean.

Marissa smiles as she collapses into bed. "From the palace's silken sheets to the rough cotton of a flophouse. That's quite a fall for twenty-four hours, isn't it?"

I pull off her shoes. "I wonder what the sheets are like in prison," I say morbidly, but she's already asleep.

I kick off my shoes and join her. When I wake up, I'll have to make my next move. Whatever that's going to be.

I'm still not sure by the time I wake up. I know immediately that I'm alone and I bolt upright. Marissa's shoes and jacket are gone, and for a moment cold waves of abandonment and betrayal rush over me. Then I spot her bag on the table where I'd left it. She wouldn't leave me here, would she? What if she'd lied about everything?

I take a deep breath, struggling to contain the panic that blooms in my chest like a flower.

Moments later, I hear the scrape of a key in the door and tears of relief prick my eyes. Marissa comes in carrying a mug of steaming liquid and a brown paper bag.

"The innkeeper downstairs grudgingly let me bring you a cup of nasty tea and I bought some bread at a bakery down the street, though I can't vouch for its flavor."

She sees my face and her forehead wrinkles in concern. "What's wrong? Are you all right?"

I nod, feeling foolish. "I'm just happy to see the tea," I tell her, my voice husky.

She hands me the mug and pulls a small loaf of bread out of the bag. "I wouldn't be too happy until you taste it."

Breaking off a chunk of bread, she hands it to me. "I woke up ravenous," she says. "I figured I'd best find something."

I'm too busy wolfing down the freshly baked oat bread to answer.

"So what's our plan?" she asks after we finish every crumb and swallow the last of the tea.

"I think our plan should start with me giving you the whole story," I tell her.

She kicks off her shoes and sits on the bed with her legs crossed as I tell her about my job for MI5 in London and Miss Tickford. When I get to the part where my father is taken, she grabs my hand.

"So you don't know where your father is right now?"

I shake my head.

"Do you know what he was doing here?"

I shake my head again. "We didn't have a lot of time to talk, but he knew who you were and told me to go to you for help." I pause. "I thought you were Velvet, only I guess you're not, really, because there is no Velvet. That was just a ruse to get me to Berlin so Miss Tickford could capture my father."

"So you aren't really a spy?" she asks.

I sigh. "Apparently not."

"Well, you're very good at it."

My lips curl upward. "Thank you. But I have no idea what to do now."

She tucks her hair behind her ears and frowns, her eyes pensive. "You said they wanted your father and me, right? We have to figure out a way to let Miss Tickford think she's going to get me. Do you have any way to get in touch with her? How did they send you messages?"

My head jerks up. "The bakery! The one on the Nürnberger Straße. It's our live drop site."

"Good. You can leave a message there. Now we just have to figure out what to say."

I bite my lip. "I could tell her that I have you in custody."

"That's a possibility." She puts a finger over her lip, thinking. "If she wants me badly enough, she'll risk poking her head out to get me. But I think it's important that she still thinks you're an ally, that she's still fooling you."

I shift and look away. Would Miss Tickford still think I was an ally after I simply disappeared on her? "We could try it," I say. "But I doubt she'll believe it. You're right, though. The only way for us to get to my father is for Miss Tickford to take us there herself. But we have no way of knowing if she is actually going to do that or not. For all we know, she's already turned him over to the Abwehr."

Marissa shakes her head. "No. I don't think so. I think she's keeping him as a bargaining chip just in case you figure out she's lying to you. And also, I think there's a likelihood that she isn't really working for the Germans. That something else is going on."

I rub the back of my neck, thinking hard. "That's a possibility. I'm fairly certain that Monsieur Elliot suspected something. He seemed to feel that there was something strange about my training."

"So it's entirely likely that you really are in LDB and that she's working alone," Marissa says. "But why does she want me so badly?"

I snap my fingers. "Of course! The formula!"

Marissa raises an eyebrow. "You mean the one we don't have?"

I cross my arms and grin. "She doesn't have to know that."

Marissa catches my meaning and smiles back. "Do you think you can write one up?"

I shrug. "I think so. I don't think she'll know the difference. Unless she is an expert, she won't know that it's fake until she takes it to a chemist."

"So we make a drop, try to follow her back to where she's keeping your father, and then make a trade."

My shoulders slump. "She may not be an expert chemist, but she is an expert agent. I'm not sure I'm good enough to fool her."

"But it wouldn't matter if she knows," Marissa says

slowly. "She's still going to take us to where your father is, only we'll have the advantage because we'll know that she knows we're following her."

In spite of the gravity of the situation, I giggle. "But she won't know that we know that she knows. . . ."

Marissa's mouth twists into a wry smile. "Exactly."

I shrug. "I think it's the best plan we have. It's better than just handing ourselves over to her."

*I hope.*

With Marissa's help, I carefully craft a message telling Miss Tickford that I have what she wants. Then I put the chlorine symbol on the bottom for good measure. If all goes well, she won't even get a chance to decode the message before we arrive to save my father and get out of Berlin.

I'm just praying that he has some sort of plan.

We pack up our things, glad to leave the stench of the inn. Outside, the spring sun shines soft and warm like a caress from Mother Nature, so different from the wintery bleakness I feel inside.

"Should we both follow her? Or just you?" Marissa asks on our way to the bakery.

Even though I'd like the company, I know it would be best if I went alone. "She's expecting *me* to get in touch with her. If something goes wrong, at least you'll know that something's amiss and be able to help. Maybe." I glance over at her. Her delicate profile is determined.

"Don't worry, Samantha. We'll get your father back."

My heart swells with gratitude, glad to have someone on

my side. I never knew how alone I felt until now. Well, except when I was with Maxwell. "Why are you doing this?" I ask suddenly. "You could be out of the city by now. You have your travel papers back."

We walk in silence for a moment before she says, "My handler hasn't been in touch with me for several days. He usually leaves messages by the statue in the Lustgarten. I've met him several times, but always in the dark where I can't see his face. He was kind, though. An Englishman. I'm worried about him."

It hits me so suddenly that I stop walking.

"What?" She asks looking around.

"My father."

Her forehead wrinkles. "Your father what?"

"My father is your handler."

She stares at me, her brown eyes wide. "How do you know?"

"He's the one who told me to go to you, remember?" I tell her. "I can't believe I didn't realize it before. You said you were working on a joint project for the Americans and the British. It makes perfect sense. Now I know why my father hasn't been home and why I could never find out anything about his supposed abduction. Most of British Intelligence doesn't even know he's here. At least, I don't think so." Who knows what Captain Parker actually knew.

"That makes perfect sense—it would explain why he hasn't been in touch with me. He was probably completely distracted by your being in the city."

We resume walking. My mind is spinning. Somehow I keep forgetting that Marissa isn't Velvet, that most everything Miss Tickford told me is a lie. We reach the corner and I point down the street. "The bakery is halfway down the block on the left-hand side of the street. There's a café across the way. Why don't you meet me there?"

She nods and her dark eyes search mine. "Good luck."

"You too."

I hurry down the street, trying to remember everything Miss Tickford taught me about surveillance. I'm fairly certain she would have thought to have someone watching the bakery, or at the very least would check for messages. I hurry up the stoop, wondering what I'm going to do if the operative isn't working today. My eyes sweep to where the blue card signal would be if I had a message. I'm relieved that it's not there. I enter the bakery and am immediately assaulted by the sweet scent of cookies, cake, and baking bread. My stomach growls in appreciation. All I've eaten is the rough piece of bread earlier. I breathe a sigh of relief when the man comes out of the back. I'd been worried that the drop site had been compromised, since he wasn't here the last time I came by.

"Good afternoon, Fräulein. May I help you?"

I look around the bakery and smile. "I haven't been here since I was a child. I would love one gingerbread, please."

He tilts his head to one side and nods. "Of course."

He reaches back to get the gingerbread and I ask, "Do you still have those little sugar cookies with the soft centers?"

Surprised, he nods. "We're using honey for sweetening now, but they're still tasty."

"I'll take a dozen."

When I hand him the money for the cookies and gingerbread, I slip him the message. He takes it without batting an eye and then gives me my change. "Have a nice day, Fräulein."

I smile and walk out the door on trembling legs. Task one accomplished. Now I just need to see if Miss Tickford takes the bait.

I rejoin Marissa, who's sitting by the window of the café. "I ordered some tea for you," she says as I take a seat.

"Excellent, because I got some cookies for you." Marissa and I drink our tea and watch the shop across the street.

An old woman dressed in black with a shawl over her head walks into the bakery, and I nod. "There she is."

Marissa screws up her face. "I thought you said she was young and pretty."

"It's a disguise. Not even an old woman would wear a shawl over her head on a nice day like today."

She straightens. "You're right. Are you sure you're not a seasoned spy?"

My heart swells with the compliment and I smile as I rise up from my seat. "I will be, after this is over."

"I'll wait a few minutes before I follow," she says. "What should we do if she gets into a motorcar?"

I remember that Miss Tickford had not one but two motorcars at her disposal the other day. "Then we've lost

her. But I am betting that she is holding my father somewhere close to the drop spot."

I take a deep breath as I stand at the door of the café.

It's time to put what I learned from Miss Tickford to the
test.

Against Miss Tickford.

# TWENTY-TWO
## WZHQWB-WZR

*Protected Source: A secret informant or agent whose
identity must remain hidden at all costs.*

Heart in my throat, I wait at the door until the woman
in black comes out of the bakery with a brown bag.
When she's several stores away, I dart out the door, staying
on the opposite side of the street and about ten yards back
so she can't spot me in the shop windows. I don't turn to
see if Marissa is tailing me yet. I'm too busy watching Miss
Tickford without seeming to watch her. She's still hunched
like an old woman, but I notice her footsteps speed up as she
gets farther away from the bakery. I'm praying it's because
she doesn't know she has a tail yet, not because she can't
wait to lure me in for the kill.

My heart is racing like a locomotive and sweat trickles
down the back of my blouse. My pistol is heavy in my purse
and I pray I can use it if and when the time comes.

And I pray my father is all right.

Miss Tickford turns a corner, and as she does so I see
her removing the shawl. I dodge traffic as I cross the street,

and then I turn the same corner. For a moment I'm confused because I don't see her, and then I spot the black knit shawl bunched up near some debris. A woman dressed in black and wearing a sheer widow's veil is walking quickly ahead. I know in a flash that it's Miss Tickford. She simply removed the shawl to reveal the widow's veil underneath; the black dress is the same.

She crosses the street quickly and then disappears into a tall brick building. I'm right. She and her men are holding my father near the bakery.

I spot Marissa on the other side of the street. Walking slowly, I point at the building I've just seen Miss Tickford go into. Marissa nods and I scout the outside, first by walking one way up the street and then by walking back down, my eyes scanning the buildings and the pedestrians for anything unusual.

Catching Marissa's attention, I make a motion that I'm going to go around the building to see if there are any exits in the back. She nods. Then I hold up the bag of cookies, hoping she understands my meaning.

My knees are practically knocking together as I round the corner. I'm fairly certain that Miss Tickford has to know that I'm following her by now—doesn't she? I'm not that good.

My only hope is that she doesn't know that Marissa is with me.

I open the door and there's a short set of steps with two doors on either side. Then a dim stairway going up. From the outside it looked as if the building was several stories tall. My stomach dips with disappointment. I have no idea which flat she has my father in. I look up the stairs, trying to ignore the panic fluttering in my chest.

I can't go knocking from door to door, can I? I start to giggle at the thought and cover my mouth.

*Think. Think.*

Would she be on the first floor or would she want to put more distance between her prisoner and freedom?

Clutching the paper bag in my hands, I make a decision and climb the stairs, one stair at a time. I reach the first landing and stand, heart pounding, between the two doors. I wait, but when nothing happens, I head up to the third floor.

Every few steps, I drop a piece of cookie.

Well, we are in the land of Hansel and Gretel, after all.

When I reach the third-floor landing, I wait for a moment before moving on. My foot is barely on the first stair when I hear the squeak of an opening door.

I freeze at the click of a pistol being cocked near my head for the second time in less than twenty-four hours.

I think I've found her—or she's found me, as the case may be.

"Good evening, Samantha. I've been waiting for you."

I turn, tension racing across my shoulders. "No need for the gun. We're on the same side."

She raises her perfectly shaped eyebrows. "Really? And which side is that?"

I hear the amusement in her voice and choose my words carefully. "Whichever side will get my father and me out of Berlin alive."

"Good answer, little one. Unfortunately, I'm not going to be able to accommodate you on that. Now, if you'll please come in."

She moves away from the door, giving me room to go in, but her gun is still pointed right at my forehead. I break into a sweat as I enter the flat. My eyes dart around the room and I take in the tattered sofa, worn rugs, and battered table. A narrow door opens into what looks like a kitchen, and through the kitchen I see the corner of a bed. It's a long, connecting flat where each room opens into the next like a chain of railway cars. Then I spot my father tied to a kitchen chair in the corner of the room, a gag around his mouth. His shoulders are slumped and his eyes regard me sadly. I know he hoped more than anything in the world that I wouldn't show up here.

"Father!" I rush across the room and throw my arms around him, not caring if Miss Tickford is pointing a gun at us. I untie the gag.

"Water," he says, and my heart breaks at the sight of his dry lips.

I glare at Miss Tickford, who shrugs. "Bernard, get our guest a glass of water."

Remembering her love of poison, I hurry to watch as Bernard, one of the beefy men who took my father, runs water from the tap into a glass and hands it to me. I hurry it back to my father, conscious of Miss Tickford's eyes on me. I hold it to my father's lips and he drinks deeply.

"We waited a long time for you to give us the signal," she says accusingly. "I thought we had a plan."

"You know what they say about that," I say. "'The best-laid schemes o' mice an' men . . .' Miss Baum was entertaining a male visitor in her room until late."

I hold my breath as I lie, hoping she'll believe it.

She doesn't.

"Then where is she now?" Miss Tickford demands.

"I have her tied up in an inn over on the Kochstraße."

Her eyes narrow and I meet them, willing myself not to look away or flinch.

"What do you want?"

"What are the chances of you giving me my father for Miss Baum?" I ask. I need to buy some time.

She grins. "Why would you want a traitor like that? A man who betrayed not only his country but his very family."

"My daughter will never believe that," my father says, and I'm gratified that his voice seems stronger. "No matter how you've misrepresented the truth or woven your deceit, she will have figured it out already, for she is far, far smarter than you, in your arrogance, will have given her credit for."

"It doesn't matter what she believes, or what she thinks she knows," Miss Tickford says. "I have the gun." She waves it at us and my throat tightens.

"That's all right," I say. "I have the formula."

My father stills. "Sam," he warns. I lay a hand on his shoulder.

Her eyes gleam at me and I can't believe that I actually thought that she cared for me. I know now that she isn't ever going to buy that I'm willing to hand over Marissa for my father, but she might just want the formula badly enough. . . .

I take a deep breath and try to sound confident. "So you want both my father and Miss Baum. That's rather selfish of you. And now that we've established that my father isn't a traitor, it follows logically that *you* are—you and your German thugs. So why did you betray your country, Miss Tickford? Why do you want the formula so badly?"

Miss Tickford stares at me, her green eyes icy.

"I'd been warned about her," my father tells me. "I received a brief memo several weeks ago that one Leticia Tickford had gone rogue and all agents in LDB and MI6 should be cautious. She used her clearance and her credentials at MI6 to set this whole thing in motion. Her objective? Blow a hole in our intelligence network and kill as many agents as possible while doing it."

"It's funny that your daughter would call me the traitor. Ha!" Miss Tickford's mouth is tight as she spews out her venom. "You and the rest of Military Intelligence are nothing short of murderers and you need to be stopped. What's really tragic is how many dead agents you and others like you are responsible for and that no one knows about. No one will ever know, because, like the cowards you are, you hide behind secrecy."

My mind is spinning as I look from Miss Tickford to my father. Why would Miss Tickford want to kill agents? Why would she call them murderers? I must get my father's hands undone. At any moment Marissa is going to create a distraction and my father will be vulnerable tied to the chair.

I stand next to him, one hand on his shoulder, the other clutching my handbag, which still contains the gun, useless as it is with my father tied up.

"But you're a spy," I say to her, racking my brain for a way out of this. "Why would you want to kill other agents?" My stomach tightens as I remember the last time I saw Miss Tickford out of control. "Lawrence," I breathe. "This is about Lawrence."

Her mouth tightens and I know I'm on to something. "You blame La Dame Blanche and MI6 for Lawrence's death."

Her eyes harden. "Lawrence was too good and kind to be a spy. They should never have recruited him. And how many others are rotting in prisons because France and England need their information? Someone needs to stop them—needs to stop them all!"

Her lips tremble and I hold my breath as the pistol shakes in her hand.

A thought hits me so hard I almost double up. "Lillian. You killed Lillian. She wasn't even an agent."

"That's not my fault," she said sharply. "You're the one who told me she was Velvet. I confronted her, and when I realized your mistake, I had to get rid of her."

I clutch the back of my father's chair for support. "You

knew she wasn't involved and you still killed her?"

Miss Tickford twitches a shoulder. "She was considering leaving Germany anyway. I just hastened her departure."

"So you murdered her." Another thought hits me. "You killed Colonel Landau, the French LDB liaison who knew Velvet's identity, didn't you. The one who overdosed on laudanum."

"Yes." Her eyes gleam as if she's proud of her work. "And that Monsieur Elliot you were so fond of."

I suck in a breath, remembering that gruff, kindly, brilliant old man. "You're deranged!" I burst out.

"England is going to pay even more when the Germans use the chemical weaponry on them. And when I sell the formula, I'll be rich enough to disappear to some South American beach somewhere and read about all of you killing one another off."

"But you have money," I say. "The apartment alone . . ."

She shakes her head. "Once the war is over, it will be sold for taxes owed. All of it, everything that has been in my family for years, will be gone." She suddenly strides toward me, the barrel of her gun seeming to grow larger and larger until it almost touches my forehead. But then she switches tactics and presses it against my father's temple instead.

"You and your father are expendable, little one. But I must have that formula. Where is Marissa Baum? I'll shoot him. You know I will." Her voice becomes more and more hysterical and my heart pounds in my ears. Now would be a *really* good time for a distraction.

I hold my breath, waiting for the sound of a pistol shot. Instead, there's a faint hammering outside and then screaming. Miss Tickford freezes and Bernard comes out into the front room carrying a weapon.

When the hammering reaches our door, Miss Tickford steps quickly behind my father, with the gun held against his back. "Don't get any ideas," she whispers.

Bernard opens the door and a young boy screams "Fire!" at the top of his lungs. The boy races down the staircase as thick, acrid smoke wafts through the hallway. Tenants push and shove their way downstairs, adding to the chaos.

*Marissa started a fire?*

*My God, I hope no one gets trapped in it.*

Miss Tickford curses and then bends to untie my father. "Bernard, get the girl." She leans toward me, her face so close that I feel her breath. She speaks very slowly, and every word sends a shiver up my spine. "One wrong move and I'll shoot his legs out from underneath him and let him burn to death. Do you understand?"

I nod.

Bernard moves toward me, but I step out of reach. "She has my father," I tell him. "I'm not going to try anything."

It's a strange procession that goes down the three flights of stairs. First myself, then Bernard, then my father followed by Miss Tickford. While others—mothers carrying small children, old men with canes, and children—rush past us, we're slow and measured in our movements. My heartbeat sounds like the ocean in my ears and I feel as if I'm walking in a dream. This can't be real.

But it is. Terrifyingly, frighteningly real.

*This has to work*, I pray. It just has to. We're only going to get one chance at this.

Furtively, I reach into my handbag and pull out the pistol. I shove it into my coat pocket, taking care to keep it out of Bernard's sight. Continuing downstairs, I place my finger on the trigger.

When we reach the exit, we're instantly surrounded by a crowd of people, and the clanging of a fire engine sounds in the distance. The streets are chaotic, noise and screaming everywhere as thick black smoke billows from the building. People are hanging out of the windows of the surrounding buildings, enjoying the spectacle from the safety of their own apartments.

A couple of German policemen try unsuccessfully to direct people away from the burning building and I keep an eye on them as I frantically look around for Marissa. Alerting the authorities to our presence would be disastrous, no matter how badly I want to escape Miss Tickford.

More people, choking and coughing, spill out of the building as Miss Tickford leads us through the throng. Fear clogs my throat; I know she's going to take us away from the relative safety of the crowd. *Where's Marissa?* My instincts, the ones I'm just now learning to trust, are screaming at me.

It's now or never.

Taking a deep, shaky breath, I turn suddenly and bump into Bernard, elbowing him in the middle. He bends over slightly and I step next to Miss Tickford and shove my pistol in her ribs. Her eyes widen with shock when she realizes what's happening.

"I'll kill him," she warns.

Without Marissa here, it's become Bernard's and Miss Tickford's guns against mine, but at this point I don't care. "If you do, you're a dead woman," I spit out. "No matter what else happens, I'll make sure you'll never be able to hurt anyone else."

And there is no doubt in my mind that I mean it.

I spot Marissa emerging from the crowd moments before she slams Miss Tickford's wrist with her own gun. Miss Tickford's pistol falls from her hand and my father snatches it up.

"Checkmate," I whisper fiercely into Miss Tickford's ear.

It only takes Bernard an instant to realize the situation is out of control. He melts into the crowd.

"Let's take a walk, shall we?" my father says.

I see resignation on Miss Tickford's face as she nods. With three guns trained on her, she has no choice but to go with us, and I bite back a victorious cheer. Logically, I know that we have a lot to do before we're safe, but at the moment, I feel triumphant.

My father seems to know where we're going and I'm content to put everything in his hands. In spite of the danger that still surrounds us, I can finally breathe a sigh of relief and let go of some of the tension that has been weighing me down ever since Captain Parker and I had our chat all those weeks ago.

"That was an ingenious distraction," I whisper to Marissa as we follow behind my father and Miss Tickford.

"It wasn't my idea," she whispers back.

Surprised, I look at her. She nods her head sideways and I turn. A young man standing in the shadows watching the chaos catches my attention. My breath hitches.

Maxwell.

Our eyes catch and hold for a moment that spins out for an eternity. The crowd feels like a great divide that can't be crossed, no matter how badly I long to go to him.

He gives me the tiniest of nods before disappearing into the mass of people.

My head swivels back to Marissa and her lips curve upward.

"What? Who?" I stammer.

"I think you would know him best as Velvet."

# PART V

*Debriefing*

# EPILOGUE
HSLORJXH

One of the things I've always loved about our London house is the garden. It isn't a particularly remarkable garden—it's not filled with classical statuary, exotic flowers, or award-winning roses. Apparently, my grandmother's many talents didn't extend to having a green thumb. Most of the plants are rather pedestrian—a nice patch of grass, a few bulbs, and your basic snowball bushes and lilacs. What the garden does boast is absolute privacy due to tall, moss-covered stone walls, along with an absolutely magnificent arbor constructed of wrought iron and covered in English ivy. The arbor shades a small table and several chairs, and nothing is lovelier than having tea on a warm afternoon while half-hidden in a fragrant embrace of green.

My father and I are sipping our tea, not saying much of anything. I've spent a great deal of time the past couple of weeks in this garden, with my father or my mother or Rose.

"You know your mother is still mad at me," my father says.

I nod. "As well she should be, really." I grin, mimicking my mother's tone exactly. "Playing spy at your age."

My father smiles back and my heart fills with happiness. His cheeks have filled out and his barber laid waste to his beard, leaving just a small, distinguished goatee. We've only been home for a few weeks and I already know that my father probably won't go off spying anytime soon. The work he'd been doing for MI6 was as dangerous as it was necessary—he, Marissa, and Maxwell had been passing information to both England and America, hoping to expedite America's entry into the war. For now, Father's simply enjoying his leave of absence, but he's an active man with a strong sense of duty and I can't see him remaining idle for long.

I sip my tea and lean back in the chair, enjoying the solitude. Glancing over at my father, I bring up the question that has been on my mind since we escaped the apartment. The question that, for some reason, felt too raw to say out loud.

I take a deep breath. "Did you work with Corporal Mayer? You said you worked with two people inside the Stadtschloss. Was Maxwell one of them?" My heart twinges just saying his name. I don't know if I'll ever be able to think of that moment on the rooftop without pain.

My father settles back in the chair and stares off into the distance, though I know he isn't looking at the clouds.

"Maxwell Mayer is one of the bravest, most patriotic Germans I've ever met," my father finally says. "He passed along information to me, yes, but never information that would put German men in danger. As a moral man, he couldn't possibly stand by and watch so many men be killed with chemical weapons, even if the German state does consider the men to be enemies. To Maxwell, people are human beings no matter where they're born."

I clench my hands in my lap. There is so much I still want to say to Max. It hurts, knowing I'll never get the chance. I change the subject.

"You know, I never understood exactly how the prince was involved."

"Did Maxwell ever tell you who his father was?"

I shake my head. "Just that he and the kaiser were good friends."

"They were more than good friends, they were like brothers. Maxwell's father was the prince's godfather, just as the kaiser is Maxwell's godfather. Maxwell went to the prince with his concerns about chemical weaponry and the prince agreed that unleashing poisonous gas on the world is reprehensible. For all the good it's done."

I remember the conversation I'd overheard Marissa having about the prince. I suck in a breath. Of course. It had been Maxwell in the alley.

How hard he must have worked to try to stop the inevitable.

Tears spring to my eyes and I look away to regain my

composure. The Germans loosed chemical weaponry on the world just weeks ago in Ypres. Even though we gave the British government the information we had concerning the weapons, the plan had already been set in motion and the damage done. Over two hundred soldiers were affected horribly and forty-six of those men died.

I remember the birds flying off into the twilight sky and wonder if anyone who had received my message even cared.

My father reaches over and pats my hand. "You did the right thing," he says, as if knowing my thoughts. "And our government does have the formula."

"So they can use it, too?" I ask bitterly. "Or perhaps develop something even more deadly?"

He says nothing, but I already know the answer. Each new weapon will develop into one even more lethal. Who knows where it will end.

Silence stretches out between us and a flock of starlings passes overhead.

"So was Maxwell really Velvet?" I ask.

My father shrugs. "He had many names. Perhaps to La Dame Blanche, he is Velvet. To MI6, he is known as Helmut. Miss Tickford sent you in a completely wrong direction, so I think everything was just guesswork on her part."

I think of Maxwell—his ready smile and the small kindnesses he showed me so many times. I think of that final act of compassion and caring on the rooftop when he let me leave, not knowing what the ramifications for his country could be.

I wonder if he is still guarding the prince and if he's still passing information to the Allies.

My mind grapples with the many twists and turns of the past weeks. I wish Marissa were here to help me make sense of it all, but she's already left to go back to the States. Father told me his part in everything, of course, but he hasn't yet told me why. Why he left us.

"Why did you take the assignment, Father? Knowing that they would tell us that you had been abducted?"

He's silent for so long that I think he isn't going to answer. Then he faces me, his eyes sad. "Nothing is more important to me than you and your mother, you know that, right?"

I bite my lip. "And yet you left."

"Yes. And yet I left."

"Why?"

"Because in protecting England, I was protecting my family. And other families. And truthfully, it feels good to know you have a set of skills that can make a real difference in the world."

Part of me is dismayed by his decision, but then I remember sitting in Captain Parker's office and being offered a chance to be a part of La Dame Blanche. I remember how torn I felt when I had to turn him down. Wasn't there a little part of me that was almost glad, afterward, that I'd been forced into becoming an agent? Aren't I considering becoming a real LDB agent now?

On the other hand, Miss Tickford was an agent and I don't want to be even remotely like her. I think of what she did to Lillian and hope she spends the rest of her miserable life in Holloway Prison. Captain Parker is also in prison. He and Miss Tickford were having an affair, which is how she gained so much access to MI6 activities. He's currently being investigated to ascertain exactly what his role was. Considering he was detained on a ship set to sail to South America, I tend to think he knew exactly what was happening in Berlin.

At least Miss Tickford had failed in her attempt to kill Monsieur Elliot. Soon after we'd left the farmhouse, his housekeeper took him to the hospital, where he was treated for poisoning. I smile to myself. It would take more than laudanum to kill someone so cranky.

A shadow crosses the table and I look up to see my mother standing in front of us, an envelope in her hand. "A messenger stopped and said I was to give this to you," she says, handing me the envelope. She turns to my father. "Come along, George. We promised your sister we'd stop by for afternoon tea. Are you sure you don't want to come?" She directs this last bit at me.

I wave at the books and papers in front of me. "No. I think I'm just going to study for a bit. Tell Rose I'll come by after she gets out of school tomorrow."

I watch my parents leave. I'm glad for a chance to be alone. I've decided to pursue my studies on my own until I either return to LDB or go to the university. As much as I love the peace and quiet of being home, I've been strangely restless since I got back and need something to fill my time.

I reach for my books and then remember the envelope. I frown upon opening it because none of the words make sense.

The hair suddenly rises on the back of my neck.

It's in code.

I pull my notebook and pencil toward me and get to work. It's a fairly easy code and my pencil flies as everything begins to take shape. I'm breathing hard by the time I write the last words on the paper: *Your friend, Max.*

I start again at the beginning.

*Dearest Samantha,*

*Since we last spoke, I've left my home and have been relocated to a country kind enough to take me in. Of course, they're more interested in what I know than in who I am, but that's understandable. After the poison was released in Ypres, I found that I couldn't stay in Germany any longer. The debriefing may take months, but I hope to be able to return to "work" soon. Do you plan on doing the same?*

*I think of you often—not the time we last saw each other in the street after the fire, but before that, on the rooftop, when you stood in front of my gun and stared me down, knowing I would* never hurt you. You were so brave to release those birds, trying to warn the world of what was to come. Once I learned what you had done, your bravery shamed me. I knew what they were planning long before that but still believed I could stop it diplomatically. Apparently, I was wrong.

I'd like your permission to visit. I know it's customary to ask the father, but what about our relationship is traditional? Yes, England is the country I have defected to, and I would very much like to continue our friendship. If I may visit, please put a rock on the third step of your stoop as a signal. I will see it. If not, if you would rather forget, I understand.

Your friend,
Max

I finish reading the letter and sit in the dappled shade, too stunned to move.

Max is here. In England.

My breath catches. How hard it must have been for him to leave and how lonely it must be for him here. My heart aches for him and I make a sudden decision.

Actually, the decision was made the moment I read his words.

Leaping to my feet, I snatch up rocks from the garden on my way to the front of the house. Then I count the steps and scatter the rocks across the third one, not caring if Bridget has a fit. Moments later, I'm sitting on the divan, twisting my hands in my lap. I tell myself that I'm being silly, that he couldn't possibly have meant *now*, but my instincts say otherwise, and if I've learned nothing else over the past months, it has been to trust my instincts.

In fact, I'm willing to bet that the messenger was Maxwell himself.

My belief is rewarded by a knock on the door. "I've got it, Bridget," I call, my heart beating wildly. I race through the sitting room and into the foyer, excitement and trepidation battling in my chest. What if he's changed?

What if he doesn't like Samantha as much as he did Sophia Thérèse?

I swing the door open and there he is. He is holding his hat in his hand and smiling in that warm, kind way he has. I don't think I had any clue just how much I missed that smile.

All my doubts are washed away by crazy, ridiculous happiness. "Maxwell."

We stare at each other, smiling. He's wearing a dark, rather rumpled suit, and it's wonderfully odd to see him out of his pressed uniform. His hair is mussed up and there's a leaf on his shoulder.

I reach out and brush it off. "Where were you waiting?"

He waves his hand. "Behind the tree across the street. I didn't think it proper to just show up. What do you say,

Samantha? May I come in?" The hope and uncertainty on his face bruise my heart as I move aside to let Maxwell Mayer step into my life.

My real one.

# ACKNOWLEDGMENTS
DFNQRZOHGJPHQWV

I'd like to thank all the people who made *Velvet Undercover* a reality, especially my agent extraordinaire, Mollie Glick, and my amazing editor, Kristin Rens, who helps me craft books that are far better than I could have done on my own. A huge shout-out to all the folks at Harper: Kelsey Murphy, Jenna Stempel, Kathryn Silsand, Caroline Sun, and Nellie Kurtzman.

I want to thank my weekly writing group of talented young adult authors for being so amazingly supportive—Cat Winters, Kelly Garrett, and Miriam Forster, your collective wisdom and friendship means the world to me. Our random conversations on bloody fairy tales, bizarre religious rituals, and strange historical customs make me a better person. Or at least one who might have a shot on *Jeopardy!*

Also thanks to Amy Danicic, who listens to me whine; Vickie Hansen, my pancake partner; and author Shirley Jump, who inspires me to keep running in spite of the deadlines. I also want to thank H. M. Brooks and Jannick Pitot who helped me translate Alphonse de Lamartine's lovely poem.

Also a big thank-you to Tammy Proctor, the author whose book *Female Intelligence: Women and Espionage in the First World War* was essential in my research and who graciously answered all my email queries.

Heartfelt thanks to my wonderful children, Ethan and Megan; my daughter-in-law, Megan; my grandgirl, Serena; and my parents, Lyle and Carol Foreman, for being awesome and not complaining about all the times I go AWOL to write.

But mostly, I want to acknowledge my hubby, Alan Brown, who read the first draft and made a big deal out of it. Thanks for being the guy I call when my car is on the side of the road.